John Dick Scott, born i███████████████ 1917, was educated at Stewart's C███████ █inburgh University where he took a█ ████ █ █n History. Married in 1941, he beca██ ██████ █ncipal at the Ministry of Aircraft Product█ ████ ██n during the war, and went on to join the Cabi██ ██ce as an official war historian in 1944.

The Administration of War Production, written with Richard Hughes, was published in 1955, followed by an account of the *Design and Development of Weapons*, with M. M. Postan and D. Hay in 1964. Scott also wrote industrial and business history, with accounts of Siemens published in 1958, and Vickers in 1962. Literary editor at the *Spectator* from 1953 to 1956, he went to America in 1963 to become editor of the World Bank's periodical *Finance and Development*.

On the creative side, Scott published his first short novel, *The Cellar* in 1947, followed by *The Margin* in 1949. Three years later came 'a love story' called *The Way to Glory*, followed by *The End of an Old Song* in 1954. His last novel, *A Pretty Penny*, appeared in 1963, and was republished as a Pan paperback three years later.

J.D.Scott

THE END OF AN OLD SONG

A Romance

Introduced by Christopher Harvie

CANONGATE
CLASSICS
33

First published in 1979 by Canongate Pub-
lishing. This edition published as a Canongate
Classic in 1990 by Canongate Publishing Ltd, 16
Frederick Street, Edinburgh EH2 2HB.
Copyright Robin Jenkins 1979. Introduction
copyright Bob Tait.

The publishers gratefully acknowledge general subsidy from the Scottish Arts Council
towards the Canongate Classics series and a spe-
cific grant towards the publication of this title.

Set in 10pt Plantin by Hewer Text Composi-
tion Services, Edinburgh. Printed and bound in
Denmark by Nørhaven Rotation.

Canongate Classics
Series Editor: Roderick Watson
Editorial Board: Tom Crawford, J. B. Pick

British Library Cataloguing in Publication Data
is available on request.

ISBN 0-86241-310-9

Introduction

The 1950s in Scotland were odd and disquieting. The country was enjoying a prosperity which it hadn't experienced for fifty years; the 'national question' and indeed the Scottish renaissance had been marginalized; in 1955 the Tories even won a majority of seats and votes. Underneath, as we now realise, things were less secure. The old business élite had shifted investment away from the traditional industries, education and training were stagnating, and political stability maintained itself by some pretty under hand methods: Tory manipulation of the home rule issue; Special Branch infiltration of nationalist organizations. Access to the British Empire had always underwritten Scottish acceptance of the Union. Now that its last post was being sounded, traditional loyalties came to seem archaic.

The quality of consciousness produced by this friction between the apparently stable and the potentially catastrophic was not immediately apparent, but powerful all the same, as James Kennaway would indicate in *Tunes of Glory* (1956). When the critic Walter Allen wrote of

> something to which the respectable, censored mind does not normally have access, something powerfully charged with love and hate, pride and violence, which, in given circumstances it might discharge in some tremendous flash of lightning,

he might have had Colonel Jock Sinclair in mind. In fact he was describing *The End of an Old Song*, which appeared in 1954. Its author J. D. Scott had been, ironically enough, the *Spectator* literary editor responsible for christening Kingsley Amis, Philip Larkin and company 'the Movement', whose more modest values and pleasures were decidedly remote from those displayed in his own novel. Remembered by Graham Martin as a somewhat dour Anglo-Scot, he had

written several novels about business and service life which
would have fitted into the Movement's definition of realism.
The End of an Old Song—A Romance—is quite different,
yet its subtitle shouldn't blind us to the fact that it is a
complex and, above all, ironic book.

Scott was by training an historian, reared in the same
grim conviviality of Edinburgh's Old College as young
John Gourlay and—a couple of decades later—myself.
He worked on the official history of the Second World War
with Richard Hughes, and evidently acquired something of
the latter's fastidiousness about chronology and historical
accuracy. Yet he chose to foreground the romantic element
in *The End of an Old Song*, as we meet young Cathy in
the old house of Kingisbyres, her lover Alastair Kerr, and
his mysterious link to the house's master, the Jacobite
Captain Keith. On the other hand, the plot begins long
after the wedding, the marriage is in trouble, and we are
being told the story by an unsuccessful suitor—the original
'unreliable narrator'. Let the reader beware. In a debate
with F. W. Bateson in the *Times Literary Supplement* Scott
had argued that the novel was 'capable of a higher degree
of organization than the drama'. This is certainly true of his
own use of the familiar elements of the romance and the
Bildungsroman to launch an extended and cold-eyed—but
always imaginative and engaging—meditation on Scottish
history and Scottish identity.

The End of an Old Song is not an overtly allusive novel,
although Scott had written appreciatively in *Horizon* of
the Scottish father-son conflict in Stevenson and George
Douglas Brown, and Alastair has more than a passing
resemblance to that other bruising materialist, young
Ewan Tavendale. More than most twentieth-century Scots
novelists, Scott is concerned with class, and in particular
with the predicament of the Scots *bourgeoisie* whom Patrick
Shaw represents. Alastair Kerr, his hero—and the term
is, for once, apposite—ought to be, as an economist, an
arch-bourgeois. Instead, the peculiarities of Scottish history
have made him a predator:

> And all the time the look deepened on Alastair's face,
> the look of a victorious commander giving permission

to loot a city, a look of brutality, pleasure and recklessness, all masked and stilled by pride.

Kerr's progress does not, however, take on the grand style
that Patrick is led by this to expect. Although he takes
his leave of Kingisbyres and Scotland with a spectacular
gesture, his future seems Prufrockian rather than Yeatsian.

The book's title alludes to the speech of the Scottish Lord
Chancellor when the country's independent parliament was
prorogued in 1707. To Alastair Kerr the old song of an
independent Scotland, represented by Captain Keith, has
long been over:

'We spit on Bonnie Prince Charlie and Flora Macdonald,
on Rizzio's blood and Mary Queen of Scots and the
Flower o' the Forest and Archibald Bell-the-Cat.'

'The end of an auld sang?'

'We spit great greeny-yellow gobs on the end of an
auld sang.'

So much for neo-Jacobitism of the likes of Compton
Mackenzie! But Alastair regards the traditional goal of
integration into the English establishment as no more
viable:

'Sir Alastair Kerr, KC, and Lady Kerr with Jeremy,
aged eight, and Curia, aged ten, on the lawn at Owlets
Pastern.' Sounds well, doesn't it? But there was a
picture like that . . . in the minds of the most diverse
people, Levantine Jews, and Irish navvies and clever
wee Scotties, for maybe a couple of hundred years.
And now we have to give it up for an apartment on
Fifth Avenue. It isn't the same thing.

The problem with Alastair is that he might become what
Edwin Muir called a 'conditional figure'—an animated
point of view. It's a tribute to Scott's skill that he makes
his oblique and shifty narrator invest him with the solidity
of Meaulnes in Alain-Fournier's *Le Grand Meaulnes*. Scott
is as precise as the Frenchman in capturing the insecurities
of adolescence, the unreasoning obsession of first love,
but to this he adds Patrick's skill as a painter of the
uncompromising landscape of lowland Scotland:

I walked up the High Street. As I had remembered
it, it had been a slum, smelling figuratively of history

and literally of extreme poverty, a horrible smell like
stale sweet biscuits. Old men, derelict and grey-faced,
with cloth caps polished black by hard old fingers, had
mooned and spat round the entries of the wynds, too
well aware of the value of attention to give it openly.
. . . And on Sunday morning the congregations of the
local churches had picked their way round frozen pools
of beery sick. It seemed different now; it had the mild
Welfare State look.

George Douglas Brown thought that the essential quality
of the best Scottish literature was 'the flashing together of
different pictures of vivid sensuousness to produce a new
compound image highly charged with meaning—actual or
metaphorical.' In his juggling with realism and subjectivity,
romanticism and worldliness, Scott achieves not only this
grotesquerie but an uncanny anticipation of the swansong of
the Union in the 1980s. If Alastair Kerr's still around in the
1990s, he's one of the unkilted realists who are wringing the
poor bird's neck.

                                        Christopher Harvie

Part One

There is the end of an auld sang
Lord Chancellor Seafield, after the signing
of the Treaty of Union in 1707

As the taxi turned out of the station a flood of watery sunshine poured erratically through the high, racing storm clouds and caught the line of the buildings ahead. They were tall stone buildings, with hard, black edges. Behind, on my right, I caught a glimpse of the flash and glitter of moving traffic. Something, some eagerness, made me open the window, and the sudden icy wind brought tears to my eyes. I shut the window hurriedly. How well I remembered it, that ferocious east wind. . . .

Edinburgh looked, I thought, incredibly foreign, stranger to me at that moment than New York, as surprising as the ruins of Berlin. How hard the buildings looked!—old, grimy, but unmellow; and when the sun went in again, everything was caught in a mysterious cold purple bloom. The taxi changed gear; we were climbing painfully towards the Castle. And it was at this moment that I saw the view, the immense purple evening view across the water to the dark hills, a view across a city, yet somehow desolate and un-European, cold and magical and almost absurdly romantic.

When I got out of the taxi I found I was shivering. I stopped by an effort of will, but the suppressed convulsive tremor made me fumble with the change.

'Very cold,' I said.

'Aye.' The taximan, who had the authentic undersized proletarian look, gave a remote grin. 'You'd better be getting in to a nice fire.' His way of speaking was curiously intimate, faintly contemptuous. But the mere mention of a fire made me look forward to the one that would be waiting for me, a hot, extravagant fire, blazing up the chimney. I was tired, had been over-working, had been restless on the journey, starting off through the London suburbs, then the

3

Home Counties countryside of weekend parties, then the Midlands, and the North, and finally, after a long time, the rolling hills, the sea, the cold freshness of Scotland.

And now it was over, and a fire was waiting for me, and I was going to see Alastair Kerr, my oldest, my closest friend.

It was cold and dark on the landing, with a bitter, dank, hostile feeling. The door in front of me was of oak, massive as the fittings of a battleship. It had a small brass plate with the name Mathieson on it, presumably the name of the people from whom Alastair had borrowed the flat. When, after a few moments, the door opened, the moment was dramatic. And there was Alastair as though the curtain had gone up, standing against a background of brilliant light and warmth.

'Patrick!' He began to laugh, as though I had been wearing absurd clothes. 'The return of the second exile.' He pulled me in, putting his hand on my shoulder in a gesture that was too light and casual to be a backslap. I blinked for a moment in the bright light, and he said: 'Hang your coat there and come in—I'm in the middle of a telephone call.' He went quickly back into the room, and I took off my coat and gloves and muffler as I heard him telephoning, first a lot of figures at dictation speed, then his voice in argument, persuasive and light but with a snap in it.

I went into the room. Alastair was lying back in an armchair, beside the blazing—the almost volcanic—fire that I had imagined, with his left leg crooked casually over the arm of the chair and the telephone receiver in his lap. Yet he had a concentrated look; a loop of his black hair had slipped across his forehead, and he was frowning, almost scowling. He had stopped talking now, and from the other end of the line I could hear a faint crackling voice, voluble and plaintive. Alastair put his hand over the mouthpiece: 'Patrick, you'll find a bottle of champagne on the windowsill, outside—bring it in will you?'

I went over to the window and opened it; the bottle of champagne was wedged into a kind of grille, as cold to the touch as though it had been on ice. Alastair, who was still listening, beckoned to me, and I gave him the bottle. He unwrapped the tinfoil and wire rapidly, and holding the bottle close to the telephone receiver, expertly released the cork. There was a loud pop and a little champagne frothed down on to the tiles. As Alastair handed me the bottle I heard the telephone voice crackle excitedly as a hot frying pan does when something cold is put into it.

'It's nothing, Jeff, nothing. My guest just shot himself. Don't give it a thought.' He paused; then added rapidly: 'No, of course not, I was joking. You worry too easily Jeff. Don't worry about these people at all. They'll be perfectly reasonable—I'll answer for that. You can call me Thursday about this time if you want to. Good-bye.' He put down the receiver.

He laughed again. He had got up and was pouring champagne into a pair of silver tankards that stood ready on a table by the fire. He seemed to be in very high spirits, but I was taken aback, almost appalled, by his appearance. The lines of fatigue and strain were furrowed into his big-boned, lantern-jawed face. His complexion, which was naturally sallow rather than ruddy, was now, except for a spot of red on each cheekbone, like dirty soap suds.

'You look a bit done in Patrick.'

'Do I? You look on the point of collapse.' He looked in the mirror which hung over the mantelpiece. He was not handsome, but his face in spite of its corroded look suggested a powerful intelligence, a dominating personality, vigour and success.

'Yes,' he said. 'I do.' He picked up his tankard and sipped, then took a long draught. I did the same. The cold, brilliant drink made its usual delayed impression. I had expected to be welcomed with champagne; Alastair always produced it on anything that could be called an occasion. As he put his tankard down he said: 'I'm whacked to the wide. I've been working too hard—as usual. I don't seem to be able to break myself of the habit.' He frowned. I had heard this before. Alastair believed that there was an optimum amount of work which any individual could do in a given time, and that to exceed this amount meant setting up a system of fatigue, loss of freshness, anxiety and inability to concentrate. He also believed—probably rightly—that he tended to do more than the optimum. There had been a story about Alastair which I had heard in the war. He had been at an important meeting, arguing his case cogently, when he had quite suddenly got up, told the chairman he had just recollected a still more important engagement, and walked out. The room he had left looked over the street, and one of the people present saw Alastair walk into a cinema almost across the way. The cinema, as it happened, was showing a particularly imbecile farce. This incident had been variously taken to indicate arrogance, irresponsibility, dislike of the chairman's pompousness, and incipient mania; actually it was, I think, a perverse flash of the grim seriousness with which Alastair forwarded his ambitions.

'Tell me,' I said, 'what's this about a Lost Weekend treatment? In your letter?'

Alastair picked up his tankard, and a red flame was reflected in it with a beautiful hard clarity.

'This is the beginning of it.'

'What,' I said, 'do you mean—?' I thought Alastair meant we should deliberately get drunk and stay that way. It would not have been out of character.

'Wait a moment.' Alastair drew a pill-box from his waist-coat pocket and took out a pill. 'And this.' He held it out to me, a very small white pill in the flat of his hand.

'What is it?'

'Phenobarbitone. It's what everybody takes. It's a barbiturate, a sedative for cases of anxiety and hypertension. You do suffer from anxiety and hypertension, don't you?—I wouldn't like one of my friends to be abnormal.'

'No,' I said. 'I'm quite normal. But I don't want to fall asleep over my dinner.'

'You won't. This is where we get a little bit more professional. You get sodium amytal when you go to bed.'

I said: 'What *is* this?' I was suddenly uneasy. Had Alastair really taken to drugs? Or was he proposing to do so? His friends had all to be prepared for sudden reckless departures of one kind and another. Once he had been driving me home after dining with me at my club in London, and had suddenly suggested that it would be nice to see the sun rising over the Welsh mountains. So we had gone right on along Piccadilly and Kensington and Hammersmith and out to the Bath Road and so on into Wales. But now he merely shrugged his shoulders.

'Nothing very terrific. It's a kind of continuous sleep treatment for amateurs.'

'The battle-fatigue thing?'

'Exactly. Personally, I'm battle-fatigued to hell.'

'How does it work?'

'The way I fix it, we'd sleep almost all day tomorrow— we can put things to eat and drink in each of our rooms and have a snack when we come to—and then we come to finally on Sunday, maybe about lunch time. You can control the thing well enough, and it's perfectly safe. And then you'll feel like the infant Hercules.'

'Do you do this often?'

'About once a month or so.'

'And it works?'

'Yes, it works. It's an alternative to the alcoholic debauch. It was worked out by a committee of drinking doctors and doctoring drinkers.'

'All right,' I said. I took the pill and swallowed it with a mouthful of champagne.

'You'd better have a bit less all round than I do. It's fine though. . . . When you come round you have euphoria. It's like a very profound religious experience. Not Christian, though. The Old Religion.' He got up, went over to the window, and threw the curtains open. A rush of icy air came in. I knew that window, opening from this building high up on the ridge of the Old Town beside the Castle, must have an aerial view over the New Town. I went over and joined Alastair.

The view was curiously disappointing. It was true that we were looking out over a wide dramatic gulf to the mile of lights, the tram cars which in their smallness and jerkiness were extraordinarily like toys, the effect charmingly neat, bright and theatrical, and the architecture of Princes Street hidden by the merciful darkness. Yet somehow it was commonplace, an arranged 'view'; it lacked the magic it had had in the cold light of early evening. A curious feeling which I had been aware of all day, a feeling of excitement and apprehension, a sense of abnormal circumstances, suddenly passed off. I had returned to a place where I had been when I was young, and I was going to have dinner with Alastair, my old friend. That was all.

It was then that Alastair said: 'I shall be seeing Harvey on Monday.' He closed the window and pulled the curtains, and I had an odd feeling, partly as it seems in the atmosphere, and partly inside myself, like the feeling that presages thunder. It is the feeling which subjects give which are locked away and handled only on special occasions.

'Oh.' Automatically I fumbled for my cigarette case.

'He's had an offer for Kingisbyres.' Across the flame of my lighter I looked at Alastair, while the information drove down into my mind like a plough, disturbing the close-packed soil of old memories, cutting some of the rootlets of my established, solid, resistant life.

'What are you—?' Before I finished my question—and in fact I don't know what I wanted to ask—Alastair closed the window with a bang, and the stream of cold air was shut off.

'I'll tell you all about it,' he said, 'but later some time.'

Alastair stood up, and a mat fell off the table on to the floor. The table had not only the disarranged air of any table after a good meal, but the truly chaotic appearance which men accustomed to be looked after give to any domestic job. The kitchen, where we had attacked the food parcels which Alastair had had sent to himself from New York, looked like a battlefield. Neither of us could cook anything at all elaborate, but it didn't matter; from the soup to the cheese straws everything had been pretty well ready to serve.

During dinner we had talked about all kinds of things, personal and impersonal, my affairs and Alastair's. Now, as he got coffee, we were talking about his, about 'the Organization', as he called it, 'the plush-linedest market research outfit in the world' as it had been described in *Fortune*. As soon as we began to talk about it I realized, not only from his surface of wise-cracking ebullience, but from an inner feeling which I sensed, a feeling of quiet and power such as one might get from a Rolls-Royce engine, that he was pleased with the way things were going, yet as unsatisfied, as ferociously ambitious, as ever.

'Took a Glasgow boy on last week,' he said, 'and only on Wednesday I saw him looking at me like he might be thinking of taking over my job. I know that look. I've seen its remains in mirrors.' He poured a little brandy into his coffee, lifted the cup, and said: 'Here's tae us, wha's like us!' He laughed shortly. 'Bankers, industrialists, colonial governors, planters, engineers—all over the world you find a Scotch success-maniac getting an edge on the locals. Getting an edge on the Jews. Getting an edge on Armenians even. Look at me! Look at you!— well, look at half of you anyway.' Restlessly he got up, went over to the window, and pulled back the curtain again.

'There it is,' he said. 'A good country to be born in— a good country to grow up in—it makes you crazy to get out and make some money and raise some hell. Don't you think so?'

'As you know,' I said, 'I'm only half-Scotch and I don't live in Scotland.'

'On the other hand you don't want to get too goddam casual about coming from a poverty-stricken, exploited, underdeveloped country. In this post-war world it's an asset. . . . Listen Patrick—the world holds no future for the English gent.'

'It's what you aimed to be once.'

'It's what the whole world aimed to be once. But that was before 1939. Speaking personally, I wasn't a particularly well-informed economist then. But I am now.'

'Tell me,' I said, 'do you remember a conversation we once had about national character?'

'I dare say I remember more than one. At one time it was quite a favourite subject of yours. Do you remember— when you used to believe Rupert of Hentzau was the rightful King of Scotland? Anyway, what did I say about national character?'

'You said it was bunk.'

'Then I was a sensible boy. It *is* bunk. Now'—almost as though he was afraid I was going to interrupt him, he looked at his watch—'it's time for the next part of the treatment.'

'Wait,' I said. 'Who's the offer from?' Alastair half turned and looked out of the window again.

'The National Coal Board. They want it for offices and a training scheme.'

'I suppose they'll knock it about?'

'They're going to enlarge it. Also it appears there's surface coal there that was never worth mining before. It's ironical.'

'Opencast mining?' I said. 'That means they'll tear the whole place open down to fifty feet?'

'Yes.'

'And have you any views about that?' Alastair jerked the curtains shut and turned towards me as though I had challenged him.

'None of my business.' His expression was one that was familiar to me, a harsh, sulky expression. 'For God's sake Patrick—we've all got the future round our necks. It's bad enough without having the past as well. Anyway, there's nothing I could do about it.'

'That's not what you're seeing Harvey about?'

'No. Of course not.' I was going to say something more, but as Alastair moved from the window to the fire I saw his face in the light, and it had a leaden grey tinge that alarmed me.

'Right,' I said, 'the next part of the treatment.' He yawned.

'Better get undressed first. Don't want to go to bed with my shoes on.'

'If you feel like that why do you need anything more?'

'Doesn't do to underdose. Come on.' He led me across the hall to my bedroom, and as I undressed I heard him washing. When I had washed I found him sitting on his bed pouring orange juice from a can into a glass.

'I've taken my dose,' he said. 'Now you take yours. You'll probably come to around eleven tomorrow, and hunger will drive you to get up about twelve. Get your-self breakfast—I've laid out. . . .' He began giving me directions, about my breakfast, and what to do when he himself came round. Then about my own procedure. 'The best thing for you, on the modified treatment, would be to take a stroll, have something to eat say about five, and then take another dose.' He yawned, threw back the sheets, and got into bed. We gossiped for a few minutes about people we knew and I heard his voice getting drowsy.

'God,' he said, 'it's beginning.' His face was visibly relaxed. 'Glad you were able to come. Must have some-one—not safe to do it all oneself.' He yawned again. 'Eat the whole box—pee the bed for sure. For God's sake see I don't. . . .'

'Of course I shall.'

'Like a happy death, this. Don't forget your own dose.'

'I won't,' I said, and rose to my feet.

'Listen,' said Alastair, 'there's one thing in my apartment in New York . . . your picture of Kingisbyres.' I was astonished.

'That water-colour?'

'Yes.' Alastair's voice was very drowsy now. 'The Captain . . . from the Captain. You know.'

'Yes,' I said. I turned off the light and moved to the door quietly. As I reached it, he spoke again.

'Patrick?' It was surprisingly clear.

'Yes?'

'I was going to talk to you about Kingisbyres. . . .' I waited a moment, then realized that he was sound asleep. I yawned deeply and made for my bed. As I got into it I found to my surprise that, for some reason which I had forgotten, there were tears in my eyes.

Part Two

I WAS JUST fifteen—approaching sixteen—when I first saw Kingisbyres House, and Alastair and I were at Nethervale School. Although we were in the same House at school, it was only about six months before that first visit to Kingisbyres that we had become friends. My earlier memories of Alastair are vague; they add up to an impression of a big, raw-boned, tough boy, with a persistent noisy sniff and a broad accent, who was always slamming doors. I disliked him. For that matter I disliked most of the boys.

Nethervale School had been founded some time before the first war with the aim of turning the sons of Scottish business men into passable imitations of the products of English schools which had as their aim the turning of the sons of English business men into passable imitations of English gentlemen. The results were unpleasing. We, the boys at Nethervale, were about half-way through what might be called the Scottish dream, or how to get from the suburbs of Glasgow to the depths of Gloucestershire in three generations. No one who cared about education, or was himself decently educated, could ever have sent his son there.

My father was mathematics master at Nethervale. He was there because of the letters MA (Cantab) which he was entitled to put after his name; that he had been a scholar of Trinity, and got a First Class in both parts of the Tripos, could not be flaunted, even by the Headmaster; it would have made even the most ignorant of parents—for if they were ignorant they were canny—suspect that there was some disreputable reason for his being at Nethervale. And this was the case. My father had gone to Cambridge from Glasgow University, and his real aim had always been to return to one of the Scottish universities and teach mathematics there. But his Cambridge year had been a brilliant one, he had missed a fellowship, and when he had been offered a post as mathematics master in a small public school he had accepted it for the time being because he believed it would give him time to do research. But it turned out that his real gift was not for research, but teaching, and above all for coaching boys who were trying for university scholarships. When he was twenty-seven he was offered a much better job in one of the leading public schools. In the following year he married my mother. But with all the characteristic Scotch dourness he had forced himself to continue to do research. I suppose it was the strain of this which had driven him to start drinking.

My mother was the daughter of a retired naval officer who lived near the school. Her father had been invalided out of the Navy while only a Lieutenant-Commander, and he supplemented his pension by writing boys' books, which he illustrated himself with drawings of sailing ships. He also gave lectures; it was through a lecture which my grandfather gave at the school that my father came to meet my mother. But not only did—School, as it were give me my being; it gave its particular shape to the first ten years of my life. The house in which we lived was one of a small terrace of Georgian houses belonging to the school and all occupied by masters; my childhood walks were along the towing path to watch the school Eight at practice; under the lime trees at the edge of the Senior Turf I soaked in the strawberries-and-cream leisure of English summer afternoons.

But there were other memories. One is of finding my father unconscious in the coal cellar with the whites of his eyes gleaming horribly through half-shut lids and a little stream of saliva and whisky still moving slowly across the purplish scarlet of his cheek. This must have been in the holidays, for I was already at a private school which specialized in preparing boys for—It had always been taken for granted that I was going on there in due course. But this didn't happen. I don't think my father was actually sacked; but the effect was the same. If it had not been for

my mother—her ability to manage my father, to conceal
his worst excesses, to plead on his behalf—the end would
have come much sooner. After a dreadful interlude working
at a crammer's in London, he managed to get himself
accepted as a mathematics master at Nethervale, and I
found myself a pupil there. It is very hard for a child to
get over a come-down like that, and I was angry and hurt
and contemptuous of my surroundings.

Yet in many ways these were not unpleasant. During the
week I lived in one of the Houses, a square hygienic-looking
building that stood among the trees surrounding the main
school building. Considering what a young cub I must have
been, I got on well enough both with the masters and
the boys. I even had a particular set of friends, although
none really intimate. My parents' house, where I spent
weekends as well as holidays, was a large square cottage
on the edge of the village. By being at home at these times
I got what was perhaps the best of my father, for his serious
drinking—except for breakdowns, which became rarer—
was now almost entirely confined to the holidays and to
weekends, and even at the weekends he managed, with my
mother's help, to remain quite presentable. The result of
this was that he had two quite distinct personalities. During
the week—if I called at home and saw him there—he was
the picture of a disappointed man, silent, irritable, and
bitter, speaking to me only to remind me that 'my present
salary doesn't run to' whatever mild extravagance I had
committed, or to remark every now and again that unless I
changed my way of life I would end up in the gutter. Worst
of all were the hours of coaching in mathematics which
he gave me every week. My father's talent for coaching
brilliant boys was remarkable, and he was good all the way
down to the level of normal ability. But he was not much
good at teaching complete dunces, and with his own son
he was useless. I remember how, as the lesson wore on, he
gradually became pale round the mouth with impatience,
frustration, and sheer rage. When drinking, on the other
hand, but while not yet drunk, he was the Professor that,
perhaps, he really deserved to have been, polite, detached,
existing on a plane a little above worldly cares.

But of course there were a lot of things which his salary in fact didn't run to, and whisky was expensive, and so in our square stone cottage on the edge of the smoky village we lived that ghastly kind of life in which, even if you never suffer from hunger, you never have a really good meal, are never chronically cold, but never have a decent fire, have shoes that keep out the rain, but take a threepenny bus ride to a man who repairs them for sixpence less. We might have spent more, but my mother, never wholly confident about the outcome of her long battle with my father's drinking, insisted upon saving against a day of worse disaster. Like everyone who knew my mother I admired her; with her resolution, which was modest and generally cheerful, she illustrated the possibility of the good man's being happy upon the rack; but this is a possibility which most people would rather have as a reserve for inspiration than as a spectacle for daily contemplation. As for me I was neither good nor happy; I fell often into a state of rebellious self-pity.

Alastair's case was very different. He was generally considered lucky to be at Nethervale at all. He came from one of the local villages where, in the holidays, he lived with an aunt who had a shop, a small ironmonger's shop. When I first knew him his manners had a raw uncouthness which I thought was deliberate, and which, he told me afterwards, *was* at least half-deliberate where I was concerned. For in me he detected that romantic social snobbery, that school-accent-background-birth-culture-snobbery, the English snobbery which differed from our indigenous and rudimentary Nethervale snobbery about the size of car owned by one's father. None of the well-off young oafs who made up this school ever ventured to express any contempt for Alastair because he lived with an aunt who kept a wee shoppie. Many of them, of course, came from families which had made their money out of shops, but these were big shops, chain or department stores, and the present generation of owners didn't work behind the counter in them. But it was not a sense of propriety which kept them quiet.

'Poor brutes,' Alastair said to me once. 'They're all scared of great-uncle Sandy.'

'Whose great-uncle Sandy?'

'They've all got a great-uncle Sandy, an old terror who still wears enormous boots and steel-rimmed specs and speaks as broad as the North Sea, who will insist on coming downstairs at tea-parties and shaming everybody by talking about the days when he and grandpa sold vegetables off a barrow. In England they'd have him locked up in a bin, or put down like an old dog; but here they daren't. People might say they were stuck-up, and being stuck-up is a crime in Scotland. That's why everybody who makes money leaves it in the end. What's the good of making money if you can't be stuck-up?'

This exposition was given, of course, after we became friends. If I mention some of the things which lay behind our becoming friends I don't want to suggest that I am explaining *why* we became friends. That, I suppose, was as mysterious as it usually is. Still, friends often do have something in common, or something which they gain from one another; and this was so with Alastair and myself. He was, as I found in the course of the first confidential conversation I ever had with him, exceedingly ambitious. He wanted to go to the Bar.

'The Scots Bar?' I asked. We were walking back to have a shower after punting a rugger ball about. I was carrying the ball and I remember the heavy sodden feel of it. The afternoon was already murky.

'No. The English Bar. I might as well have a go at it. If you do well you make a lot more—if you don't what's the difference?' Because of this ambition of his I had a kind of fascination for him. I represented the country he was setting out to conquer; in me he could study the kind of knowledge which I had brought with me from —— and which was regularly renewed by my holiday visits to English relations—and which perhaps he might learn from me how to use. Above all the snobbishness, that English snobbishness which I defiantly cultivated and flaunted, and which Alastair detested with all the force of Scotch democratic puritanism, aroused him as Susanna roused the Elders. For my mother, who was untainted by this snobbishness, Alastair conceived an admiration and a fondness which drew him to her whenever school routine allowed it. For me Alastair had the attraction of someone who was determined to rise to the top of the world from which I had been ejected, and who by the strength of his determination seemed already to belong to it. But he had something else as well; he was on visiting terms at Kingisbyres House.

Kingisbyres was the big house of the village in which Alastair's aunt had her wee shoppie. It was a seventeenth-century house, built on the site of a much older keep, but it was in all the guidebooks mainly because of Bonny Prince Charlie's Coat. Bonny Prince Charlie's Coat was the subject of a celebrated legend. The story was that the Keith of that day, one of the very few lowland lairds who were 'out' in the Forty-Five, was at a levee at Holyrood House when he noticed a stain on the coat that the Prince had just put on. He pointed it out, and the Prince smiled, took the coat off, and handed it over to him with the words: 'Keep it, Keith, and one day the King will come and muck out his byres in it.' 'His chamber will aye be ready,' Keith replied, and sent instructions accordingly. And the room was prepared, and was kept ready, with a fire and a warming pan in the bed every night, and the coat in a wardrobe, 'from that day to this', as the guidebooks said, 'awaiting the arrival of a Stuart King, to "muck out his byres".'

At the time of which I am writing a descendant of this Keith was still the Laird of Kingisbyres. It was he, in fact, Captain Keith, who had provided the money for Alastair to go to Nethervale. Apart from the headmaster, the headmaster's secretary, and perhaps my father, I was the only person who knew this. There was always this slight air of mystery about Alastair, and about how he came to be at Nethervale—which actually cost as much as a good school—and Alastair did nothing to dispel this mystery. When he told me that it was Captain Keith who paid his fees he swore me to secrecy.

We were sitting, or rather crouching, in the lee of a dry-stone dyke on the moors; the wind was hissing across the heads of the tufty moorland grass, but because we were supposed to be on a run we were only wearing shorts and thin short-sleeved shirts. We were each, I remember, smoking a cigarette very fast, as though for a bet, because we were already late, and because custom and honour required that everyone should stop and smoke a cigarette during a run. Because of the chattering of my teeth, and the wind, I had had great difficulty in getting mine lit at all.

'I expect,' I said, 'that Keith's got plenty of money to throw about.' I had a rather vague idea that it was less humiliating to accept charity from a rich man, and especially perhaps from a spendthrift rich man who perhaps hardly knew what he did with his money.

'He hasn't,' said Alastair. 'He's poor. He lets the shooting, of course, but it doesn't bring in much.' Alastair's teeth also by this time were chattering; his face was blue and his legs were crawling with gooseflesh, but he hadn't finished. 'Not that he g-g-'—he controlled his chattering with an effort—'gives a damn about money.' As he got up and started to trot on I noticed how enormous were the holes in the heels of his socks.

Not long after this conversation Alastair asked me to join him on a visit to Kingisbyres. He told me that Captain Keith asked him once or twice each year, and that the invitation had always asked him to bring a friend, if he cared to, but he had never done so.

It was a Sunday afternoon in the summer term when we went. Sunday afternoons were the only time, at Nethervale, when there seemed to develop silence and a feeling of private life, and on a hot summer day the sense of isolation among the trees—the main school building had once been a private house wrapped away in its woods upon the edge of the moors—was, by contrast with the clattering door-slamming turmoil of the week, almost monastic. I remember the heavy smell of conifers in the sun, and of damp woodland drying out, as we cycled along the drive, and the contrast as we emerged at the lodge gates and turned upwards on to the moors, where the breeze hardly ever dies completely away, and the air is intensely clear and cool, yet with a flavour in it, a very subtle flavour, like spring water.

Then, after we had climbed up on to a high open plateau

on the moor, a kind of inverted saucer naked to the wind, we reached the almost imperceptible crest, and started running down to Kingisbyres. The village of Kingisbyres lay in a little valley; I had passed through it often; it was a sheltered little place, rather pretty and cosy with its neat stone cottages and a graceful bridge over the river. There were no mines here to spoil the countryside and enrich its owner. The house lay beyond, half a mile up the hill, isolated behind a high shabby greenish stone wall that ran beside the road for hundreds of yards, and by great ramparts of trees. The lodge-gates were set back across a vast sweep of weedy gravel, and even the shade and the smells as we began to cycle along the drive seemed to have an altogether different quality from Nethervale. At Nethervale everything was well-kept in a utilitarian way: the surface of the drive for instance, or the grass borders of it; the fences; the woods themselves, where the undergrowth was cut back, fallen elm boughs removed, and saplings replanted. Nethervale House itself, a half-hearted Victorian Gothic edifice, although very large, somehow failed to attract attention. Everything was impersonal, institutional, open to the day; it was hygienic, and even in the holidays it had the look in every corner of a place frequented by many people.

Here at Kingisbyres the drive was rutted and weedy, the woods overgrown and choked, dark even under the sun, holding the house and its grounds like the dark skin of a plum. As I turned into the drive and began to cycle through the woods I was impatient and excited. For my imagination had fastened upon this house. During my first years in Scotland I had been passionately anti-Scottish, hating the dourness, the unsmiling lack of grace, the vulgarity and pushfulness which I found at Nethervale, and projecting my hatred upon the whole country. Later I had come to see a more complex picture; kindness, sharpness, bawdy wit in the working people with whom I had few contacts; the history of a graceful, violent, aristocratic past with which I had no contact at all. It was to Kingisbyres that I looked for this contact. It was a dramatic surprise to emerge from the trees and to see the house itself, a high dark shape, a little gaunt, yet domestic, standing on its eminence against the background of the hill which sheltered it. It lived up to my imagination, making upon me a striking impression, an impression of isolation and self-containment and yet at the same time of homeliness and even of welcome. Seen from that distance, it seemed not particularly large; close at hand it grew again, until, as we approached the high narrow steps which led to the main door, it appeared august and formidable, a house only just emerged from a medieval keep, a castle only half-domesticated.

The door was opened to us by an old man in a white linen jacket and very baggy dusty-looking striped trousers. He was tall and upright about the shoulders, with big gnarled hands, and for a moment, recalling what Alastair had said about his poverty, I thought this was Captain Keith himself. I was just about to shake hands with him when I remembered that Alastair had mentioned once that Captain Keith was looked after by a servant, called Henstridge, who had once been his batman. Afterwards I blushed to think of the gaffe I had almost made; later still I came to see that Kingisbyres was a realization of the social novice's dream—a place where you could shake hands with the butler, drink your tea from the saucer or your port from the decanter without its being remarked as anything but a personal eccentricity.

'The Capting,' Henstridge said, 'is in the loibry.' He had an old-fashioned, adenoidal, aitch-dropping, cockney accent, such as I had not heard for years, and a manner of confidential respectfulness which contrasted strikingly with the mixed sourness and familiarity of the servants employed by the school. But he announced us formally, even with an air, as we entered the library and met our host.

My first impressions of Captain Keith were disappointing. Half-consciously I had expected someone tall, stately, dreaming; the reality was a neat, wiry, squirearchical personage in a grey check suit. Both his gestures and his speech had a jerky, military quality, which gave him an alert, on-the-spot air.

'Let's go out,' he said. 'Pity to be indoors on a day like this.'

My disappointment grew; it was a schoolmasterly remark, such as one was accustomed to hearing at Nethervale, but unworthy of its present author. But as he turned towards the door—preceded by a small thin spaniel—the coat of his jacket caught something that stood on the edge of the table—I didn't quite see what it was, perhaps a small ashtray—and knocked it to the floor. I made a move to pick it up, but before I could do so Captain Keith put his toe at it and lobbed it deliberately across the room into the fireplace, where it crashed into the fireirons with a great rattle. At the same moment he gave me a quick, odd look, conspiratorial and yet derisory, and laughed.

'I think *that* defeated the goalkeeper,' he said, and it seemed to me that after all he was not ordinary, and I was pleased. And as we made our way along a narrow passage, down a steep twisted flight of stairs, and out through a stone-flagged garden-room, on to a lawn at the side of the house, my initial disappointment was further lightened. The house had some atmosphere that was worthy of its legend, communicating its sense of the past in a series of faint stirs and recognitions, just as, when one reached the lawn, there were breaths of wallflower from the beds under the windows, of mown grass, of herbs or perhaps of heather, and the curious indescribable heavy smell that a yew-hedge on our left gave off under the hot sun.

We walked slowly round the house talking about cricket. I fancy that it was I who introduced this subject, in the belief that it was 'suitable'. After a few moments the Captain asked Alastair whether *he* liked cricket, and Alastair said no, he played it because it was compulsory but it bored him.

'I played it at school,' said the Captain, 'but to tell you the truth'—he smiled at me, as it were apologetically but also a little mockingly—'I thought it gey dreich. You know what that means? It means rather dreary.' Although I was a little disconcerted at the idea that I was being laughed at, I also felt that we had got somewhere, broken through one of the paper walls which must be got through on the way to friendship or even acquaintanceship.

And this proved to be the case. The Captain began to

'show us round' more specifically, walking us over to the Italian garden, pointing out there a window from which a great-aunt had climbed when she eloped; and there a well the water from which by tradition gave women the gift of fertility. The well-head was built of roughly hewn stones, one or two of which had fallen and lay half-sunk in the roughly cropped grass. The whole thing looked like an eighteenth-century water-colour.

'People used to come from all over the countryside for a bottle of the water—brides used to drink it on their wedding day. It's even gone to Canada—a local girl who went out there sent back for a bottle for her sister-in-law. It worked too.' I smiled, tentatively, but the Captain apparently did not see my smile: at any rate he didn't smile himself. But after a moment he laughed suddenly, an impressive, braying, hereditary laugh: 'Haw, haw—haw, haw, haw.' I didn't know what to make of this.

Suddenly, as though in reply to his laughter, a bell rang, sharp and crystalline and brief. We resumed our tour, without loitering now, and when we completed it, and found ourselves suddenly on the same little lawn, tea had been laid out in the shade of a garden shelter, and three deckchairs had been set up. The canvas of the shelter and the chairs was faded to a blanched greeny shade, in which the original stripes could be discerned only with difficulty. Kingisbyres on the whole, I thought, was rather surprisingly shabby. The tea itself was heroic, oatcakes and farm butter and new-baked scones and jam and cream and rich dark fruitcake. It was so obviously a 'schoolboy's tea', and I thought rather sniffishly, as I sat down, that it was really more suitable for boys of twelve than for ourselves, but as it turned out we all three did very well, and in the end I had eaten prodigiously and drunk six cups of tea.

It was then that Captain Keith said that he would show us the King's Chamber.

'I expect you would like to see the King's Chamber?' The question—if it was a question—was addressed to me. Alastair had seen the King's Chamber before. When I said yes, I should like very much to see it, we got up out of our deckchairs. It was then, before we had even entered the house, that something happened. The place where we were standing—the little enclosed lawn—was suddenly stirred by a faint breeze, warm and perfumed with the scents of the moors, which rustled the yew hedge and touched my cheek. I saw both the worn stone of the old house and the panorama of the moors, their timeless pattern of receding planes, and suddenly my mind was caught by a vivid sense of the past, of the actuality of the scene which had occurred between Keith and the Prince, of its independence of the views that people held about it. For an instant I could almost see in my mind's eye the scene which had never happened—the arrival of King Charles at Kingisbyres. I saw the King as a man still young, but with that fine melancholy Stuart air transmuted into a professional graciousness, greeting his faithful Keith of Kingisbyres by putting his elegant gauntleted hand on his shoulder with a kind of tired cynical kindness.

The moment of enlivened imagination faded with the breeze, and as we went into the house it faded still more. Yet it did not fade entirely—or at least it left behind it the possibility of a return—and it was only the King's Chamber itself which finished this. For this room, somehow vaguely ecclesiastical, tapestry-hung, and smelling of polish with its carved four-poster bed which was kept always made and ready, the fireplace in which, in winter, a log fire burned day and night, seemed more like a museum than like a living reality, while the coat seemed merely an exhibit in an exhibition of costume through the ages.

I was more interested in Captain Keith himself. He was business-like, giving information in his clipped soldierly voice as though he were a paid guide, perhaps a retired sergeant-major in a military museum. His small moustache, his short-cut stubby hair bristling iron-grey, his rather faded look, as though, like his deckchairs, he had been left out for years in the sun, his jerky precision and his blunt-fingered hands rummaging in a tobacco pouch— they were all very military, all very much 'typed'. Only his laugh, his pealing 'haw–haw–haw' was something rather special, perhaps acquired like the coat from Prince Charles Edward.

Apart from this he seemed oddly unconnected with what he was showing us, curiously impersonal. Then at one point he looked at Alastair, who was puzzling over a document which hung in a frame on the wall, and began twitting him about his difficulty in reading the Latin. His voice was rough and loud and jolly: ' "and further thereto shall be entitled and empowered"—that's pretty easy, heh, imagine letting an ignorant old soldier teach you Latin.' He might have been any old gentleman going through the well-worn forms of entertaining a couple of schoolboys to tea. Only I realized that as he translated he was not in fact looking at the elegant faded script, but that he knew the writ by heart.

He showed us all over the house, mixing anecdotes of his own childhood with legends that went back to the seventeenth century. Cheerful, a little garrulous in his slightly harsh staccato voice, he was on the whole a good raconteur. The time passed quickly; when we finally arrived back at the little room in which we had first found him, Alastair and I suddenly realized at the same moment that we should be very late for supper.

'Oh, that's all right.' He was fumbling with the stopper of a decanter on a tray of drinks which had been set down on the table. 'Tell them I detained you. They won't mind.' There was arrogance in his remark; it was hard to say whether it was cynical or innocent. In any case, what he said was of course perfectly true; to have been detained by Captain Keith of Kingisbyres was an excuse of almost impudent perfection.

'You'll have a glass of sherry before you go?' We accepted, Alastair reluctantly because his aunt was 'Temperance', and myself blushing with pleasure. It was, if not perhaps the first time that either of us had ever been offered an alcoholic drink, certainly the first time that the offer had been made apparently casually and as a matter of course. The Captain handed us our glasses. We were all standing beside the tray of drinks, on which, among the bottles, decanters, and so on, was also the jug from which the Captain had just poured water into his whisky. As he lifted his glass he made a quick gesture and said: 'Gentlemen, the King!

You know what that means? It means the "King over the water"—I passed the glass over the water, you see.' Since I was standing beside the table, I too passed my glass over the water, responded 'The King', and took a mouthful of sherry. It tasted, I thought, disagreeable but interesting. Then it seemed to me that Captain Keith was looking at me with a curious, quizzical expression, and I suddenly wondered whether he had, after all, merely been inquiring whether we knew the famous Jacobite toast. Or had he actually proposed it—seriously—half seriously? And had he taken my gesture of response—made half in mere idleness, half out of a kind of curiosity to see what it felt like—in the same way? In my uncertainty I suddenly blushed, consciously, burningly. Alastair, who was standing so that the Captain could not see him, scowled at me and drank his sherry in an uneasy silence.

As we began to cycle home I was very polite to Alastair and said that it had all been very interesting and I had enjoyed myself very much. He received these courtesies glumly, and after a time he said: 'You made a fine fool of yourself drinking that toast.'

'He meant me to.' Very angry because I was embarrassed and self-conscious, I hated Alastair's heavy and disapproving face.

'Away, man,'—Alastair used such contemptuous Scotch phrases with devastating effect—'he was only showing you how it was done.'

'No, he meant me to.' Weakly, I could only repeat this unconvincing phrase.

'You mean he was serious? He was seriously drinking a toast to what's his name—Rupert of Hentzau? Rudolph of Bavaria?'

'Perhaps he was.' Braving Alastair's scorn, I had stuck to my guns, but I was surprised to learn from what he said next that I had apparently shaken him.

'Well if he was then he's cracked, and you needn't make him worse.'

'Don't be such an ass. How could *I* make him worse?' I allowed my embarrassment to turn happily into irritation. 'He's not a child. What if he is cracked, anyway? What if

I do make him worse? What's it got to do with you?' There was a brief pause as we cycled beside one another; then Alastair looked across with his heavy, hard look.

'It's got this to do with me,' he said. 'He's maybe my father.'

'What rot!' I said, but my voice sounded thin and uncertain. Alastair's suggestion, whether credible or not, suggested a whole world of concealed relationships, hidden actions, guilty secrets; a world of things like my father's drinking, an adult, frightening world. So Alastair's statement gave me a profound shock. 'What on earth makes you think that?'

'Oh, I haven't got a case that would sound well in court.' As he spoke I realized that Alastair was nervous, and this disconcerted me almost as much as his original statement. I had never seen him in any kind of abnormal emotional state before.

'The first thing is, he really is poor. He's not in a position to be paying for me at school. So why does he?' Alastair paused. We were coasting down a long gentle slope at the time; no effort was required, hardly even the effort of steering the bicycle. When he went on it was with the same kind of controlled speed as the bicycles. 'And then about my parents. My aunt is my aunt all right—I mean my mother was her sister. I know all about that. And my mother was married to my father. I've seen her marriage certificate. My father is supposed to have deserted her and gone back to sea—he had been a ship's engineer before—he came from Greenock. You see my mother left Kingisbyres soon after war broke out, to go into munitions. She went to England—at least, she was supposed to have—there was some mystery about that. And Captain Keith was in England then—he was wounded in the retreat from Mons. And my aunt won't ever say anything about my father, though of course that might be because of the way he behaved. . . . But then there's the other side of it—Captain Keith I mean. More than once, when I was very young— about five—he came to my aunt's house, and I heard them talking for a long time, and it was something serious—you can tell from people's voices, can't you?' He looked at me for confirmation, and I nodded; we were both near enough to childhood to have that clear recollection of that special quality in adult voices.

'Oh, and there's all kinds of things,' Alastair burst out. 'Things people have said to me in the village, and the way Captain Keith himself treats me—honestly, there is something funny. I know there is, and what else could it be? It's obvious enough, when it strikes you.'

I was deeply stirred and excited, but I hardly knew what I felt, let alone knew what to say. Fortunately I was saved by a hill, and for some minutes we needed all our breath for pedalling. And now I began to wonder whether what Alastair had said was true. When he had spoken first he had convinced me by a kind of shock effect, but now that was wearing off and I became doubtful. I didn't think that he had been making it up—that idea never crossed my mind; but I wondered whether he had made correct deductions from the evidence. There were things that made me think that he had. The first point I was clear about was that Alastair was an altogether exceptional person— exceptional on account of brains alone if on account of nothing else—and an exceptional origin seemed natural for him. My second argument was a contradictory one— that the origin was not very exceptional. That such things happened I knew very well. There was a village not so far away, at the gates of a great house, of which it was said that, however many people were about, you saw only one nose—a prominent nose having been the characteristic feature of successive earls and their progeny. Moreover, I was prepared to accept the evidence I had not heard in detail. Every child knows that the whole adult world is a vast conspiracy of silence, and although at the age which Alastair and I had then reached we had pretty largely broken into this conspiracy, we still remembered what it was like to be outside it.

When the conversation was resumed I quickly turned it to another subject. Looking back, I wonder how I can have been so gauche. It was, in a way, against my own wishes, for I valued Alastair's confidence and was flattered that he had given it to me. It was simply that I found the conversation difficult and embarrassing and after my first few attempts did not know how to conduct it. Alastair was however not in the least hurt or disappointed. Anyone at Nethervale School capable of being hurt or disappointed by crudity and lack of ease would long since have committed suicide.

TWO

THAT SUMMER holidays—the first after Alastair and I had become friends—we spent a lot of time at Kingisbyres. Alastair was of course living at home, and we, as a family, never had any regular summer holiday because it was at this time that my father did most of his drinking. This no longer made us a particularly unhappy household—it only made us immobile. In previous summers I had gone with my English cousins to the sea; but this year my mother had agreed to let me stop at home. Both my parents approved of my friendship with Alastair. His mathematical ability made him my father's favourite pupil, and that was that. With my mother the position was more complex.

'I am sure Alastair will do well in the world,' she said to me one day. 'I hope he will do good in it.' When I told Alastair of this, he smiled and said: 'If I do well I shall owe much of it to your father; if I don't do good it won't be your mother's fault.'

On our visits to Kingisbyres we did not always enter the house. Captain Keith had given us the freedom of the policies—as the grounds surrounding a house are called in Scotland—and we used this discreetly, making friends with the two keepers and religiously avoiding any disturbance of the grouse. I expect it is an illusion, but in my recollections of this period it is always summer, hot but with cool intermittent breezes from the moors, and with the noise of running water almost always audible either clearly or in the background. We found a place in the river where the water, after miles of sun-warmed shallows, suddenly collected in a deep clear golden pool, and we dived there— it was nearly ten feet deep at its deepest, yet not broad enough for more than a few strokes—and lay on our backs at the bottom, holding ourselves down by the edges of the

great smooth stones, and looked up at the circle of brilliant
light which was the surface. This pool lay in a little gulley,
it was completely shut away, sheltered, secure, and private.
To have it to ourselves, to know that it was guarded by
keepers, was to have a little taste of what privilege might
mean.

But often, too, we went to the house. Sometimes we went
round to the little courtyard by the old coach-house, where
in the evenings Henstridge sat polishing shoes, and while he
went through an immense ritual with damp rags and methy-
lated spirits and chamois leather, he told us, in his old-
fashioned cockney voice, very shocking anecdotes about his
life as a young guardsman in Edwardian London. Yet by far
the most important time was the time we spent with Captain
Keith himself. As we got to know him better my first
impression of him began to change. I no longer saw him
as a stereotype of the retired-soldier-country-gentleman.
That, of course, with his pepper-and-salt or check suits,
his breeches, his faded old green hat, his barking way
of speaking and his stumping way of walking, was what
he still looked and sounded like, the more so since he
was impatient about small things, and used to flush with
annoyance and swear under his breath at a lost tobacco
pouch or a jammed window or a deedbox that wouldn't
open. Sometimes, at such moments, he was completely the
retired colonel of the cartoons. But after a time I realized
that what appeared as impatience was only something to
which he had given this appearance; really it was a kind of
physical flamboyance, which, for the rest, showed itself in
his habit of semi-deliberately dropping things on the floor
and then kicking them across the room. And although
he had this retired-colonel *appearance* he didn't have the
interests that go with it. Except as a matter of convention,
he didn't care for fishing or shooting, he wasn't interested
in the army and never thought of himself as having been a
soldier. He was however a very good landlord, passionately
interested in the welfare of his tenants and in local politics
in so far as they contributed to this.

But his main interest, at least the interest about which
he mainly spoke to us, was the history of Kingisbyres.

And he spoke about this a great deal. As I swam in the deep pool of the river, so I swam in the deep pool of the past. It became intimately familiar to me. Alastair did not share this interest; at least he derided it, calling it morbid and sentimental. When I pored over old papers he called me an archivist, and when I began cleaning the collection of old weapons he called me a museum curator. Both were terms of contempt. Yet he usually gave me a hand in such tasks. And he listened to the Captain's stories with respect, and sometimes something more.

'We're standing on the foundations now.' The Captain measured a distance with his eye. 'Yes, that's right. We dug them up once—you can see where the trench was. The cottage probably faced that way, so the back wall would be *there*.' He jerked his finger at a spot on the rough whinny grass. And there, where he pointed, a man had been shot, with his wife and two children for audience, and his cottage had been burned to the ground to give the firing party light to see by, and the walls knocked down so that it would never be worth the trouble of rebuilding. The man who had been shot, so the record said, was a 'pigman to the Laird of Kingisbyres', and the men who had shot him were Covenanters.

'It doesn't really say anything,' Alastair said, 'about *why* they shot him.' We had spent a lot of time deciphering the faded ink on the dry, brittle paper. The Captain smiled.

'Probably he'd saved up a stockingful of silver pieces.'

'Do you really think it might be just that?' Cautiously, because he did not want to appear naïve, Alastair expressed the shocked doubts which we both felt.

'It isn't the kind of thing you learn about the Covenanters at school, eh?' The Captain smiled again. Sometimes he seemed disturbingly shrewd, as though he could read exactly what was in our minds.

'I didn't mean that exactly. . . .' Alastair hesitated, since in fact that was what he had meant exactly. 'Well, I suppose in a way I did. I mean one doesn't have to accept the Whig version of history wholesale in order to—to—' he hesitated again, for the phrase 'the Whig version of history' was

an impressive one which he expected to do his arguing
for him.

'You should always remember that history is written
by the side that wins. It's one of the advantages of winning.' The Captain did not appear to have heard Alastair's
attempts at learned qualifications.

'Well in this particular case they didn't win. It was at any
rate a draw.' Alastair looked at the Captain as it were for
confirmation, although this was unnecessary, as we had all
studied the same source, the only source, so far as we knew,
that existed of knowledge about this microscopic piece of
history. The leader of the band who had shot the pigman
had been taken prisoner and brought to Kingisbyres House,
where he had been found hanged from the highest branch
of the highest tree in the policies, 'doubtless' as the record
urbanely put it 'having taen his own life either from remorse
or from apprehension of the justice quhilk wd. be servit
to him'.

Alastair quoted this now, with a quiet, baleful relish, and
suddenly began to laugh. The Captain's haw-haw-haw rang
out but died quickly in the breeze that blew across the little
plateau on the side of the moorland valley on which we
stood, this deserted, modestly idyllic spot where a murder
had been committed, but Alastair's echoed it, almost on
the same note, a laugh that did not at that moment seem
only a curious survival, but an expression of pride and
exultation and power. And suddenly the infection caught
me, and I laughed too, feeling what it would be like to exact
vengeance, to be secret and powerful, to be feared. But for
me this feeling was spoilt by doubts, by uneasy movements
of conscience and reason. I prided myself on being civilized,
and this feeling was uncivilized, barbarian, alien to that
European world of thought and art, where men pursued,
not dominance, but knowledge and happiness, and where
I liked to imagine that I was, or one day would be, at
home.

In this world neither the Captain nor Alastair had the
slightest interest. The Captain showed me one day, but
quite casually, the manuscript of a diary, kept by his
great-great-aunt Christian Keith, who had been born in

1801. It covered, he said, the years 1815–25, when she
had married. Over the next few days I read this diary
with an interest that grew to fascination. For one thing
I fell in love with the diarist, whom I saw develop from an
observant mischievous schoolgirl into a charming ironical
blue-stocking. I traced in her too the development of a
particular circle of society, a little provincialized by lack
of travel during the French wars, but after 1815 roaming
widely over Europe, collecting pictures, reading, thinking,
talking, creating gardens; with a taste but no craving for
distractions; a society closely allied to, but still distinct
from, that of England; perhaps with less money but a
lustier enthusiasm for such things as the French library,
the gazebos and ha-has upon which, in particular, Christian
Keith, my dear charmer, had lavished her ironical love.

'I've been told it's interesting,' said the Captain, 'but
apart from descriptions of how the place was laid out in
those days, I never saw much in it.' His sympathies in
the past lay elsewhere. I found Henstridge at the silver
and inquired who was coming to dinner.

'Mr Irvine of Airth.'

'Airth?' I said. 'You mean the ruin?'

'That's as may be,' said Henstridge.

'Who is Mr Irvine of Airth?' I asked Alastair.

'He's Donny Irvine of the garage.'

'Donny Irvine?' I knew Donny Irvine quite well; he was a
great ally of Alastair's. I had never seen him out of overalls.

'Yes. The Captain worked it out. The noblest blood in
Scotland flows in such of Donny's veins as aren't choked
with oil.'

'He's coming here to dinner tonight. The silver's being
done.'

'He often comes,' said Alastair. 'The Captain likes a
good crack with Donny. I was here with him once in the
holidays. We had a fine old time. I wouldn't have called
Rupert of Hentzau my uncle—although of course he may
be my uncle. Any time the middle classes are admitted,' he
added cruelly, 'I'll put in a word for you.'

Occasionally we met other visitors, and if they were
neighbours, or people such as Mr Crerar, the Captain's

lawyer, who might possibly know the truth about Alastair's relationship to the Captain, I watched them closely for any sign. But no one ever gave any, so far as I could see. Mr Crerar was always preoccupied and negative; Charles Crimond, the Captain's only near neighbour in the county, was a lofty, loud, rude young man who ignored both of us completely; and upon the Clandillons, who seemed to be the Captain's oldest and closest friends, Alastair made an immediate impression in his own right.

At that time Alastair and I were deciphering and copy-ing some accounts—factor's cash books and such things—which the Captain had recently found in an old box. They dated from the early eighteenth century, and were not of any professional historical interest. But to me they were fascinating, and even to Alastair, because they were 'prac-tical' they had some appeal. We worked in the garden-room, which had folding glass doors, which when they were opened left one side of the room almost entirely exposed to the sun. It was into this room, while we were doing this work, that the Captain one day showed the Clandillons. Lady Clandillon came first, like some great bird landing on the water, and simultaneously calling to its mate. She was in fact talking animatedly both to her husband and to the Captain, while also asking us a stream of questions about what we were doing, but without waiting to hear any answers she suddenly moved over and stood looking out of the windows, quite silent and still, as though the bird had landed and come to rest. Lord Clandillon was tall and stooping; he had a rather dandiacal air, but he was very ugly, with a receding chin, a coarse, toothy mouth, and pale blinking eyes magnified by small, thick, old-fashioned glasses. He had a good, high forehead, rather impressive. In different clothes he might have looked like a self-educated workman of the best type. In fact his peerage was an Irish one of respectable antiquity; he was a great coal- and land-owner, and Cabinet ministers shot over the famous moors he owned about fifteen miles away.

'A couple of budding historians, I see.' His voice was genial and deliberately ordinary; quite different from his wife's aviary shrilling. 'May I see?'

Alastair, who was transcribing from a thin folio roughly bound in sheepskin, smiled and handed it over. Lord Clandillon ran an eye down the column of entries, and began turning over the pages.

'This is very interesting!' He gave a toothy, nice, 'interested' smile; it was impossible to tell whether he was interested or not. 'But there's a wrong total,' he said after a moment. Alastair looked at him with interest.

'Page 27,' he said. 'Is that it?'

'Yes. How did you know?'

'It's the only wrong one.'

'I see.' Lord Clandillon laughed. 'So you did them all?'

'Yes.'

'Oh Heavens,' said Lady Clandillon, suddenly taking part again, 'just like Harry! You know, he can't see figures without adding them, and multiplying them, and taking the square root. It's a sort of nervous tic, only it's his secret pride, isn't it my love?'

'Yes,' said Lord Clandillon. 'It is.' And he gave a dry ironic smile, which, I found later, belonged to his private personality, which he did not often unveil; this smile was the way in which he registered amusement amongst his intimates. 'I can add up pounds, shillings and pence together,' he added. 'Can you?' He made this boast with great yet somehow mysterious simplicity.

'A bit,' said Alastair.

'It's a trick often found in association with low intelligence, you know. Still, it's useful. In any walk of life. Are you thinking of anything in particular yet?' He smiled, this time a public smile, attached to the kind of question public men are supposed to ask.

'I was thinking of the Bar,' said Alastair.

'The Bar.' Lord Clandillon nodded. 'A quick mind, hard work, and a good constitution—I imagine you've got these—you might do a lot worse.'

'Most people,' said Alastair, 'say I'll starve.' This was true. The English Bar was a career so far removed from us, and traditionally so risky, that Alastair's ambition was looked upon with incredulity.

'I don't see why you should!' Lord Clandillon appeared

surprised. 'It's hard at first, of course, but people get on.
. . . Most of the people I know seem to keep the wolf from
the door.'

'Edward, for instance!' Lady Clandillon, who had been
looking out of the window again, appearing almost unconscious, gave her sudden aviary scream, startling us all.
Lord Clandillon laughed, and the Captain joined in. I wondered who Edward could be, imagining a relation of Lady
Clandillon's, rich, clever, handsome, immensely successful
but not vulgarly famous.

The conversation turned, Alastair's moment was over,
but as it turned out, it had lasted long enough for Lord
Clandillon to remember him. Or would he have done so
anyway, because he was the Captain's son? Another point
to be mulled over, later on.

That was Alastair's moment, but a few days later, as it
happened, I had my moment too. I was summoned to the
library, and when I entered, blinking in the gloom—I had
come in from outside—the Captain was standing at the
window, with another man who was holding in his hands
a small unframed oil-painting.

'Ah, here he is!' The Captain's staccato was perhaps
even more pronounced than usual. 'Patrick—this is Mr
Agmondisham. He likes the little picture you found.'

'It's an attractive little thing, isn't it? Captain Keith tells
me you came across it in a boxroom?'

'Yes.'

'Were there any other pictures there?'

'One or two.' I hesitated for a moment, but the romantic
vision could not be suppressed. 'Why?' I asked. 'Is it
valuable?'

Captain Keith laughed. 'Eh, well, Patrick, my dear
chap—'' He sounded embarrassed. But Mr Agmondisham,
although he laughed, was not embarrassed.

'Well, that's rather what we were thinking about, you
know!' He smiled at me. 'It's—ah,' he murmured apologetically yet firmly, 'rather dirty. . . . If we had some distilled water and a linen rag?' He glanced at the Captain.

'Distilled water? I expect we could manage that.' He
rang, and Henstridge entered.

'Henstridge—could you produce some distilled water?'

'Distilled water? Yes, sir.' He turned to go, just as he would have done if he had been asked for, say, furniture polish.

'Well, just a moment, man, how are you going to distil it?'

'Well, I thought perhaps one of the big kettles sir, and a length of brass pipe?'

'Yes, that would—or, wait a moment—I'll come with you.' They went out of the room together, more like two friends—and perhaps even like two boys—than like master and servant. Mr Agmondisham was examining the back of the canvas through a glass. After a moment he put the glass away into his waistcoat pocket.

'You're interested in paintings?' He smiled, but his voice of social inquiry was so casual, bland, and polite that I thought he must be making fun of me.

'I suppose so. I don't know much about them.' It was Nethervale at its least engaging. I probably scowled. Then it occurred to me that perhaps after all he was not making fun of me, and I blushed. 'What about the hole in it?' There was an ugly rent in the canvas in the corner of the little flower-piece. I had thought it completely spoilt.

'Oh that's not serious. It can be patched up so that most people would never know it had been damaged.'

'Are you an—expert?' I meant, was he a professional expert, but I did not know how to put it. It moved me to think of the damaged little painting, which I had rescued from neglect, having the science and the art of the restorer lavished upon it, and I spoke with reverence.

'I'm a dealer.' He smiled again, looking at me. I was disappointed. I had vaguely imagined him as having something to do perhaps with the National Gallery, or perhaps the Victoria and Albert. As a dealer he seemed to me not quite gentlemanly, like a cricket professional. Yet I could not quite accept this; there was something about Mr Agmondisham, something about his clothes and voice and manner, which impressed me more than anyone I had ever seen, for much more than Captain Keith or Lord Clandillon he seemed to me someone that I could aspire to imitate, so that I might myself, in some distant future, be so profoundly self-assured, so intelligent, alert, so worldly, and yet so sensitively in communication with something unworldly as he had been when he had been examining the little flower-piece. Suddenly I realized how unworthy and provincial my disappointment had been, and without further knowledge I was prepared to accept the idea that there were picture dealers of a kind of which I had never dreamt, pursuing an avocation exciting beyond the dreams of romance and ambition.

When Mr Agmondisham left—several hours later—he gave me his card and asked me to call on him 'when I was in London'. At that time I had never been in London; an invitation to call on someone when I happened to be in London—before Mr Agmondisham extended it to me— would have seemed as unreal as an invitation to call on someone when I happened to be in Tokyo. Yet as soon as Mr Agmondisham asked me, a visit to London seemed, although still not easy, a perfectly possible and natural thing. In meeting Mr Agmondisham, in fact, in meeting the Clandillons, in being at Kingisbyres, Alastair and I were both receiving a vital element in a privileged upbringing; we were mixing with people to whom the things we wanted were commonplace, to whom our ambitions seemed, not wild, but actually modest, and in whose presence our dreams took on an actuality, less ethereal and more prosaic, but not less exciting, than their condition of childish vagueness.

Our education continued in different ways. One day, in the village, Alastair and I called on Donny Irvine at the garage, and found him, as we generally did, in the yard at the back, with his nose in the bonnet of a car. But the car was unusual; it was an Aston-Martin.

''Morning, Airth,' said Alastair.

'Aye, Alastair.' Donny raised his head. He was accustomed to being addressed by Alastair 'by the title of his estate', although he would not have liked it from anyone else except the Captain, whom under instruction he addressed as Kingisbyres.

'That's a bonny thing,' said Alastair softly.

'Aye, she's a lovely wee bit of work.' He wiped his face with the back of his oily hand and squinted into the bonnet, 'Though,' he added, 'since I'm no' trying to sell her to you, I don't mind saying she's a right hoor for petrol.'

'She's yours, then?'

'Aye. Part-exchange for yon big Humber.'

'Part-exchange!' Alastair whistled vulgarly. 'What happens when the sealing-wax you put in melts and the Humber comes to bits?' Donny put his head into the engine and made no reply. There was silence for a few moments.

'If you let me have a wee hurl in her,' said Alastair in a wheedling voice, 'I would pay for the petrol.' Donny looked up and gave a brief theatrical laugh.

'Ah ken Ah'm daft,' he said, 'but Ah'm no' that daft.' We stayed for some time, chaffing and gossiping with Donny, breathing in the rich petrol-reeking air, but although nothing more was said, I saw Alastair's gaze linger on the low-slung powerful car.

'I'm going to drive that,' he said as we came out, 'or die in the attempt—and don't say what you're thinking of saying.' The following day I didn't see him, and although we met on the day after that he said nothing about the car. On the third day, however, he rang me up in the morning.

'Are you prepared to put your life in my hands?'

'The Aston-Martin?' I asked. 'How did you do it?'

'Donny has some business in Edinburgh. We're going in with him. He's promised to let me drive most of the way back.' We called at the garage after lunch, and Donny was ready to go. He was a man in his early thirties, fat from over-eating and lack of exercise, shrewd about his car-dealing, but in some ways surprisingly boyish. He was one of those people who, although not given to reading anything else, was always reading and quoting Burns—both the published and the unpublished works—and Alastair had acquired the habit from him. They used to quote things like 'Holy Willy's Prayer' or 'The Two Dogs', verse about.

It was another uncharacteristic hot, sunny, clear day, and the road that we took at first over the moors was broad and smooth, but quite quiet, and providing a view a long way ahead. No doubt most drivers would have taken it fast; Donny, who was a professionally good driver, took it very fast indeed. But he drove easily, in a relaxed way, laughing and talking bawdy and slowing down every now and again to wave to girls, who, I noticed, were responsive as they would not have been if we had been driving a prim saloon. His business in Edinburgh did not take long—I wondered afterwards if it had been more than an excuse— and he ran us to a place in Leith where the proprietor was a friend of his and we had fish and chips. While we were eating, Donny and his friend told stories of the time when they were our age—or so they said, though I imagine they were antedating—stories which reminded me of Henstridge's anecdotes about his life as a young soldier in London; they had that wonderful, that liberating note of genial curtness about sexual pleasure, as of something both treasured and taken for granted. So, I thought, I too would live one day, perhaps in the not-far-distant future, and this feeling, this sense of the possibilities of the future, was for that afternoon, like a final glass of wine which gives the glow of drunkenness.

We started back and as soon as we had got clear of the suburbs Donny pulled up.

'"Wilfu' man mon hae his way,"' he said to Alastair, 'but tak' care with the clutch.'

I knew that Alastair *could* drive a car—as I myself could not—because he told me that Donny had let him; but I doubt whether his driving experience at the time added up to more than about twenty or thirty miles, and that mostly in played-out old cars on deserted moorland roads. He started off very slowly, as an experienced driver driving a strange car would do. And indeed he handled the car very well, driving after the first ten minutes or so with increasing smoothness and fluency. Meanwhile the sun was sinking, but the evening had not yet turned cold; only in the open car there was a kind of keenness that seemed to work in the blood. We sang and sang again and waved at girls and children and even at surprised-looking old men and women; we passed through a damp-smelling wood, and at last we were up on the high rolling moors again, the open, yet secretive, dark purple Covenanting moorland.

And all the time the speed of the car was increasing. I would not say imperceptibly, because I was very conscious of it, and as I observed Alastair there was a peculiar set hard look on his face that told me very well that he knew what he was about, but smoothly and easily, so that there was no moment at which one could say: 'We are now going very fast.' Yet by the time we had reached the particular stretch of road along which Donny had driven so hard that morning we *were* going fast; not so fast as Donny had driven earlier, but fast enough to make Donny's long hair stream out flapping in the wind, for my heart to pound violently, and for my stomach to give me the sensation that it was being left behind at corners. And all the time the look deepened on Alastair's face, the look of a victorious commander giving permission to loot a city, a look of brutality, pleasure, and recklessness, all masked and stilled by pride.

Nothing happened; yet when at last we turned the corner into Kingisbyres village the actual physical loosening of screwed-up muscles was almost painful. Some things of that afternoon—the salt-water smell of the chip-shop, the charming smiles of the girls we waved to, the look on Alastair's face, and the atmosphere of the whole of it, the feeling that we had with Donny of being adult and relishing it and being on our own—these I shall remember always. They remain for ever as a concentrated flavour in my being.

THREE

WHEN THE SUMMER holidays came to an end Kingisbyres faded out of my life; or rather not out of it altogether,
but into something vague on the edge of it. There is
something mesmeric about life at a boarding-school; it
is hard to look over the wall and see what is going on
outside. And for both Alastair and myself this term was
an especially absorbing one. Alastair was settling down with
my father to the grind of coaching in mathematics which
he would need in order to have a chance of a Cambridge
scholarship. So far my father hadn't given him a great deal
of coaching. Alastair had been working mainly at classics
and history and other subjects for which he would have less
time when he began mathematics seriously. Now my father
at last began to devote to him that gift of teaching which had
for so long been spent unworthily, that insight into another
mind, that patience and ability to inspire with enthusiasm
which he had poured out like water into the desert of
Nethervale. Alastair began—as he told me later—to have
his first glimpse into the enchanted garden of mathematics,
and he was in consequence not altogether of this world.

This had an effect on my own life. Because of his pre-
occupation with Alastair, and Alastair's powerful response
to it, my father had less time to worry about me. I was
no longer told once a week or so that I would end up
in the gutter, and the ghastly coaching sessions, which
had in any case been getting fewer and fewer, now came
altogether to an end. I took the opportunity to go, from
my father's point of view, completely to the devil. Half
through inattentiveness and half through despair, he gave
his permission for various schemes of mine, so that during
the chemistry and physics periods, for instance, which had
always been a useless torture of boredom, I officially did

extra French while actually sketching the heads of my classmates and doing elaborate charcoal doodles which I affected to believe were works of genius. It was at this time that I decided to be an artist, but for the time being I withheld the decision from my father.

My mother, however, knew about my plans. Too deeply impressed by her own experience to be very sanguine about life, she was on the other hand quite without bitterness, and without the fear that goes with it. If I, having considered the matter carefully, wanted to be an artist, she would help me to achieve my aim, for it was a matter of duty to help people to live their own lives. This duty was however compatible with playing a part in shaping those lives. My mother was not a profoundly religious woman, but her feeling for certain virtues was religious in its tone. The qualities about which she felt in this way were a queer mixture of the basic Christian virtues and the moral characteristics of what she called 'the best type of naval officer'—meaning her own father. Charity and uprightness were the chief of them; comradeship and modesty played a part, and good manners played a part too. 'Mean', 'underhand', 'self-seeking', 'pot-hunter', 'inconsiderate'—these were my mother's condemnations, given infrequently, reluctantly, ponderingly, as though she tried moral qualities with her tongue, but damningly. She used the word 'worthy' without irony.

Alastair and I had tea with her every Sunday afternoon in term-time. My father was asleep in his study, and we three sat in the drawing-room with that rare comfort, a blazing fire, and with a rich tea for Alastair and myself. The small room lit by uninstitutional flames was a refuge; and there my mother carried on a long, long tussle with Alastair.

'But why not the Civil Service, Alastair? Though I suppose you wouldn't fancy being tied to a desk.' She hated the Bar; a career for the self-seeking, for pot-hunters competing in glibness, defending the guilty, prosecuting the innocent—underhand!

'I don't care to be tied to three thousand a year.' Although he spoke without a smile, Alastair was not altogether serious. A year ago he might have been; the same remark could then have issued as a flame from the furnace of his ambition. But a long series of such conversations had taught him self-consciousness, given him an irony to direct against himself as well as against others, enabled him to bring his sense of humour into the drawing-room.

'But my dear—three thousand a year is a great deal of money!' My mother's sense of irony was not especially sharp—as a form of humour it was perhaps just a little underhand. In the firelight I could see upon her handsome lined face the special look she had for Alastair, a little uncomprehending, anxious, yet something else too—admiring, I suppose.

'I tell you what, Mrs Shaw—I'll accept a judgeship the very first time it's offered to me. It often means a great drop in income, you know—but it's all right to be a judge, isn't it?' Sitting at a stool by her feet, he looked up at her solemnly.

'To be one of His Majesty's judges,' said my mother, 'is a very great honour—and to be an impertinent little boy at the age of sixteen is a very great disgrace.' She laughed; for if her sense of irony was not especially sharp it was not abnormally blunt either.

So the term passed, and at Christmas-time it snowed heavily so that the moorland roads were often impassable, and Alastair and I did not see so much of one another as usual. He told me later that when he wasn't working he and some of the Kingisbyres village boys had built a toboggan run on the steep hill behind the village and held races on it. One of the competitors, thrown off at a steeply banked corner, had broken his collar-bone; another had had his ear torn off. Alastair himself showed me an appalling purple-green bruise on his thigh, but his time, he said, was on average two seconds better than anyone else's. I asked after the Captain—and Henstridge—more out of politeness than anything, since the summer days when we had spent so much time at Kingisbyres seemed a long way off, and also I couldn't imagine what, in that quiet life, could provide news. Alastair answered in the same offhand way that he had seen the Captain once or twice and he seemed to be all right.

Yet towards Easter my imagination began to go out to Kingisbyres again. I had the idea that I would like to paint the house, and at once a kind of vision of it came into my mind and would not be dislodged. The weather now was cold and blustery and wet, with storm-clouds scudding across the moors, and snow still lying in big patches on all the high ground. Sometimes, out on one of the Spartan runs which still claimed us, I would see a group of fir-trees, high up on a hillside, shrinking before the wind in the midst of a patch of greyish snow and I would suddenly envisage Kingisbyres as a Transylvanian hunting lodge, its light blazing out to welcome some fur-wrapped prince and his friends as their sledges were galloped across the snow, and the wolves howled in the forest. And then, sometimes, in association with Kingisbyres, I would suddenly have, almost overwhelmingly, the sense of the past, not so much of a particular episode or period of history, as of some essence of the past of Scotland, its dark, fated, cruel quality, and the contrasting strain that ran through it of lightness and grace and gaiety; and even then it seemed to me that this historic past was like a kind of collective subconscious, something to which the respectable, censored mind does not normally have access, something powerfully charged with love and hate, pride and violence, which, in given circumstances, it might discharge in some tremendous flash of lightning.

Anyway I wanted to paint Kingisbyres, so I suggested to Alastair that we should cycle over on one of the first days of the Easter holidays, so that I could make some sketches. As the term drew nearer to its end this expedition began almost to obsess me, and in the end I insisted upon going over on the very first morning of the holidays. Only if it had actually been snowing heavily could I have found a more unsuitable day for outdoor sketching. The weather was Siberian, bitterly cold, with an icy wind and a brooding steel-grey atmosphere. But Alastair and I, like everybody else in those parts, were used to such conditions. When I called for him I was wearing so many clothes that I had difficulty in cycling; they included, apart from woollen underwear, an old suit of heavy flannel pyjamas and alternate layers of Shetland and cashmere sweaters, a Balaclava helmet, three pairs of socks and a pair of boots borrowed from one of the gardeners. Alastair was much the same except that instead of a Balaclava he was wearing a tattered shawl wound round his head and tucked under a very old army coat. We looked like Napoleon's two Grenadiers in the retreat from Moscow.

And, by the time we arrived at the place I had chosen for my first sketch, a point rather distant, looking across a shallow depression, so that one caught the proportion and grace of the old house, Alastair and I were actually overheated. With admirable concentration I sketched for an hour and a half, while Alastair, sheltered by a corner of a dry-stone dyke, read mathematics. When I came to I was very cold indeed; in fact, I had to give up because my hands would no longer carry out my wishes even to the limited extent to which, as an artist, I was accustomed. So we decided to eat. It was characteristic of us as we were at that time that we had brought food with us. It was only about a mile to Alastair's home, and his aunt would, of course, have been delighted to feed us. Out in the open, after a period of immobility, we were chilled to the bone, our teeth were chattering, and we both burned our tongues trying to warm ourselves with tea from the thermos. But after a term of school, with the pressure of people round us all the time, it was peaceful to be in the Kingisbyres policies, which were at this point only a piece of improved moorland, wild and empty, with the intermittent whistle of the wind in the firs near us, and the curlews calling— a desolate and characteristic sound—as they wheeled and turned down wind.

After we had eaten we moved to another vantage point and I began a fresh series of sketches. For a time Alastair continued his reading, but quite soon he gave up, saying that he was still hungry and that we ought to go now to the house for tea. From this new position however we could see the main door, and, since there was a car which we did not recognize in front of it, we supposed the Captain had guests for luncheon who were unknown to us. We decided to wait until they had gone. But with this waiting the spirit went out of us; soon I was only pretending to sketch, and a little later I gave up even that. Our talk became desultory, and was fading out altogether when Alastair saw someone we knew. For that matter we knew everyone that we were likely to see.

This was Tosh—I never knew either his real name or his surname—who, although not unemployable, was simple and did not often hold a job for very long. He was a very gentle, shy creature, whom we often saw on the moors, plodding along on mysterious errands with his dog at his heels. He was mildly suspected of poaching, and he had certainly taught Alastair and me, in a most expert manner, how to set snares and 'guddle' for trout, but the keepers did not take him seriously. They knew that his wants were easily satisfied; as a matter of fact, just because he was simple, he benefited more from the Captain's charity than other unemployed men whose genuine needs were less limited. We waved and went to meet him, running to warm ourselves up. At the same time he changed his course to meet us. He was not shy with us, because he had known Alastair since he was a baby, and in fact I think he liked to be with us, but he was naturally solitary, and would not have joined us if we had not waved first.

'Aye, Tosh,' Alastair greeted him and fell into step. Tosh looked at him sidelong, gave an evasive nod and an inarticulate mutter, and continued to march along with his head downcast, as he always did. For a man who spent nearly all his time out of doors he had a curiously pale, delicate face, and now he blushed deeply, as he often did when anyone addressed him.

'Whae's caur's yon at the hoose?' Alastair, who had of course spoken broad Scots in the village as a child, could switch it on still when he wanted to, and generally spoke to Tosh in his very broadest.

'Never heen it. Nae freenh caur onyway.' In addition to his antique accent Tosh had an impediment in his speech which caused him to pronounce the letter ess as aitch; because I had had some experience of listening to him I understood that he was now saying he had never seen the car before, and that it didn't belong to any of the Captain's friends. The conversation continued as we made our way to the lodge gates. Often I didn't understand much of what Tosh said, and perhaps Alastair didn't either, but then he spoke very little, so there was no strain. When we reached the gates, the tall gates with the great half-circle of gravel which set them back from the road, and which would have been so much more impressive if it had not been green with weeds, we stood by them talking for a moment. But we had already parted, Tosh to go to the village and ourselves to go back to the house, when the car appeared. It was a capacious Daimler, very highly polished, a kind of car that makes me think of funerals. As it reached us it stopped, and I saw there was a chauffeur driving and a middle-aged man and woman in the back seat. The woman, who was on our side, had already opened the window, and, addressing Tosh, who was nearest to her, she said: 'We do turn right for the village, don't we?'

Caught off his guard, and failing to understand the quick, high, English voice, flustered indeed by its imperiousness, Tosh was at his worst. A kind of spasm ran through him, his gaze jerked from his boots to the questioner's face and back again, and his long pale face turned scarlet. He looked at that moment much more simple than he in fact was, yet at the same time he had a curious air of hurt dignity, like a clergyman who had been crudely accosted. After a moment he gave vent to a strangled incomprehensible mutter. At the same moment Alastair stepped forward and said: 'Yes, turn right here and take the right-hand fork about a quarter of a mile down.' The woman looked at him sharply.

'Oh—thank you.' She withdrew abruptly into the interior of the car, the window through which she had been speaking rose rapidly, and the gravel spurted under its wheels as the big car turned away and in its instant acceleration seemed to spurn us indignantly.

'I wonder who *she* is?' Alastair looked after the car in faint puzzlement, and waved absent-mindedly to Tosh, who was making his way off into the freezing gloom. 'Rude old bitch anyway.'

'Perhaps,' I said, 'she thought you were making fun of

her—imitating her way of speaking.' Alastair stared at me for a moment, then laughed.

'My God, do you suppose she did? We must all have looked daft.' We looked at one another, and Alastair's stained and tattered army coat, the retreat-from-Moscow effect of the grey shawl wrapped turban-wise round his head, struck me afresh, as no doubt my huge boots and girth struck him. We began to giggle.

'And Tosh mopping and mowing,' I said.

'We must have looked like the village idiot multiplied by three.'

'And then my best company voice issuing from this shawl like the voice of God from the burning bush.' We were still laughing as we began to run, or at least to waddle along the drive as quickly as our clothes would allow us. Henstridge let us in to the back quarters after we had tapped on his pantry window. He laughed when he saw us.

'You look like you was straight out of the trenches.'

'We feel even worse,' I said.

'Quite strangers too.' He was pleased to see us; he liked company and he found the locals very slow. We chatted for a moment while Alastair and I took off some layers of clothes. Then:

'Who were those people who just drove away?' said Alastair.

'Ah,' said Henstridge, 'Mr and Mrs Harvey.' Rather noticeably he said nothing more.

'Where do they come from?'

'Glasgow, I believe.' His voice lost its friendly intimacy and took on its formal, upper-servant's gentility. 'I believe Mr Harvey is the 'ead of some business in Glasgow.' He spoke as though it would be beneath him to know for sure. Since Henstridge's knowledge of any of the Captain's acquaintances was in proportion to their social grandeur—his knowledge of the Clandillons, for instance, was encyclopaedic—I deduced that the Harveys must be socially insignificant.

'Biscuits, it is, I think.' Henstridge relented a little. 'And they're very wealthy, so I'm given to understand. They say 'is granny started making them in some cottage around these parts. In need, I dare say she was. And now—now we come calling at Kingisbyres.' Henstridge rose, and looking at himself in the long narrow mirror which was fastened to the wall, he squared his shoulders, flicked some crumbs off his waistcoat and ran his big knobbly hand over his hair. It made one recall the young soldier he had once been, getting ready to go on guard perhaps at St James's Palace.

'Now, if you like,' he said, 'I'll show you up. The Captain will be glad to see you. 'E's a bit down recently so see you cheer him up.' In a rather lower voice, as we approached the heavy baize-covered swinging door that led to what he called 'the front of the house', he added: ' 'E 'as 'is troubles too, as the sailor said to the girl.' Then he pushed the door and we were the Captain's guests and Henstridge would no longer speak to us familiarly.

We found the Captain sitting in front of the fire in the library, which smelt of cigar smoke. Not having seen him for some months, I noticed a change in his appearance. He looked older, and smaller, and he sat as though he were crouching up to the fire as I never remembered his having done before. He made me think, for a moment, of a monkey, huddled and wretched in an English winter. Then he got up and greeted us and the impression wore off a little. He was undoubtedly glad to see us; he asked us what we had been doing and when I said I had been sketching the house and proposed to do some water-colours, he was delighted.

'Will you give me one Patrick, to hang alongside my great-aunt's daubs in the drawing-room?'

I made some modest but quite sincere disclaimer.

'Of course they'll be good enough. My great-aunt once told me that until she was middle-aged she spoilt all her water-colours because she could never get out of the habit of sucking the paint off her brushes.' He laughed. 'And she was only a suckling when she painted the house.'

One way and another we passed a very happy afternoon. The Captain, by contrast with his appearance when we first came in, seemed very gay; he laughed a great deal, delighting in the animal spirits of two boys bursting with health and energy, one of whom had a mind of formidable power. When we got ready to go, he decided to walk down to the village with us.

'The pipes in the hall will burst again in the thaw if I don't go and talk to Simpson myself. Should have gone before. But I'm getting to be a donnert auld bodie. You know what that means? It means an old person whose wits are wandering, you know.'

For some reason, as we went through the village we stopped at the war memorial. It consisted of a big plaque let into an outcrop of rock, and showed, in rather blurred bas-relief, a dying soldier tended by an angel. Above there were the figures '1914–1918', and below the words 'They shall not grow old, as we that are left grow old', and a list of names. I saw the Captain's eyes run down it.

'They were mostly killed in 1917,' he said. 'All useless butchery.' His voice became contemptuous and angry. 'We could have negotiated with the Kaiser, you know, but that fellow Lloyd George wouldn't have it. I suppose they teach you at school that the Kaiser was a complete villain?' He spoke, challengingly, to Alastair.

'They don't teach us anything about him,' said Alastair. 'We don't do modern history.' His flat, matter-of-fact statement would have stopped some people, but not the Captain.

'All that scrap-of-paper nonsense!' he exclaimed. 'Don't let yourself be deceived by that. The Kaiser was a silly enough fellow in many ways, but he was an honourable man.' The Captain pursued his train of thought in silence for a moment. Then: 'Anyway he was good enough for the Germans—they're not likely to get anyone better. As for Grey—' He gave a kind of snort and fell silent again. We walked on; I knew that after a few moments or a minute or so, the Captain's thoughts, like a stream emerging from underground, would reappear in speech. And, sure enough, they did so.

'I sometimes wonder at what point the mess became incurable,' he said. 'Now you're interested in history, Patrick. Tell me, d'you think if we'd shot Dreyfus—shot him at the very beginning, you know—' Then, seeing my puzzled face, he broke off and gave his loud, braying laugh.

After this return to Kingisbyres I expected that we should be resuming our regular visits. But first the Captain had bronchitis, and then something happened which caused an interruption. I had been sketching by the river when Alastair, who was with me, suddenly took it into his head to cross it by some rocks which we used in summer. I saw at a glance that the particular boulder which was the key to the crossing was submerged under two inches of racing brown water.

'It'll be much quicker,' said Alastair, but I knew that in fact he had been bored with sitting while I sketched, and only wanted a diversion.

'Don't be such an ass,' I said. 'You can't do it.' It would have been wiser to have been less curt.

'What will you bet me?' From his voice, and his polite, almost caressing smile, I knew that he was now determined, and I was about to say crossly that I wouldn't bet, when it occurred to me that I might mark my disapproval of his folly by making him pay for it.

'Fifty Balkan Sobranie,' I said. This expensive brand of cigarette was our favourite luxury; such a bet was an unprecedented gesture.

'Right,' said Alastair, and jumped up on the first rock. As I looked at the swirling, foam-covered, hostile-looking water I wanted to call him back, but I knew of course that it was too late, so I dropped my sketching things and scrambled up after him. There was only one point of real difficulty in the crossing, a jump down on to this boulder landing on the left foot, and a long step off it, all of which had to be done in one continuous movement. It was easy enough when the top of the boulder was clear, and even now Alastair was almost successful. He jumped beautifully, placing his foot high to allow for the current, and taking off again quite easily, but the stone on to which he was jumping was wet with spray, and his foot, poised tensely for a moment, slid off. The next moment he had fallen heavily.

There was, he argued afterwards, no serious danger; at the worst he might have broken a leg. But as he disappeared for a moment into the flood, I felt panic-stricken. I thought he was probably stunned; I had a kind of vision of him on a mortuary slab, with blood still trickling out of his ears. In fact, he came up at once, and was swept into a shallow where, after a desperate plunge, I grabbed him and pulled him out. He hadn't broken anything, but he was badly bruised and had to be taken home, retching and swearing, in a passing lorry.

For several days he was too stiff to go about, and though I continued my sketching at Kingisbyres, I did not go to the house without Alastair. In any case the weather was improving, and if I cycled over in the afternoon I was able to go on painting almost in comfort, quite late into the afternoon. I enjoyed this concentration, and by the time Alastair was around again I had completed one water-colour drawing which was the most ambitious work I had ever undertaken, and of which I was exceedingly proud. I was very anxious indeed to present this to the Captain.

We accordingly called at the house for this purpose, but did not fulfil it as I intended. Almost as soon as Henstridge opened the door to us I knew that something was wrong; there was something briskly ominous in his manner.

'The Captain,' he said, 'has influenza now. If it *is* influenza. The doctor's with him, and we're expecting the nurse at any moment.' He cocked his eye at the row of bells which hung like an elaborate frieze along the top of one wall of his pantry, and which, despite the electricity which was run off the falls in the river, were still worked by an elaborate system of wires actuated by long, velvet-tasselled bell-pulls.

'What might it be,' said Alastair, 'if it isn't influenza?' He spoke sharply, for although he enjoyed Henstridge's mannerisms at ordinary times, he was sometimes impatient with them, and now he was, I felt, suddenly anxious.

'The doctor's afraid of pneumonia.' Boys of about the age that we were then, boys who have led sheltered lives, with little contact with death or serious illness, or any other great trouble, although they may be callous sometimes from thoughtlessness, retain a childishness which is easily shocked and alarmed, and a kind of tremor ran through me when I heard the word 'pneumonia'; instantly I saw myself, in my Sunday suit and a black tie, attending the Captain's funeral. Yet at the same time I noticed how Henstridge had reacted to the snap in Alastair's tone by dropping the manner which he had displayed at our entry. Not for the first time, but more strongly than ever before, I was aware of this snap of authority in Alastair.

In the brief silence that followed one of the bells rang loudly, startling us all, even Henstridge, who was expecting it.

'That'll be the nurse,' he said, and he went quickly out of the room, glancing automatically in the mirror and straightening his tie.

'Has he got any relatives to come and take charge?' I asked the question partly out of genuine concern, but also with some idea of easing the slight nervous tension. But as so often happens when anyone speaks for such a reason, I had said something which I would not have said if I had thought. Since our original conversation we had never spoken about the possibility of Alastair being the Captain's son. It had been in my mind, for one reason or another, often enough, but from lack of nourishment it had become very small and far-away—quite real and distinct, but like something seen through the wrong end of a telescope. Now that it had suddenly bounced up again, it seemed more than lifesize.

'He's got a brother in Kenya,' said Alastair, 'but apart from that his relatives are wrapped in mystery,' and he gave something like a very brief humourless laugh.

'You don't know—' I said. 'I mean there's been nothing—you've never learned anything more?' I was troubled and embarrassed, but I forced myself on, because it seemed to me that now the subject had suddenly sprung on us like this we had to meet it, it would be cowardly to try to evade it, cowardly or perhaps rather gauche and improper. It was part of my ideal of the civilized life that fitting words should be found so that everything should be discussed rationally and with dignity.

'No. I've never learned anything more.' Alastair made the same brief grimace, only this time it was a little more like a genuine laugh, although wry and puzzled rather than amused. 'Sometimes I think one thing, sometimes another. But honestly I just don't know.' He spoke the last words very slowly, as though they summed up the results of many hours of brooding. Then in a changed voice, self-consciously brisk and hard, he added: 'After all, for practical purposes it doesn't matter. It's only a matter of interest.' He went over and looked out of the window: it opened on to a paved courtyard, which was surrounded by what had been laundries and bakeries, which were now used mainly as stores or potting sheds, and which, even in their comparative delapidation, were spacious and well-proportioned. 'It would be a different matter if there was any chance of proving myself *legitimate*.' His voice, despite its guarded quality, was not so much bitter as petulant.

'What difference would it make to you to have the prospect of inheriting this place one day? You don't want to live here, do you?'

'No.' He spoke impatiently. 'Of course I don't want to live here—I've more to do than be a museum curator. You know I want to go to the Bar—if I get the chance. But think of the difference it would make if I had even a little money of my own—even a few pounds a week. Let alone all the connections, and the friends, and the influence!' I realized that although Alastair was prepared to work very hard for success, he felt that it was his birthright.

Henstridge came in again.

'The nurse—' he said. 'Seems competent,' he added after a moment in his judgmatic, world-weary, upper servant's manner. 'And now we might 'ave a cup of tea. The doctor's 'ad some, and one of the girls will take a tray up to the nurse. I've known nurses that would expect to be waited on by a man, but this one looks sensible. Of course, if I wasn't single-handed, and seeing that a nurse's job is a very responsible one, it's a job I might give to a footman, supposing we 'ad a young one I was training.' He looked at me to see that I was taking this in. In his youth, before he had joined the army, Henstridge had been a pantry boy, and later, until he seduced one of the maids, a footman in a vast establishment that moved with the seasons between

London and Yorkshire, and he knew that I delighted in
the stories he told of this vanished society, its barbaric
wastefulness, its nice etiquette, its hieratic rigidity, its
microcosmic ambitions, feuds and loves, its professional
snobbery. But this afternoon I was not to have the pleasure
of hearing any more about the relative positions of nurses
and footmen.

'No,' said Alastair. 'Thanks very much, but we'd better
go. I'll telephone tomorrow. You'll be very busy.' This was
a plea which Henstridge seldom heard, and which he could
not bring himself to argue with. As we cycled down the
drive we discussed the Captain's illness briefly and in some
connection or other I mentioned Henstridge.

'He's in his element, isn't he?' said Alastair sourly.

'He's upset all the same.'

'Oh, I dare say. Only I get a bit fed up with him now
and again. And'—Alastair looked across at me—'just then
I didn't feel I could stand a long conversation between you
and him about whether it's part of an under-housemaid's
duty to empty the groom of the chambers' chamber-pot.'

'Oh, I don't think it would be,' I said. 'That's a personal
servant's job. I expect the groom of the chambers would
have a boy training as a valet to do things like that for
him.'

'Think of a job like that,' said Alastair, 'and here's you
nothing better than an artist.'

Next day, when Alastair telephoned—which he had to do
from his friend the butcher's, since his aunt was not on
the telephone—the Captain was no better, but he had not
developed pneumonia. Nor, though he was very ill, did he
do so. Alastair telephoned every day, but by common con-
sent we did not go near Kingisbyres again until towards the
end of the holidays. During this period Alastair and I did
not even see very much of one another. Alastair, I imagine,
worked at his mathematics and engaged in various ploys
about the village. He was still accepted by the village people
as being one of themselves. The people in the villages round
Nethervale regarded the school with a mixture of contempt
and envy. Contempt, because they knew, in their shrewd

way, that it was an inferior kind of place, a second carbon copy of an English public school; and envy, because they knew too, of course, that it provided stupid boys with opportunities that only a tiny handful of their own most brilliant boys would enjoy. So long, then, as they could regard Alastair's 'English accent'—which still would have seemed Scotch enough South of the Border—as something which he cleverly assumed in order to fool the anglicizing machinery of Scottish snobbery, they accepted it. Indeed they rather admired it, and invited him to perform on it occasionally when they wished to be entertained. So he played football, drove the butcher's van, and—although he did not tell me this until later—began to take part in other village pastimes.

As for me, I spent a lot of time sketching elsewhere than at Kingisbyres, cycling long distances to find 'subjects' of the kind that the old art master at school had taught me to look for. I also bought my first painting, a small academic landscape which I found folded up in a junkshop and paid half a crown for. I cleaned it, using distilled water and a linen rag as I had seen Mr Agmondisham do, and later still made some experiments in repainting a bit where the paint had been rubbed off. It was my first venture in restoring with oil paint, and I enjoyed it so much that I began to keep an eye open for damaged canvases to practise on.

I had become so absorbed in this activity that in the end it came to me as something of a shock to realize how long I had been out of touch with Alastair, the Captain, and Kingisbyres. It was the sight of Tosh which brought it home to me. I was walking along one of the moorland tracks when I saw him still some way off, approaching diagonally, with his gaze characteristically downcast, and the air of a man deep in thought, striding out as though on some definite and urgent business. As always, the dog followed a pace or two behind, nose down, like its master. We were on converging courses, and bound to meet. The prospect of a conversation with Tosh embarrassed me, but there was no alternative, and when we were about twenty yards off we exchanged a sketchy salute, and a moment later I said, 'Aye, Tosh,' exhausting thereby my ability to speak the language of the people. Tosh gave the faint strangled noise which stood with him for a greeting, his eyes still modestly cast down. But after a few paces I realized that conversation was unnecessary, and we walked in a silence which after a time became contented and companionable. I wanted to ask about the Captain, and was getting ready to try to make myself comprehensible when he got in ahead of me. For a moment I couldn't make it out at all; to me it sounded something like 'Whittle we awday when Kinghbyrhh ihnay here?' Then I realized that—following the old custom—by 'Kingisbyres' he meant not the house but its owner, and he was asking me how we would all get on when he wasn't here.

'Where's he going?' I said.

'Africa.' Pleased to be giving news, Tosh shot a quick, almost sly glance at me.

'Africa?' Taken aback, I no doubt spoke sharply and incredulously. Then an idea came to me. 'To Kenya, is it? To stay with his brother?'

'Aye, maybe.' Tosh's voice was completely non-committal; he had retreated into his shell again.

'For how long?' I said.

Afraid that I disbelieved his whole story, or perhaps afraid that he had been mistaken about it, Tosh was now wilfully vague and vacant. He made no attempt to answer the question, but after a few seconds said, 'Aye . . . weel . . .,' raised his hand in the same half-salute, smiled in the direction of my feet, and turned away. The dog, which had fallen several paces behind while we were together, closed up with the inconspicuous precision of a destroyer escorting a battleship.

For perhaps a hundred yards I walked on, annoyed with myself for having handled Tosh badly. If I had not spoken sharply he could, I was sure, have given me more information. Then suddenly, perhaps because of something in Tosh's manner, I became uneasy, with that apprehension about changes, that nervous conservatism which is as characteristic of the young as their wish for movement and excitement. In my walk with Tosh I had moved nearer to Kingisbyres village, and now I changed my direction so as to reach Alastair's house by the most direct way. By the time I entered the village I was almost running.

In the shop I was welcomed by Alastair's aunt in her usual manner.

'Oh, Patrick, I'm glad to see you! And won't Alastair be pleased you're here! He was telephoning you earlier, and he's fairly been wearying for you to come. Come away in now.' She beamed at me. Miss Craig was a small, round woman with hair that was still reddish and had once been beautiful; she still had the smooth, creamy complexion. To me she was always extremely nice, and her welcomes, with their repeated 'Come away in', sometimes sounded almost maudlin. She was in fact, like many Scotch people, extravagantly, sometimes almost insanely, hospitable—it was always extremely difficult for any casual visitor to get out of the house without taking a meal—but there was, I was beginning to realize, another side to her character. She had always looked after Alastair extremely well in every way, and he was, in an undemonstrative way, very fond of her. But their relationship was anything but straightforward. One noteworthy thing was that although Miss Craig appeared to have had even less schooling than might have been expected, and was curiously uninformed, Alastair would argue with her as an equal, throwing himself passionately and with all his ability against her immovable prejudices. Below all her 'cheeriness' I sensed a personality as strong, and perhaps as twisted, as the heather.

A door opened above.

'Auntie, is that Patrick? Tell him to come up.'

'There now! Impatient isn't the word.' Miss Craig gave me her full-cream smile. Then, raising her voice, she said, 'I *am* telling him, what do you think?' and laughed. But her next words were spoken quietly to me: 'He's upset about the house.'

I was going to ask a question, but at that moment the door flew open and Alastair stood there.

'Where in God's name have you been all day?' He was frowning, and I felt the force of his personality like the heat from a furnace when the door is opened. 'Now you're here you might at least come upstairs.'

'Well,' I said as I entered his room, 'what *is* all this about Kingisbyres?'

'What have you heard?'

'Tosh told me the Captain was going to Africa. I suppose it's to convalesce?'

'Convalesce! A long convalescence! He's going for three years.'

'Three years! And what's to happen to the house?'

'It's to let. And who do you suppose it's to be let to?'

A flash of illumination struck me.

'Oh my God—not the biscuit people?' I was taken aback by the depth of my feeling of revulsion.

'Exactly,' said Alastair, 'the biscuit people.'

During the heavy silence that followed Miss Craig put her head round the door and said: 'Now you'll take an egg to your tea, won't you?'

'Oh,' said Alastair, 'an egg. Yes. Yes. I suppose so.'

'Oh yes,' I said, 'an egg—yes, I mean yes, thank you very much.'

'What can they want to live at Kingisbyres for?' I said. 'Surely they must see it's unsuitable.'

Alastair made an impatient gesture, and his frown deepened. He muttered something.

'What?' I said.

'I said I didn't know what you had to be so snobbish about.'

'My objections to the Harveys taking Kingisbyres aren't personal. They're aesthetic.' Alastair made a grunting noise of profound disapproval. My hurt momentarily changed into annoyance.

'And what about yourself?' I said. 'You're in a screaming temper yourself. What about?'

He made the same grunting noise, and his frown deepened into a scowl.

'Well,' I said, 'go on. *What about?*'

Alastair, who was standing beside his dressing table, had his back towards me. I noticed that he was fiddling with one of a pair of china ornaments. Suddenly, without any warning, he hurled it with terrific force against the wall, where it shattered.

'About nothing.' He turned towards me, and his face was twisted. 'I'm just angry, that's all.' The second ornament smashed against the wall, and Alastair contemplated the wreckage. When he spoke again his expression was normal and his voice curiously restrained, almost gentle. 'I'm just angry,' he repeated. 'Just angry.'

WHEN I HEARD that Captain Keith was going to Kenya and had let Kingisbyres to the Harveys, I believed that I should never see either Captain Keith or Kingisbyres again. Being young, I thought in terms of sudden endings, complete breaks, new beginnings. It did not even occur to me for some time that as a matter of common courtesy Alastair and I should call upon the Captain before he left for Kenya; still less that he would invite us to do. My deepest, secret feeling was that the Captain, in letting Kingisbyres, above all in letting it to the Harveys, was betraying a trust, a trust of which I was myself a kind of co-trustee. This was of course very absurd, but for one thing, I still found it hard to understand that a man in Captain Keith's position might simply be unable to afford to keep up a house like Kingisbyres, and that as for the Harveys, he was lucky to get a tenant at all. In a fit of cross-grained, adolescent bitterness I refused to admit that the Captain himself might—indeed must—be unhappy. I looked upon him with hostility, and, perhaps because of a subconscious recognition of my own absurdity, felt that he must be hostile to me.

It was therefore with great surprise that I received a note from the Captain himself, thanking me for the water-colour of the house, and saying that he would have to 'take his great-aunt's daubs' off the wall, since they weren't fit to hang with mine. He also thanked me for the kind inquiries I had made during his illness, said that he was now much better, but, as I would have heard, had been advised to spend some time in a warmer climate, and asked me to come to tea. The day he proposed was, as it turned out, the second Sunday of the new term. It was a very courteous note, flattering in its terms, flattering even in its existence—since the Captain seldom wrote letters at all—and it mollified my feelings very much, without however altogether driving out a residue of hurt and resentment. Alastair, of course, had been invited as well. He had now closed up about the whole business, and would say nothing about it, except once when he remarked that it would be a pity not to be able to go swimming in the Kingisbyres pool during the summer holidays. Since we were both hiding our feelings we could not discuss the matter.

But I was curious about the Harveys and one day an idea occurred to me. As I was coming out of the art classroom on the first day of term I saw a Third Form boy called Mooney about whose origins I dimly remembered my father saying something. I called him over.

'Mooney,' I said, 'your father owns all those teashops in Glasgow doesn't he?' He looked up, taken aback to be addressed by a Senior.

'Uh-huh.'

'Don't say "uh-huh", say "Yes, Shaw".'

'Yes Shaw.'

'That's better. Your father has worked hard all his life opening one teashop after another, and he doesn't want to hear you say uh-huh, as though you were all still in Cowcaddens. You'll remember that, won't you? Now for Christ's sake don't say uh-huh.'

'No Shaw. I mean, yes Shaw, I'll remember.'

'Good. Now tell me, do you know the Harveys, the biscuit people?'

'Yes, Shaw.'

'Personally, I mean. Do you know anything about Mr Harvey and Mrs Harvey?'

'Yes, Shaw. Mr Harvey's an old friend of Dad's—'

'Not "Dad's", Mooney. "My father's".'

'My father's. They were in business together once.'

'I see. And Mrs Harvey? Is she a friend of your mother's?'

'No. Not really. I mean she never comes to tea or anything. She's English. She's Mr Harvey's second wife, but they've been married for ages. Mr Harvey's first wife was the one that was really a friend of my mother's.'

'I see. And is the story true, do you know, that Mr Harvey's grandmother started making the business by selling biscuits in her cottage somewhere near here?'

'Oh yes. I'm sorry, Shaw, I forgot that. But I'm sure it's true. At least I've forgotten where it was, but it's true about the cottage. They use a cottage for their trade mark you know, and it's a picture of Mr Harvey's granny's cottage—the real one. I've heard—my father say so.'

'Thank you Mooney. You've been very helpful. So I'm glad I was able to help you by telling you not to say uh-huh.'

I did feel that Mooney had been helpful, and when I saw Alastair I gave my translation of the information. When I told him I had got some information about the Harveys he said at first he wasn't interested, but when I said in that case I wouldn't bore him, he scowled and said he supposed he might as well hear it.

'It's true about granny and the cottage,' I said. 'Harvey himself is a successful business man with no social pretensions. But when his first wife died that woman we saw got hold of him, for his money presumably. I imagine she refused to have anything to do with his old friends and she's been working on him for years to drop them. She's English.'

Alastair made a Scotch noise in his throat.

The journey to Kingisbyres on the Sunday was a gloomy affair. Over it there hung the rather dreary sentimentality of doing for the last time something that one likes doing. In any case neither of us had ever enjoyed these Sunday visits in term time so much as the easy, informal, habitual visits of the holidays. We felt Sundayfied, and constrained. Anyway Alastair and I were not at this time on quite the best of terms; or perhaps I should say, on quite our usual terms, which were rudely argumentative. Some coolness had come between us, a coolness of obscure origin connected with our feelings about Kingisbyres. The result was that we arrived at the house in a cold, ruffled, disagreeable mood; at least that is how I felt. Henstridge received us with complete formality—another characteristic of these Sunday visits—and led us up to the drawing-room in silence. There was something funereal about this silent procession. We turned a corner into a small hall, and I saw once again the painting of a Keith who had been a general. It was not a very good painting; but it showed the general playing with his dog, a spaniel, and somehow the artist had caught the sense that he really was playing with it, indifferent to having his portrait painted, a smiling, homely, yet dignified man. Below this, in a glass case, hung his sword draped in frail dusty black. It seemed to sum up Kingisbyres, the intimacy, the dignity, and the sword.

Then we were shown into the drawing-room. The Captain was not alone; there was with him in the drawing-room a woman and a girl of about fifteen. It was with a slow, echoing shock that I heard the Captain introducing Alastair and myself to Mrs Harvey and her daughter Catherine.

'Alastair and Patrick,' said the Captain, 'are neighbours of mine here, and so will be neighbours of yours.'

Did Mrs Harvey look askance at us for an instant before she registered a polite greeting? Probably I only fancied this, for Mrs Harvey was too experienced socially to betray any recollection of our last meeting. Alastair thought, so he told me afterwards, that she hadn't recognized us. But I did not believe this, and I do not believe it now. I believe that our acquaintance with Mrs Harvey was vitally influenced by her first impression of us as two weirdly dressed tramps, consorting with the village idiot, or to put it in more picturesque terms, as a couple of peasants at the gates of the castle as the chatelaine drove out in her coach. But an instant later those impressions of Mrs Harvey were submerged.

'Oh do tell me'—for the first time we heard the voice of Catherine Harvey—'are there many young people around here? I've been absolutely aching to know.' Her eagerness bubbled over into a laugh, in which, as in her voice, despite the gaiety and assurance, there was something hectic. I looked at her sharply. Her features were not striking—attractive rather than pretty—but she was dark, with striking eyes. And what was even more striking about her was her vividness, the instant impression that she gave of animation, of energy, of personality, an impression which was not less

but more exciting, because she was in the puppy-fat stage
of girlhood, and because she was dressed with extremely
severe good taste in the slightly dowdy and juvenile manner
which her mother knew to be correct for a schoolgirl visiting
in the country.

'There are plenty,' I said, 'where we are, at Nethervale.'

'Nethervale?' Mrs Harvey gave a brilliant ravaged smile.

'Nethervale School,' I added.

'Oh it's a *school*—I see—yes, of course.' She laughed,
a harsh noise, but she had registered that we were at a
school which she did not recognize. Then, at once, she
asked Captain Keith about a woman in the village who
did the Kingisbyres laundry. I could not have been more
completely dismissed if she had ordered me out of the
room, and for a moment I had that gathering sense, that
oddly delayed recognition of the socially inexperienced, that
I had been snubbed. I was, of course, hurt and angry, but
perhaps my lack of social experience saved me from being
even more hurt and angry, and in any case I felt that Mrs
Harvey's having snubbed me placed her as nothing else
would have done. From that moment onwards I was never
able to take her completely seriously.

'Agnes?' The Captain was saying. 'Oh, I'm sure you'll
find her very satisfactory—very good at her work, you
know, and very obliging. Unfortunately she's going to
Canada for about three months—she has some nephews
and nieces there, and she's going to visit them.'

'Isn't it funny, they always have nephews and nieces in
Canada! I had a cook who left me about two years ago to
go on a Canadian tour. I offered to keep the place open
for her, but she said she really didn't know how long she
would be!'

'Rather sporting, I think,' said the Captain, and both
the stylized Edwardian phrase and a kind of dry vagueness
in his tone indicated to me that he found Mrs Harvey
embarrassing. There was the briefest pause. 'In Agnes'
case, I mean,' said the Captain, 'for she's getting on in
years, and she's never been farther than Glasgow in her
life. Must be over sixty, I think.'

'She's sixty-two,' said Alastair, entering the conversation

for the first time. 'I know, because she's a friend of my aunt's.' He spoke in a voice which I knew he intended to be cold and challenging, but which only succeeded in sounding rude. I could almost see Mrs Harvey wince.

'Oh, Alastair,' said the Captain, 'why don't you and Patrick take Catherine out and show her round—Mrs Harvey and I have a number of small business matters to clear up which I expect you three would find very boring.' He smiled to Mrs Harvey. 'Alastair and Patrick know more about this place than anyone else.' Mrs Harvey gave a brief non-committal smile, she hardly seemed to have heard what it was the Captain had said.

As soon as we had closed the door of the drawing-room behind us Catherine Harvey turned round to me: 'Oh, I'm so glad to have met you! And now you must show me everything!' As she spoke she gave a loud high-pitched laugh, a gurgling kind of laugh that was full of life and charm, yet which seemed to me even then a little wild and nervy. At the same time, with a quick gesture she put her hand momentarily on my sleeve between the elbow and the wrist. I had a curious sensation, as though the beam of a searchlight had passed across me, but the next moment Catherine had turned away from us and was walking rapidly across the hall, looking back over her shoulder, and although we were following immediately behind, saying: 'Oh do come on. I've been aching to get out—I thought I'd die of boredom if I had to sit in there another minute.'

'Let's go down to the river,' I said, 'to the pool, and then along the bank and up to . . .' So I began to plan an expedition, catching from Catherine her excitement, beginning, as I answered her questions, also to catch a little her trick of laughing at nothing. At first I had been disconcerted and put off by the traces in her voice and manner of her mother's voice and manner. But after a few minutes I no longer noticed these, for whatever her mother's attitude might be, Catherine was not only friendly—she was forcing the pace of intimacy. But all the time, as she and I chattered, I was aware of Alastair at our side, withdrawn, frowning, blackly silent. I noticed Catherine glancing at him once or twice and already, it seemed, I knew her well enough to know that she was capable of making some direct challenge to him, but she did not, and after we got outside he overcame his mood sufficiently to be able at least to reply to questions, although monosyllabically.

Yet when we reached the top of the bank that ran down to the river, above the deep pool where we swam, and which now, because the river was still in spate, was full of swirling peat-brown water on which patterns of saffron-coloured foam formed and broke, we all three jumped and slithered down like children. And here in this miniature mountain valley, this little rocky cleft in the moors, where the air was charged with the heavy hypnotic noise of the waterfall above the pool, and the patterns of foam forming and opening like hands and weaving and reforming added to the hypnotic effect, we found ourselves in a place shut away and isolated even from the lonely moors. A change had come over us; it was no longer a situation of Alastair and I on one side, and Catherine Harvey on the other, each side being a kind of expeditionary force, on the one side for Captain Keith and on the other for Mrs Harvey, but rather that we three, even although there was opposition between Alastair and Catherine, were in some way united.

'This is where we swim,' I said, and suddenly with a new pang realized that our swimming here, which I had thought of as a right, was in fact a privilege which we had lost. Even if we came here as Catherine's guests, which, in view of Mrs Harvey's attitude, I thought unlikely, it wouldn't be the same thing.

'Do you really swim in there? It looks so cold and *beery*.' She gave the loud, nervy, yet also genuinely amused laugh which was her special manifestation.

'That's only because the river is high.' Alastair's voice was curt and heavy, but it was the first remark he had contributed at all, and it marked a further development in the situation.

'Would you swim in there now?' Suddenly admiring and submissive, Catherine made what an older generation called sheep's eyes at Alastair. And Alastair responded. Glancing casually at the pool, he said in an offhand voice: 'I wouldn't mind.'

'Go on then.' Catherine's voice was transformed; no longer admiring and submissive, but challenging. Alastair flushed darkly, and, taken aback for a moment, looked at her. Then, almost before I realized it, he had taken off his jacket and flung it on the ground. When he pulled at his collar the button flew off violently.

'Oh Alastair,' said Catherine in a sugary voice, 'don't be absurd.' She too, was a little flushed. Alastair hesitated; the rhythm of his determined gestures was broken. Looking at him, I was suddenly conscious of the short half-visible downy hair on his face; that horrible condition of adolescence, neither one thing nor the other, like a nobleman's bastard! Even then I felt it. He picked up his jacket with a lumpish, sulky air, and we all began to climb the bank again in an indeterminate way. At the top Alastair, with a half-audible mutter, turned away abruptly and left us.

'Where's he gone?' Catherine sounded astonished; she apparently did not connect Alastair's behaviour with her own.

'I don't know. I expect he'll join us again shortly.'

'I suppose you and he are great friends?'

'I suppose we are.'

'Does he always behave like this?'

'Like what?'

'I mean walking off like that and beginning to tear his clothes off—' Catherine giggled, and then, putting on a severe and priggish expression, added, 'and being rude to Mummy in the drawing-room.'

'Was he rude?' I was angry. 'I thought your mother—' Catherine grabbed my hand.

'If you say a *word* against Mummy I shall walk straight back to the house and never speak to you again.' She had turned round and was facing me, looking up, a plump plain schoolgirl with—at the moment—a rather red face, but with a vividness and candour that drew me irresistibly. In that moment I fell under the spell.

'I wasn't *going* to say a word against your mother—naturally—I wouldn't dream of it. All I meant was, Alastair's rather touchy, that's all.'

'What was all that about the laundress being a friend of his aunt? Who *is* his aunt? What about his parents?'

'He's an orphan. His aunt's called Miss Craig. She keeps a shop in the village.'

'I believe you're pulling my leg.' Catherine looked at me suspiciously.

'I'm not, honestly.'

'Well, I mean, why doesn't he go to the village school or something? Is he a scholarship boy?' Actually there were no scholarships at Nethervale except for a couple of wretched twenty-pound-a-year things for the 'sons of officers', but some sense of discretion prevented me from telling the truth; I felt certain that if Catherine were to learn that Alastair's fees were paid by Captain Keith she would be on to the problem like a terrier on to a rat, and that would be undesirable.

'Yes,' I said.

'Oh, I see. What does *your* father do?' Catherine's voice was sharp.

'He's an unemployed lavatory attendant.' She looked at me for an instant. Then she laughed, the same laugh.

'I think you're quite mad,' she said, and her large dark eyes snapped at me caressingly. 'What does he really do?'

'He's a schoolmaster at Nethervale. He teaches mathematics.'

'Are *you* good at mathematics?'

'No. It's Alastair who's the mathematician.'

'Never mind about Alastair. It's *you* I'm interested in.' Catherine looked at me again, and a kind of ecstatic terror seized me. For I now realized that she was flirting with me. I had been slow to realize it not only because of natural timidity and backwardness, but because I believed that girls of fifteen at expensive boarding-schools led a cloistered existence devoted to lacrosse and holiday visits to Dresden. Catherine, however, was flirtatious; if there is another word for describing her behaviour it is 'coquettish'. These are old-fashioned words, and there was in fact something old-fashioned in the frank pleasure that she took in attracting interest and admiration, in her unadolescent ease and pleasure in sex. At that time hearty companionship between young people of both sexes was the approved modern attitude, at least in the circles in which I had been brought up. I was to learn a great deal more about Catherine's attitude; but at that moment, during that first tête-à-tête, I was not in a discerning mood. I was filled with a combination of the exquisite satisfaction which a man derives from the attention of an attractive woman, and the sense of inadequacy, amounting to terror, which a boy experiences in a social situation where he doesn't know the rules. However, if there was one thing I could do it was talk, and already I was helplessly caught in the business of 'entertaining' Catherine, talking to her as for a bet, mixing information about the history of Kingisbyres with elaborate wordy compliments, making her laugh, and going all out to win her interest. And as we talked we walked along the top of the steep bank of the river, now in sight of the house, but soon, I knew, dipping into another of these miniature valleys where we should be alone and hidden. I was desperately conscious of the girl beside me, in the lemon-yellow cardigan and pale-grey pleated flannel skirt, so schoolgirlish, so very, very correct, and of the clash between the cliché upper-class *jeune-fille* clothes and the flash and crackle of the personality. The path took the turn downwards towards the river; there was a flight of rough steps overhung by silver birches, turning sharply with the curve of the bank, which at this point was almost a cliff. It was here that, stepping ahead of her, I took Catherine's hand—it was a small plump hand with tapering fingers, elegantly shaped but surprisingly rough and weather-beaten—and helped her over one of the steps which had gone askew. As she stepped down beside me she smiled, in invitation so open and so charming, that I found the courage to draw her towards me and kiss her on the lips. She smelt faintly of newly washed wool and of something which I afterwards discovered was Johnson's baby powder. Although she did not open her lips, she *did* press her body against mine. After a moment however she broke away and said:

'I wondered whether you were going to do that.' Her voice was absurdly complacent.

I made to kiss her again, but she evaded me.

'Not now,' she said, and laughed. 'When did you decide you wanted to kiss me?' As she asked me this question in a business-like tone of voice Catherine took my hand.

'As soon as I saw you.' This was not true, but I knew it was the right thing to say. We began to walk along the path together.

'Did you think I was attractive?' This—words rather than action—was what I was good at: I began to tell Catherine how attractive I thought she was. After a few moments she gave a lively squeal of delight, threw her arms round my neck, kissed me, and said: 'You do that frightfully well, you ought to be on the stage.' Not for the last time in my dealings with Catherine I was taken aback. But again she broke away at once, and said: 'And now you can tell me about Alastair if you like.' In fact I did not like: I was much too occupied with adjusting myself to the revolutionary situation in which I found myself; but before I had time to say anything at all Catherine added: 'I'm sorry, but I don't like him.'

'He wasn't absolutely at his best today.' I hoped this line of conversation wouldn't be pursued.

'I suppose he's very clever?'

'Yes. Very. But what made you suppose it particularly?'

'He has that clever, Scotch, glum look.'

'He isn't glum, honestly.'

Catherine shrugged impatiently.

'Well, you know what I mean. And it was very rude going off like that. I suppose he's no time to waste on girls?'

'Oh yes,' I said. This was a charge on which I could defend Alastair with confidence. 'He's supposed to be very successful with girls.'

'What girls?'

'Well, girls in the village, in the holidays.'

'Village girls!' exclaimed Catherine. 'Making love in the pigstyes, I suppose.'

It was at this moment that Alastair came back. He scrambled down the bank and jumped down beside us, and there was an uncomfortable moment during which I wondered if he had overheard Catherine's last words, perhaps even the conversation preceding them. But apparently he had not; at any rate, it appeared at once that his mood had changed.

'Well,' he said, 'I hope Patrick has been entertaining you.'

I recognized the dig at my well-known talkativeness, my anxiety to please.

'He's been very nice,' said Catherine, emphasizing 'He's'.

'I'm sorry I had to leave you.' Alastair's tone was very unlike the sulky gaucheness he had displayed in the drawing-room. This tone was something new; I had noticed it occasionally during the previous month or two. It was as though the sessions with my mother, the visits to Kingisbyres, the meetings with people like the Clandillons, had suddenly 'taken'; but this was not quite the case, for my mother had certainly never intended that blandness and ease should be used as a weapon. 'But I wanted,' he continued, 'to go and look at something that Captain Keith was talking about. I'm interested in the history of Kingisbyres, you know.'

'Well,' said Catherine, 'you might have shown it to me. After all, I'm going to live here!'

'Yes of course,' said Alastair. 'You're really part of the history, aren't you?' He spoke with the same bland smile, and now the implications were as clear as they were derisory. At least, they were to me; if they were clear to Catherine she did not betray it. With a politeness and social control equal to Alastair's own she began to ask questions about the history of Kingisbyres, and before long we were engaged in a quite serious discussion of it.

Talking this way we walked back to the house. No doubt, to anyone overhearing us, the conversation would have sounded quite normal and friendly, but I knew very well that Alastair and Catherine were hostile and critical of one another, fencing, feeling for one another's weak spots. When we got back to the house the big Daimler that we had seen before was standing in front of the door, and Catherine said: 'Oh, Daddy's arrived.' And when we got into the drawing-room, there in fact was Mr Harvey, a

thick-set stoutish man, rather impressively immobile as to
his body, but with hooded, restless, observant eyes. Beside
him stood Charles Crimond, ostentatiously of the outdoors,
with his red cheeks, meaty hands, and shabby loud tweeds;
by contrast Mr Harvey looked white and manicured and
citified. Both of them had glasses in their hands, as had
Mrs Harvey and the Captain. It was long past tea-time; we
had never thought of it. As we entered, the conversation
appeared to be lively; on Crimond's lips I heard the word:
'. . . knew him at Rugby.'

'Catherine!' Mrs Harvey welcomed her daughter with
a screech. 'Come, darling, and meet Mr Crimond—he's
going to be a neighbour of ours—or rather we're going to
be neighbours of his—and he knows the Whitwells!'

Catherine greeted Crimond with bubbling enthusiasm,
and he, for the first time since I had known him, changed
his behaviour from a kind of heavy contemptuous off-
handedness—modified by certain gestures of conventional
respect when he spoke to the Captain—to a loud gallantry.
But I wasn't able to observe this performance as closely as I
wanted to, because meanwhile the Captain was introducing
Alastair and myself to Mr Harvey. As I felt the small plump
hand, the quick eyes rested on me for a moment and the
lips were withdrawn in a restricted, pursy smile.

'Ah,' said Mr Harvey, 'so you're the artist, are you?
Captain Keith has just been showing us your painting of
the house.' He spoke with more of a Glasgow accent than
I had expected. I made some suitable remark.

'It's very good,' said Mr Harvey. 'I recognized the house
at once. And are you an artist too?' He turned to Alastair.

'No,' said Alastair, 'I'm not.' If Mr Harvey's manner
of complacent patronage had been a little more marked,
Alastair might have been able to take it as an absurdity;
but Mr Harvey escaped being absurd. Alastair's layer of
blandness, still thin, had been penetrated, but Mr Harvey
was too obtuse, or more probably too indifferent, to react
to his bleakness.

'And what are you then?' The smile operated again,
briefly.

'At present I'm specializing in mathematics.' This time

Alastair sounded pompous as well as bleak. It was an unhappy combination, and no doubt he recognized this.

'Mathematics! And what use are you going to make of that? Are you thinking of engineering?'

Alastair always took such questions as a challenge.

'No,' he said, 'I'm going to the English Bar.'

'The English Bar!' Mr Harvey's mouth was slightly more pursed than before; then he laughed a little. I think that he had suddenly realized that Alastair's coldness was deliberate. 'I suppose you've been reading the life of Marshall Hall, eh, or someone like that?'

I felt my heart give a jump, for I knew that to Alastair this question would appear as an insult, and I was afraid of what he might say. Before he could speak, however, Mrs Harvey suddenly claimed her husband, and at the sound of her voice he immediately turned his back upon Alastair without giving him any chance to reply. As for Mrs Harvey, she completely ignored both of us, and tried to draw the Captain too into the conversation. He, however, did not appear to have heard her; his face was completely expressionless, and after looking at him for a moment Mrs Harvey turned away, perhaps believing him to be a little deaf. As soon as she turned away however he smiled to us and said: 'You two must stay on after the others—I've something to say to you.' Then he turned and joined the Harveys and Charles Crimond.

There was now a general movement of departure. Crimond went first, pressed by Mrs Harvey to call upon her as soon as she was established. His spaniel— he competed with the Captain in breeding spaniels—rose from the end of the room and joined him and he cuffed the dog with an affectionate dog-lover's gesture.

'He's just waiting to be a proud papa.' Crimond's loud laugh beat upon us as he bent down and pulled the long ear. 'Doesn't look very worried, does he!' He gave a kind of conventionalized leer at Catherine. 'You must come over and see the litter.'

'Oh I should absolutely *adore* to,' said Catherine, 'but I shall be at school, you know.' She rolled her eyes at him, and my heart contracted with jealousy. I now felt completely miserable, for I had never been either socially snubbed or made sexually jealous before.

'She ought to be there now,' said Mrs Harvey, 'but she's had whooping cough. Girls'—she pronounced it 'gels'—'are a frightful nuisance really.'

The remark was addressed to Crimond who smirked and exploded into: 'Oh I say, come Mrs Harvey—' and so on, as we all made our way out of the drawing-room. I went along, feeling desolate, because I wanted a chance to speak to Catherine, and Alastair came too because the Captain nodded to him to do so. He and I were bringing up the rear, when about half-way downstairs, Catherine suddenly said that she had forgotten her gloves. Crimond, walking ahead of her with Mrs Harvey, made a convulsive turn, but Catherine had already turned back and caught my eye.

'I'll get them,' I said.

'Perhaps you won't be able to find them.' As soon as we entered the drawing-room Catherine drew up and faced me.

'Patrick—would you write to me sometimes? I get terribly bored and lonely at school.' With her exquisitely spontaneous coquetry she put her hand on my forearm again and smiled up to me. A little incoherently I said that I would. But then the jealousy that had been building up in my heart over-flowed.

'Have you asked Charles Crimond to write to you too?'

Catherine opened her eyes.

'No, of course not. Surely you're not jealous of Charles Crimond?'

It was not easy to deny this convincingly.

'You mustn't be. Honestly. I know scores of people exactly like that.' She spoke contemptuously and impatiently. 'It's just that he's a neighbour—I have to be polite. But you're different. No one's ever spoken to me like you did this afternoon.' Almost anaesthetized with pleasure I made a gesture to take Catherine in my arms. But she smiled and drew back.

'No,' she said, 'there isn't time now. Next holidays you shall. You must come and see me the instant I get back.'

'I don't think,' I said, anxious to have my second worry put down, 'that your mother likes me very much.'

'She doesn't know you yet. She confused you with that horrible Alastair person.' I began to say something, but Catherine pulled me impatiently towards the door. 'I know he's a friend of yours, but I can't help it, I think he's the most hateful person I've ever met. Now we must go down.'

'Your gloves,' I said. Catherine pulled them out of her bag.

'If I'd really left them,' she said, 'someone might have seen them before I got out of the door.'

When we reached the hall, the party was standing about waiting and chatting. This entrance hall was one of the 'features' of Kingisbyres. It housed a collection of Scottish arms and armour, and the walls bristled with swords and halberds and Jedburgh axes. The Captain was talking about these, and while Mr Harvey looked bored enough, both Crimond and Mrs Harvey appeared to be taking an interest; no doubt each considered this interest proper to the roles, of chatelaine of Kingisbyres, and of sporting country gentleman, in which they fancied themselves. Perhaps, on the other hand, they were only sucking up to Captain Keith; at any rate, when he asked Alastair to bring down a sword to illustrate something that he had said, it seemed to me that their interest suddenly waned. Alastair scrambled up on to a large marble-topped table and lifted a sword off the hook on which it hung. It was a beautiful weapon, a basket-handled Highland sword in its scabbard, with a damascened blade, and I myself, with some rather reluctant help from Alastair, had oiled and polished it only a few weeks before. He turned round, with the sword and scabbard in his hand, as Catherine and I reached the foot of the stairs. The Captain was standing beside the table with the Harveys, with Crimond a little in front of them, in a group facing it. As we reached this point Mrs Harvey turned and greeted Catherine, and her father and Crimond also half-turned towards her. Turning their attention away from Alastair in this way at the very moment when he was about to show them the sword was a piece of rudeness which was characteristic of all three of them. I had just taken it in when Alastair drew the sword from its scabbard.

He drew it, with a long sweep of his arm, in one movement, so that suddenly the light flashed all along the naked blade, and I heard the menacing whistle in the air. We were all startled, but the Captain, Catherine, and I had at least been looking at him, so that we were half-prepared. But the others had not; they turned with a start, and as the blade swept upwards it caught their eyes and jerked them helplessly after it. There was a moment in which everyone in the hall was staring up at the sword with a kind of fascination, and Alastair was looking down upon us, smiling.

'Damn it,' said Crimond, 'do be careful with that thing.' But he was probably the least angry of the three.

'One has to do it like that,' said Alastair, 'or else it jams.' He spoke mildly and reasonably, but he was looking, not at Crimond, but at the Harveys, and it may be that they had in that moment a glimpse of the truth—that it was an armed enemy who stood over them. At any rate no one said anything further, and everyone examined the sword with an appearance of attention.

'I let him get away without an answer,' said Alastair, 'and may I burn in hell for it!' His voice was low; he was in a murderous rage. We were on the way home.

'Yes,' I said, 'he is disagreeable.' I was engaged in the process of falling in love with Catherine. It was almost a physical sensation, a kind of tingling feeling all through my body. I wanted to think well, or at least as well as possible, of her parents, hard as it was to do so.

'Disagreeable!' said Alastair. 'They're poison. They're cyanide. I hope their biscuits choke them. In fact—' Alastair was talking himself out of his anger. 'I'll put a curse on them. That's a fine old Scottish custom. It should appeal to you. Make them one of our Best Families, too.' He began to intone, his voice seeming to echo a little from the high mossy wall of Kingisbyres, which we had not yet left behind us. 'May their biscuits choke them, their usurped house fall on them, and may God withhold his

mercy from them on the great Day of Judgment.' Alastair
paused, and added: 'That goes for Crimond too. He's not
worth a separate curse.'

'No,' I said, 'he really *is* the end.' About Crimond I could
wholeheartedly agree.

'Although,' said Alastair cruelly, 'your little piece in the
yellow sweater didn't seem to think so.'

'She's got to be civil to him. After all, they're going to
be neighbours.'

'So are Mrs Harvey and I. But she didn't offer herself
to me.' Alastair, I could see, was in an excited, belligerent
mood, a mood which I knew and which was marked by
cruelty and a special kind of coarse humour. 'Of course,'
he went on, 'I don't belong to the landed gentry. At any
rate Mrs Harvey doesn't know of such claims as I may
have. And Mr Crimond does belong. I think, don't you,
we might call Miss Harvey and Mr Crimond the nubility
and landed gentry?' With Alastair in this mood I could not
confess to him my feelings about Catherine. So I tried a red
herring.

'Crimond doesn't really belong to the landed gentry,' I
said. 'I mean his father was a shipbuilder, you know, in
Clydebank.'

'And I suppose,' said Alastair, 'that you look down on
him for that, as though you were fancying prize stock.
The Keiths have owned Kingisbyres for ten generations
or more, so they get a hundred marks; Crimond's second
generation, so he gets ten; and the Harveys get nothing so
far. You're playing their own idiotic game!'

'And whose game are you playing?' Suddenly angry, I
launched a counter-attack which had been building up in
my mind for some time. 'Who wants to go to the Bar
and make twenty thousand a year and end up as Lord
Chief Justice? And what then? I bet you do just like the
Harveys and the Crimonds—buy a place in the country—
probably in Scotland.' A brilliant idea struck me. 'Why,'
I said, 'you'd buy Kingisbyres if it was on the market.'
For answer Alastair, who was cycling perhaps half a wheel
ahead of me, suddenly and without warning pulled his front
wheel across mine. We were not going particularly fast at

the time, but naturally there was an almighty crash. As it happened, I fell across Alastair, and got off with a jarred wrist; he himself, however, scraped his left cheekbone on the road, and as he sat up the blood started welling out, and he mopped it with a handkerchief.

'That was a damned silly thing to do,' I said. But it was merely a comment. I didn't feel angry or even annoyed; in fact, I felt much calmer.

'It was, wasn't it?' Alastair mopped his cheek again and examined the result on his handkerchief. 'But I felt I needed it.' I nodded, and we began to disentangle the bicycles. They were undamaged; we had been lucky.

'All the same,' he said, 'you're wrong about Kingisbyres. I may be ambitious, but I'm not sentimental. The idea of Scotland as a country is archaic, really—everyone who makes any money ceases to be recognizably Scotch in two generations. Look at Crimond—there's nothing Scotch about him but his boorishness. I'd rather be honest about it. I won't retire to Scotland to found a line of Old Rugbeian lairds. I'll retire as an Englishman to the South of France and keep a lot of whores.' We got back on our bicycles and set off again, but now, with our feelings changed by the collision, we could say more of what was really on our minds.

'It's rotten about the Captain,' I said. Carefully secured in its case on the back of my bicycle was a Highland pistol which had been removed from the dead hand of its owner on the field of Culloden. This had been the Captain's parting gift to me, a small return, he had said, for the painting I had given him. To Alastair also he had given a parting gift—a handsome if slightly battered desk which had stood in the corner of the library, and which Alastair had once, in the Captain's hearing, compared favourably with the rickety table in his room at home. This had given to Alastair, as the pistol had to me, a peculiar pleasure. It was a handsome possession, of a kind which suggested status; he liked it in itself because it was an efficient mechanism for keeping papers and so on; and as such it ministered to the achievement of his ambitions.

'Yes,' said Alastair, 'it is pretty rotten,' and for a few

minutes, perhaps, we emerged from the normal selfishness of youth and saw the events that were occurring as they must appear in the eyes of the Captain.

At any rate, a little later I was able to say: 'You don't think that Catherine's a bitch, do you?'

'So that's the way it is.' Alastair looked at me ruminatively but kindly. 'Who knows?' he added. 'I bet she leads you a hell of a dance, anyway.' Soon after this we reached the gates of Nethervale, and adult life was cut off from us as the noise of the sea sometimes is when, walking away from it, one turns a corner.

FIVE

YET ALASTAIR and I had now reached an age when, even in school, we could no longer be quite shut off from the noise of the sea. There was a lot of talk now about careers. Fully half our contemporaries were leaving Nethervale at the end of the term, when the summer holidays began. Seventeen rather than eighteen was the usual age for leaving Nethervale, since most of the boys were going straight into their family business. Of the remainder a number were usually going to study medicine at Glasgow or Edinburgh, while a small and privileged handful were going to either Oxford or Cambridge, there to seek the Rugger Blues which, short of their being capped for Scotland, would be the crown and culmination of their careers. As the term advanced and decisions were taken it became clear that those in our form who were staying on for a further year would need a good deal of mathematical coaching. For Alastair this was unfortunate, since it meant competition for my father's time. There began to be discussions about whether Alastair *should* stay on for a further year, or whether it would be better for him to go to Edinburgh University for a year and try his Cambridge scholarship from there.

My career was also in question. For some years past my father, if asked whether I had anything in mind, had been in the habit of saying, 'Well, he's thinking of medicine.' I had no idea of the origin of this myth, but whoever was asking would look at me without surprise and make some such encouraging remark as that he had never seen a starving doctor. But for some time it had been obvious that I was peculiarly ill-qualified for this well-fed profession. I was outstandingly bad at physics and chemistry; I had no interest whatever in a doctor's life; and I was now in fact set upon being an artist. I told my father this one Sunday in his study. It was after lunch, and he was sitting by the fire with a bottle of whisky and a glass beside him. He had a book on his knee, but he had ceased to read; he had begun to enter the alcoholic's Nirvana. It was the best moment at which to approach him. With less drink he would have been unapproachable; with more, he would later have denied responsibility for anything he had said.

'Hello,' he said. 'Sit down.' In this state he was kind and a little formal. Another drink or two and he would treat me even more formally and perhaps even more kindly, as though I were a stranger whom he was particularly glad to see.

'It's about this business of being a doctor,' I said. He put his hand out to pour another drink, but withdrew it without doing so.

'Yes?'

'I'm no good at any of the subjects.'

'So my colleagues tell me.'

'And I don't want to be a doctor.'

'What do you want to be?'

'I want to be an artist.' Put baldly like this in the atmosphere of my father's study, it sounded painfully ingenuous, even to me. My father's hand again started its movement towards the bottle, and again stopped.

'I see,' he said, and I knew, as clearly as though I were seeing it on a screen, that he was thinking of his days at a crammer in London, and seeing me condemned to a lifetime of cheap digs, shoddy food, and contempt. This mood was terribly catching; I found myself thinking that my father's moustache was whiter, more straggling than usual; his bony legs under their crumpled weekend flannels thinner than ever. Funereal ideas passed through my mind. As so often happened I had caught from my father the feeling that life was at best a poor affair; but I also had the feeling that, if this were so, I might as well live it my own way.

'What exactly would you want to do?' my father added. 'Teach?' Exactitude was the last thing that had any place in my desires, but I knew that I didn't want to teach.

'Possibly,' I said, 'but the training would be the same, anyway.'

'I suppose you would want to go to the Art College in Edinburgh?'

'Yes.'

'Have you found out what it costs, and so on?'

'Not in any detail.' Relieved that he would not have to face any painful financial business, my father poured out thee fingers of whisky and drank two of them.

'Surely,' he said, 'it's a very risky career, unless you do teach?' This, which from another man at this stage in the conversation would have been the opening of an attack on my project, meant nothing from my father. He had passed over one of those mysterious lines which mark the progress of drunkenness, shed his sense of failure and anxiety, and was merely making conversation. Soon, as he had done ever since I was eight, he would be politely pressing me to take a glass of whisky.

These discussions of the future, then, kept me aware of the world outside Nethervale. Also I had entered into a correspondence with Catherine Harvey. My first letter to her had been written in a shy and backward mood, and had been stilted and precious and no doubt extremely silly. But it seemed to have pleased her—after all, she was not yet sixteen—and the letters she wrote to me had all the naturalness, the gaiety, and the coquetry which, in its candour and lack of mawkishness, was this remarkable girl's special quality. She sent me a photograph, a snapshot, in one of her early letters, and her gypsy-maiden face was so alive that it seemed almost to be moving as I looked at it. My letters to her were worked over through long hours, and copied out sometimes three or four times as improvements occurred to me, and with brilliant impromptus—laboriously worked out—in the margins. There was a good deal about Kingisbyres in her letters, about what her mother was doing to the house—all the main furniture had been taken over under the lease, but the Harveys were entitled to redecorate and furnish some of the rooms—and, always, the assumption that Catherine and I would be seeing a lot of one another at Kingisbyres during the holidays. The prospect made me almost ecstatically happy, but at the same time embarrassed me. For the idea of going to Kingisbyres without Alastair seemed to me shockingly disloyal, and there was no suggestion in Catherine's letters that Alastair would be welcome there. In my earlier letters to Catherine I had mentioned Alastair's name freely, saying what I could to make her like him, and hoping that if I said enough she would at least accept him as my friend. But it didn't work out.

I remember one particular thing that went wrong. Alastair was, this term, competing in what is called the Bursary Competition of Edinburgh University, the open competitive scholarship examination. Of course, everyone entering any such examination makes a careful survey of old papers, spots recurring questions, and tries to work out which are likely to come up again in his own year. Coaches such as my father are experts at this. Alastair however had carried the matter further; he had made a kind of statistical analysis of all the questions in all his subjects back to 1918, and as a result composed model answers to several questions which he regarded as good bets. He had done this analysis only half seriously, since he liked doing such things in any case, but I made a story out of the episode in a letter to Catherine in the hope that she might impressed.

'Your story about Alastair,' Catherine replied, 'was awfully funny, but I think that's just because *you* were telling it. Actually it's just the kind of fearfully painstaking and thorough thing I should expect of him—I really can't think why you should have someone who does such dreary things as a friend. Anyway, I think it's unsporting. The girl who's head of my form here is fearfully religious and always prays before examinations and I said to her that was unsporting because what about complete heathens like me? So she said she would pray for guidance and I said to her I thought even that was a bit doubtful. She said firmly it could never be wrong to pray for guidance, and she did, and the guidance was to pray before examinations and pray that I would do well too. Well that was last term and in the exams at the end I came out second instead of third, and now Amabel is wondering if perhaps she isn't a Saint.

I'm sure in his own way Alastair feels very superior too, although I can't imagine why.'

And of course it was true that Alastair felt superior. In one particular way this worked to my advantage. He was already deadly tired of the atmosphere of school; his background no less than his abilities made him feel that it was absurd for boys of our age to be shut up together, besotted about rugger and cricket, inveterately foul-mouthed while rather grimly innocent of real sexual experience, and tending to develop furtive passions for younger boys. He therefore approved of my being in love with Catherine Harvey, and when I told him she expected to see a lot of me at Kingisbyres, and hinted at my reluctance to go there without him, he savagely ridiculed my sentimentality.

'You go to Kingisbyres,' he concluded, 'and give your little friend what she wants.'

The term, like all terms, seemed endless, but as usual I woke up one day to the fact that it was nearly over. The thought brought a kind of panic with it. Catherine had now become a dream to me, and in my worst moments I wasn't sure whether I had strength to face the reality. During the last few days I could hardly eat, and on the last Sunday of term I was afraid that my mother would notice this. But if she did she said nothing, and the day inexorably arrived when I set out for Kingisbyres, making the familiar journey for the first time alone. I had been asked to luncheon, and Catherine had given me some advice about my behaviour.

'I'm sure Mummy didn't really take agin' you,' she had written, 'except that you're mixed up in her mind with Alastair and how rude and queer he was. So if you don't remind her about Alastair and talk to her and amuse her and behave in your most *courtly* way I'm sure she'll love you. She's very interested in the history of Kingisbyres now and perhaps you could tell her things about it, only with a great deal of finesse you know because naturally she doesn't want to be made to feel like an intruder.'

So, in the regulation grey flannel suit, rather short in the sleeves and trousers, but which was nevertheless the most presentable clothing I possessed, I rode over the moors, summoning up all my reserves both of courtliness and finesse. As I grew near to Kingisbyres my nervousness increased. I was nervous of the place itself, so familiar and now to be so strange; of the servants, so different, I felt sure, from Henstridge; of Mrs Harvey and her high metallic voice; but above all of Catherine, this strange girl with whom I was so vulnerably in love. And in fact I saw changes even before I got through the gates. The great half-circle of gravel was not only free from weeds, but new gravel had been laid, and the drive, formerly so rutted as to be difficult to negotiate on a bicycle, was now smooth and neat as a municipal park.

I was utterly unprepared to find Catherine sitting on a tree-trunk round the first corner. As I turned the bend she rose to her feet and looked at me with a smile that was almost a laugh, and before I fully realized what had happened I had nearly run her down. And I had a most curious feeling, because I hardly recognized her. It was true that she was wearing tweeds, and that these made her look older than the yellow sweater and grey skirt in which I had last seen her. But that was not the real difficulty; it was simply that I didn't really know her face. It was composed, as she looked at me now, of curves and planes, of shapes and relationships, which were almost strange to me. Of course I had seen her only for an hour or two, and that almost three months ago, but had I not fallen in love with her? Surely I must have looked at her with some care. And her photo-graph, which I had examined with religious attention every day? Then after an instant it seemed that I saw her face again from a new angle, in a new focus, and I knew it.

Already I had got off my bicycle, but this journey's end was a little difficult, because a bicycle has either to be held or leant against something, and as there was nothing to lean it against I had to hold it rather awkwardly while Catherine leant across and kissed me lightly on the lips. As she held her face up to mine I saw tiny droplets of water in her black hair, and her dark golden skin was bright with the cold, and I felt a touch of her cheek, cold, and then of her lips, warm and with a kind of spring in them. This kiss was familiar rather than intimate, and its ease and candour ravished me almost beyond words.

'Oh,' she said, and she put her hand on my sleeve, 'I'm so glad to see you! Let me look at you!' And standing there smiling, almost laughing, she examined me briefly. 'Are you feeling shy?' The almost clinical note of the question amused me, and I was able to laugh.

'Yes,' I said.

'Oh, well, don't worry.' Catherine spoke as though shyness were an irritating minor complaint, like toothache. 'You'll get used to me.'

'Not easily,' I said. Catherine stopped smiling.

'You don't know what it's like,' she said, and her voice was serious, even heartfelt, 'to have someone saying nice things, and being polite, and setting me up in my own esteem, after months of everyone being jolly, or rude, or antiseptic in school.'

'Do you hate school?' I said. She had sent me a photograph of her school, a hygienic-looking place on the Berkshire Downs that made me think of racing stables, and now I thought of her as being conventionally unhappy there, and I suddenly boiled up with sentimental sympathy. I saw Catherine miserable, perhaps weeping—

'Oh no,' she said. 'Actually I rather like it. It's only that in some ways I'm not very well adapted to being a schoolgirl.' She spoke quite impersonally. 'Now,' she added, 'we ought to go along.'

I now saw a bicycle leaning against a tree, and Catherine pushed this out on to the drive and mounted it. By the time we came to the house I had recovered my voice, and we were talking quite happily. Only when we entered it did I feel something like a check, for we went in from the little lawn with the yew-hedge where the Captain had given us tea on my first visit to Kingisbyres, and so into the room, called the garden-room, which had been used for storing the sun-bleached old deckchairs on which we sat. Now this room—itself painted and new looking—housed a whole suite of 'garden furniture', a vast swinging seat under an awning, new deckchairs, long basket-chairs on wheels, a large folding table, golfing umbrellas, tennis and badminton and croquet equipment, all split-new and smelling of the shop. This sight had the effect of stirring up again resentment of the Harveys, and my resentment had in turn the odd effect of causing me to make a good impression upon Mrs Harvey. For instead of being nervous and talkative and inclined to show off, I apparently manifested a dignified reserve.

'Mummy thinks you have nice manners,' said Catherine later on. 'And I told her how you lived at —— and were supposed to have been going there and she said that no doubt explained it.'

Mrs Harvey was a tall woman, with big and rather clumsy bones, hair which was greyish-auburn when I first knew her, but which had once been red, and a weather-beaten kind of complexion. With her angularity, her physical dignity, and her suitable tweeds and shoes, it must be admitted that she looked the part of the chatelaine of Kingisbyres. By origin, as I learnt later, she was the daughter of a solicitor in the North of England, a man who had quarrelled with all his associates until he was reduced to a miserable job administering a derelict charity. Mrs Harvey herself had been working in the Conservative Central Office when she had met the widowed Mr Harvey during one of his visits to London. I felt a hardness in her, not a hardness like Alastair's, the hardness with which a man meets rivals, but something cold, selfish, and furtive. She spoke to me, perhaps, as amiably as her harsh, loud voice would permit; but it was not only pleasure at the thought of being alone with Catherine which made me welcome her announcement that we were going out; it was relief at getting away from her mother.

'Mummy—we're going out so that I can show Patrick the tennis court and things.' In her voice there was some of the harshness, even some of the loudness of her mother's, although I felt that what lay behind them was different.

'But Catherine—Patrick may want some more coffee!' There was a note of genuine, not merely social protest, in Mrs Harvey's voice. 'And I daresay he likes to sit quietly for five minutes after a meal, like a grown-up person, even if you want to run about like a hoyden.' She smiled at me now, conventionally, and I smiled back in the same way, but I realized that Catherine's restlessness, her strain of wildness, were a cause of worry. Indeed, the suddenness of Catherine's announcement, the impatience of her tone, had startled me a little.

'Of course he doesn't—do you, Patrick?'

'As a matter of fact,' I said quite truthfully, 'I don't.'

'Well,' said Mrs Harvey, 'don't let Catherine bully you. She's a frightful bully, you know. She bullies *me*'—Mrs Harvey smiled in recognition of the unexpectedness of anyone's bullying her—'but don't let her bully *you*.' She was, as I dimly sensed even then, making a kind of appeal to me, seeking in me an ally against something that she feared in her daughter, already beginning, as I was later to discover, a pattern of relationship with her daughter's friends.

'Certainly not,' I said, and smiled, for I had no idea how ludicrously hollow this boast was. Catherine merely laughed, took my hand, and led me to the door. Then, as I closed it behind us, she turned round to me, raised her arms round my neck, and opened her lips. It was a long-drawn-out kiss, both sensuous and passionate, the first truly adult kiss of my life, and for a moment I literally did not know where I was. Yet as soon as it was over, although I felt it was unworthy, I thought of Mrs Harvey emerging from the door by which we stood, or, even more likely, a servant coming to remove the coffee-tray. I must not, I felt, show myself less reckless than Catherine, yet it was with some apprehension mixed with my happiness that I bent to kiss her again. But she drew away from me.

'No. Let's go out now.' And, taking my hand again, she began to walk with me across the little hall in which we were standing, led me along a narrow corridor, and then down the broad stone stairs and so into the cold, echoing hall in which Alastair had drawn the sword. And all the way, and out through the door, and down the worn steps—on which a wounded man, falling from his horse on a snowy night too weak to knock, had once bled to death—she chattered again about school and the new tennis court. And she led me to this firmly, ignoring the tepidity of my interest, the impatience which I now felt to be alone with her in some undisturbed and convenient place. The site of the tennis court had in fact been chosen with some taste, a patch of what had been rough lawn, hidden from the house and not interfering with any of its immediate surroundings, the parterres now clipped and neat, Christian Keith's Italian garden with all its stonework already repointed, the sundial now restored to its column, the small lake tidied and cleared of rushes. The little piece of lawn was now a tennis court, an oblong of newly laid turf surrounded by steely wire-net, with bright lines and yellow-varnished net posts.

'You do play tennis, don't you?' Catherine turned upon me almost suspiciously.

'Yes,' I said, 'but not very well.' In fact I was quite good; I wanted to surprise Catherine.

'I'm rotten,' said Catherine indifferently, 'but Hero, that's the girl who's coming to stay with me, she's not bad.'

'Is there a girl coming to stay with you?' I asked. 'You didn't say anything about it in your letters.'

'Didn't I?' Catherine looked surprised. 'Oh well, I suppose I didn't because it's only just been fixed up.' I felt hurt, I hardly knew why, partly because, I suppose, I had somehow calculated on monopolizing Catherine's attention, and partly because of the casual way in which she had revealed that I was not going to do so.

'Tell me about her,' I said.

'Hero?' Catherine sounded surprised again. She always, as I was to find, expected one to know all about her friends without being told. She was one of those people whose conversation was always full of names, Hero, Anthony, Graham, Sally, John, Gerald, and if one were to say, 'Who's Gerald?' she would look surprised and a little annoyed and say, 'Why Gerald, of course, Sally's brother, surely I've talked to you about *Gerald*,' and pass on. 'Well Hero's at school,' she said, 'and her parents are divorced and she lives mostly with her mother in Sussex because she's crazy about horses. Her father lives in Curzon Street with his mistress who's a most disgusting woman, so Hero says.'

'What's her other name?'

'Prime-Challis.'

'Do you mean to say she's called Hero Prime-Challis?'

'Yes. The Prime-Challises are a very old Cambridgeshire

family.' Catherine reacted to the incredulous note in my
voice by speaking in her stickiest social manner, which I
found both absurd and intimidating.

'But she doesn't live in Cambridgeshire?'

'No. I told you, she lives in Sussex. But she wants to
live in Leicestershire. She's terrific about horses. She just
absolutely lives for hunting. I'm sure you'll love her.'

'I expect so,' I said, although not even my love for
Catherine could blind me to the extreme improbability of
my loving Hero Prime-Challis.

'And then,' said Catherine, 'there'll be Charles Crimond,
and lots of people we can have over for the day.' She
surveyed the scene with satisfaction. 'We've improved the
place quite a bit, don't you think?' she added at the end of
the survey. Suddenly my feeling about it welled up again. I
felt fiercely loyal to the shabbiness of the old Kingisbyres
and angry against the invasion from stockbrokerland.

'No,' I said, 'I think you've suburbanized it.' It was a
great deal more than I had meant to say, and I was taken
aback by my own unexpected frankness. I half expected
Catherine either to be mortally offended or else to burst
into tears. But she merely looked a little disconsolate.

'I don't think we have, really,' she said, rather slowly.
'But of course people will think so, because of who we are.
Mummy didn't want to take this place at all, you know.'

'But?' I said.

'But,' she said, 'Daddy wanted to. It was always here-
abouts that he wanted to buy a house. It was near here, you
know, that—that'—suddenly Catherine looked at me and
laughed—'the family fortunes were founded, you know.'

'Really?' I said.

'Heavens,' said Catherine, 'I should have thought the
whole neighbourhood knew all about *that*. Well, anyway,
we did, making things and selling them at the door, all very
humble-like. It was still just a local business when Daddy
took over. He built it up to what it is now.'

'I see,' I said.

'And he likes to be here and have people remember—'
Catherine broke off and gave a kind of wail. 'It's awful
really. There was an old man the other day who called me

Cathy! Scotch people always seem to be sentimental and familiar or else resentful and sullen. They don't seem to know how to be in-between like people in England!'

'Would you rather live there?' I asked. Catherine looked at me in astonishment.

'Well of course! Wouldn't you?' I remembered the eternal cricket match, the strawberries and cream, the peacefulness, and the loud, assured, polite voices.

'I don't know,' I said.

'I think you're quite, quite mad.' Catherine took my hand and pulled me after her. 'Now let's go somewhere where we shan't be disturbed.'

I led the way to a loft above the stables. It was one of many places to which, in this over-large house, no one ever came. But because the boiler for the greenhouses was down below, it was warm, and Alastair and I, by dusting a couple of old car seats we had found there, had made a kind of retreat of it. From the beams there hung harness, so old and dry that it was like cardboard, and where we had pushed them into a corner lay a heap of objects which I suppose no one but ourselves had seen for half a century—a tennis racket with no strings in its narrow oval frame, a single tree for a riding boot, a coachman's top-hat with its cockade, dusty, faded, tinder-dry. Here Catherine and I sat down on one of the car seats and began, a little awkwardly, but with great good will, to kiss one another.

I was so surfeited with happiness that I was able to remember that Catherine and I were very young, that no one could be expected to take our love affair at all seriously, and that in the normal course of events it couldn't last very long. I thought myself very adult and perceptive to have had such a flash of objectivity. I would have been surprised if at that moment I had learned that my love for Catherine was an adult love, or at least that if it was to give me only some of the happiness of an adult love it was to give me a full share of the wounding unforgettable pain.

SIX

'WELL,' SAID ALASTAIR, 'it's you, is it? The boy volup
tuary in person. Come in.' He sniffed as I went past.
'Scented from the boudoir. And how's Catherine?'

'Very well,' I said.

'I'm glad to hear it.' He went ahead of me into the
living-room, declaiming as he went:

> There Cathy tight, a lassie bright,
>> Besides a handsome fortune—
> Wha canna' win her in a night,
>> Has little art in courting.

It suddenly occurred to me that he was in very high
spirits. When he had finished he turned towards me. 'And
speaking of handsome fortunes, you owe me ten shillings,'
he concluded. For an instant I didn't know what he was
talking about, and then, apart from his words, his irre-
pressible smile of triumph informed me. He had bet me
ten shillings that he would be first in the Bursary Competition.

'Well,' I said, 'congratulations!' And his smile, which
he still couldn't suppress, made me realize how fond of
him I was, and in a moment we were shaking hands and
dancing about, and for some reason laughing uproariously.
Yet in the midst of it all I suddenly felt Alastair to be almost
a stranger to me. To be first in the Bursary Competition—
well, someone was first every year. But to have won a bet
on it—that was the act of a man conscious of not yet being
in touch with his limitations. Miss Craig came into the
room.

'Don't you go breaking anything,' she said. 'Carrying on
like two big weans!' Alastair went across and put his arm
round her shoulders; it was a gesture of affection, but he

97

allowed a little of his weight to rest on her, so that after a moment she had to knock his arm away.

'He was just telling me the good news,' I said.

'Aye,' said Miss Craig, 'we're very cock-a-hoop today.' Too conventional to rejoice openly in Alastair's success, at any rate so long as Alastair was doing this himself, she like Alastair was too pleased to be able to suppress a smile. 'Now,' she added, 'you must just away through and mind the shop while I put the girdle on. Mrs Mathers and Miss Goodyear are coming to tea.' Alastair and I went through to the shop accordingly. Minding it was a light task, and as Alastair managed it it consisted mainly in gossiping with customers until his aunt came through to join in. Now, as we went in, Alastair sat on the counter beside a pile of cardboard cartons.

'This makes it quite definite that you won't be staying on another year at Nethervale?' I asked. Alastair pushed aside a bundle of tea strainers that hung beside his face, and nodded.

'That was getting to be pretty certain anyway. In fact your father said when I spoke to him that perhaps he should have put me in for a Trinity scholarship after all. I wouldn't have got it, but for the experience.'

'Even if you'd got it, you wouldn't have gone up?' I was now so much determined to go to Edinburgh when Alastair did, so much looking forward to spending a year there in his company, that even a hypothetical threat to the possibility disturbed me.

'No.' Alastair shook his head. 'They don't want people coming up as young as I am. They want them more mature. So I'm to go to Edinburgh and mature. You must come and mature along with me.'

'Oh God,' I said, 'I hope I can.'

'Well, look here,' said Alastair, 'my stock must stand pretty high with your father at the moment. Suppose I were to make some kind of tactful approach to him?'

'That's not at all a bad idea,' I said. It was only long afterwards that I reflected that it was characteristic both that Alastair's first use of the power of success should be to help me, and that he should so quickly leap to use this power. Mrs Mathers and Miss Goodyear came in together. I knew both of them well; they were Miss Craig's particular friends. I had often had tea with them here already.

'Well Alastair!' said Mrs Mathers. 'First in the Bursary Competition! It's as good as your head in a wig already. Soon you'll not be speaking to your old friends.' She was a big motherly-looking woman, said by Miss Craig to be a true friend in adversity, but by my own observation exceedingly jealous.

'I hope to be passing sentence on them before long,' said Alastair. But even while he was making this riposte Miss Goodyear was moving in.

'Oh Alastair,' she said, 'what a big day this is! Oh I'm so pleased for you and your auntie. She must be gey proud of you.' She peered up at him, her eyes misty with short sight and happiness.

'Oh I hope not,' said Alastair. 'I mean, not too proud, I hope.' He gave a kind of cough and shuffled a little with embarrassment. For dealing with Miss Goodyear he had no technique. She was too kind and gentle to be repelled in any way, too simple to be teased. 'I'll just snib the shop door,' he said quickly, 'and we'll go through to tea.'

'Oh Ella,' I heard Miss Goodyear saying as we went in, 'this must be a proud proud day for you!'

'Well,' said Miss Craig cheerfully, 'pride goeth before a fall, they say, so we best keep quiet about it.'

'I see we're celebrating, all the same,' said Mrs Mathers, and she nodded towards the table, on which, with many other things, stood a large pink cake. 'Still,' she added, 'it's a poor heart that never rejoices. And there's never been a laddie first in the Bursary Competition from Kingisbyres before, not that I mind, anyway.' Mrs Mathers was not herself a Kingisbyres woman. She had only come to Kingisbyres from Falkirk thirty years before, on her marriage. 'Now, in Falkirk I mind we had several. Counting Glasgow as well as Edinburgh, that is. There was one family had one son first and one son fourth, I think it was. The one that was first is a very big bug in the Civil Service, I believe.'

'I wonder,' said Alastair, as though to himself, 'which I

would be better as—Lord Chief Justice or Master of the Rolls?'

'Of course,' said Mrs Mathers in a gloomy voice, 'being first in the Bursary Competition is no guarantee of anything.'

'It's a guarantee that Alastair's a fine, clever laddie!' Miss Goodyear put in bravely. Her voice rang with emotion.

'Aye, but he's a long way to go yet. And a lot of hard work ahead of him.' Mrs Mathers' voice suggested to me that she was not herself fond of hard work.

'Who's for some more potted tongue?' said Miss Craig. 'Mrs Mathers—pass your plate.' We all began on a second helping, which was in effect compulsory, of potted tongue. It was only a good deal later, when we had made our way through a salad of hard-boiled eggs and tomatoes, tinned peaches and cream, new-baked scones and butter and honey, ginger snaps and the pink cake, that Mrs Mathers opened a new subject.

'I hear,' she said, breaking a ginger snap crisply between her fingers, 'that you're in with the Harveys, no less,' and she gave me what she would have described as 'a look'.

'I know them slightly,' I said.

Alastair shot a sardonic glance at me.

'Well,' said Mrs Mathers, 'it's more than the rest of us are likely to do. Personally,' she added, 'my granny was left well enough provided for no' to have to sell biscuits at the door. Maybe that's why I still have a civil word for folk that knew her.' She withdrew into a Sibylline inscrutability. There was a moment's silence, for Miss Craig, Alastair, and I were in the dark.

'I didna' really ken the old lady,' said Miss Goodyear. Her voice was unhappy and almost protesting.

'But you knew this Mr Harvey's father—him that's dead a year or two back?' Mrs Mathers led her like a lawyer in court.

'Ooh aye,' said Miss Goodyear. 'I kent him weel.' Almost a generation older than the other two, she spoke a good deal broader. 'He was such a kind man. And I kent this Mr Harvey—Willy—when he was a wee laddie, before they

went away. So when I saw him in the street I thocht I
would just have a word, ye ken. But he'd got into his car
when I got there, and there I was, face to face with her. So
I felt I had to speak to her—it would have been rude.'

'Don't you worry my dear—it wasn't *you* that was rude.'
said Mrs Mathers.

'I hope Mrs Harvey wasn't?' Miss Craig, although a
truly kind woman, was as determined to hear this story,
which Miss Goodyear didn't want to tell, as Mrs Mathers
was to make her tell it.

'No,' said Miss Goodyear. 'She wisna' to me.'

'She just said they were in a hurry, but they must all
have a lovely long talk some other time.' Mrs Mathers'
voice was a gruesome parody of Mrs Harvey's. 'But tell
what happened then,' she added.

'Maybe I shouldnae have said onything aboot that,' said
Miss Goodyear, and she looked pleadingly at Mrs Mathers.
'She didna' mean me to hear.'

'With that skirling English voice of hers!' said Mrs
Mathers. 'Did she no'!' I saw her take a deep breath to
renew her imitation: '"It's only another old person who
saw you in your first bawth dawling."' In spite of the
grotesqueness of the imitation, I could hear Mrs Harvey's
voice. Yes, I thought, she could say that, and as I looked at
Miss Goodyear's pathetic simple old face I thought that anyone who could be rude to her must be singularly merciless.

'Well,' said Alastair, slowly, 'the English bitch.' Mrs
Mathers gave him an approving glance.

'It's a comfort,' she said, 'to have a man around to say
what a lady shouldna'.'

We were walking across a large field in which a couple
of marquees provided the only shelter from a bitter wind.
A few yards away from us a man with purple hands was
arranging brushwood, and in the middle distance another
man with a megaphone was making an announcement to
a small group of people on horseback. Behind us a very
short line of very seedy-looking bookies were putting up
blackboards. It was the local horse show. The party was
small; it consisted only of Mrs Harvey, Catherine, and

Catherine's school-friend Hero, a girl of insolent smooth prettiness whom I had met for the first time today, and who had not so far uttered any words unconnected with horses. She had done very well in the jumping, but had expressed no approval of her mount, procured for her through the agency of Charles Crimond, whose voice could be heard, every now and again, addressing competitors by megaphone in a manner in which a tolerant patronage was shot through with flashes of bad temper.

'You know,' said Mrs Harvey, 'I love these little local events, when everything is so intimate and friendly. And I do so like being where there are horses.' She smiled to Hero. She was, I thought, doing gallantly, because as for the intimacy and friendliness, there were people there whom she would very much have liked to know, but they had none of them yet called on her; while as for the horses, when Hero's mount had shied at a piece of paper, Mrs Harvey had jumped like a shot rabbit.

At this point we were making our way to the tea marquee, and it was just outside it that I saw the Clandillons. Lady Clandillon, who was to present the prizes, was obviously horse-coping, standing in conversation with a man who looked like a cross between an army officer and a barrow boy. The two were talking gravely, intently, and rapidly, like a physician in an emergency consultation with a surgeon. Lady Clandillon, with her hands thrust down into the pockets of her coat, was kicking at a piece of turf with a curiously awkward unconscious gesture. Beside her her husband was talking to two people, obviously a substantial farmer and his wife, and the smiles on the two rather dour faces, the gratified and slightly flustered air of the woman, would alone, without the Clandillons' clothes, have been enough to stir curiosity in an avid observer of the social scene. Such an observer stood beside me.

'Who are those people?' said Catherine.

'The Clandillons,' I said.

'Mummy—Patrick says that's the Clandillons over there.'

'Is it dear?' Mrs Harvey gave the briefest of glances, distinguished from the slow devouring gapes which other passers-by were directing upon the focus of attention.

'Lady Clandillon,' said Hero to no one in particular, 'hunts with the Pytchley.'

As we moved forward I had two hopes, one that the Clandillons might recognize and greet me, and the second that we should not see Alastair in the marquee. The first was a dim hope, for I was worldly-wise enough to know that people like the Clandillons suffer from social myopia, and, in fact, as I passed I was humbly unsurprised to see that they were immersed in conversation. But at least Alastair was not in the marquee, and I was saved the embarrassment of not being able to invite him to join us.

I was under no very serious delusions about the position which I occupied in Mrs Harvey's eyes. It was one in which I was a little bit better than tolerated and something less than welcome. It depended entirely upon the influence which I might exert upon Catherine. That I had some influence Mrs Harvey recognized; it was an unfortunate but undeniable fact. She may not, at that time, have seen Catherine's character in a clear and steady light, but she had had some glimpses of it, and these had taught her that if it were not I who was to influence Catherine, it might be someone less innocuous, someone who might encourage Catherine's recklessness and independence, who might realize the potentiality of disaster that resided in her. But accepting me as harmless did not mean accepting Alastair, particularly as, by a piece of good fortune, Catherine disliked him.

It was when we were coming out of the marquee that we saw Alastair; he was talking to the Clandillons. He must have said something amusing, for they were laughing. The incident was somehow isolated from its surroundings; it looked like a photograph in *The Tatler* in which Alastair didn't look out of place. The three of them had the look of intimacy which people laughing together always do. We passed quite close, but none of them saw us. For that matter Mrs Harvey gave me the impression at the time that she had not seen them.

The afternoon drew to its chill conclusion; the prize-giving was performed with an unobtrusive professional haste by Lady Clandillon. The faces round about were now all faintly purple with cold. As soon as Hero had played her part we made for the car, clumping stiffly over the muddy tussocks. It was a relief to be in the car out of the wind, and I had no attention for the figures still clumping along outside. But as we were just approaching the gate that led out of the field which had been lent for the occasion Mrs Harvey suddenly stopped the car and said to me:

'Isn't that your friend Alastair over there? Won't you ask him to come back to tea with us?'

So there began a new phase. Alastair was now welcome again at Kingisbyres, since he figured as a friend, or at least a protégé of the Clandillons.

'She doesn't like me any better,' said Alastair, 'but'—and he allowed his voice to broaden into the local *patois*—'she jist has to thole, puir bitch.' And he gave me a malignant smile.

'But,' I said, 'why do you go there if they don't like you and you don't like them?'

'Patrick! I can't hide it from you—I've fallen madly in love with little Miss Surcingle.' He leered at me horribly. 'My little bowler-hatted beauty in her old but well-cut breeches.' He rose to his feet. 'Now let's go,' he added. We had been sitting on the lichen-covered base of one of the Covenanting memorials on the moors, having met there and being now about to embark on one of our long, discursive, argumentative walks. On this particular day the Kingisbyres party had gone visiting; it would be the first day for almost a week on which we would not see the two girls. For Catherine and myself Alastair's presence was, apart from anything else, a great convenience. It meant that Hero was taken off our hands, and that we were able to be alone together. Alastair had looked after Hero with great amiability and with a masterful ease and dexterity. He laid himself out to be agreeable, to entertain and charm her, and he succeeded surprisingly. I myself couldn't make the girl out. She was always rather impassive, and I thought her self-centred and cold. Her prettiness, too, seemed to me over-regular, oriental; if one could have thought of her as anything but an English sub-débutante, it would have been as a haughty Chinese princess. Alastair however struck sparks from her; he amused and astonished her with verbal fireworks and foolery and high spirits. He even talked to her seriously sometimes, shocking her by quotations from Marx, which was his latest interest, and saying that he was a Communist. I had never seen him in such form. He had been that way ever since he sat the Bursary Competition. His self-confidence, his sense of power, his ease, his ambition, and perhaps also his recklessness, were all growing, and sometimes during the last few days I had seen Hero looking at him with a kind of wonder. She did not fall in love with him—he was too far removed from her and from the people she was accustomed to for that—but she was fascinated, and happy to spend her time with him.

Almost as surprising as this surprising friendship was the continuing hostility between Catherine and Alastair. After a week in which they had seen quite a lot of one another, they were still barely friendly even on the surface. Catherine, when she was alone with me, never passed by an opportunity to make disparaging remarks about him; in his company she often behaved towards him with childish rudeness. He on his side now adopted towards her a teasing, taunting, yet polite air, very far removed from the 'glumness' and lumpish incivility of which, nevertheless, she continued to accuse him.

Now as Alastair and I started our walk along one of the old drovers' tracks that wound across the moors I realized that he had not answered my question. Why, having levelled the score with Mrs Harvey, did he continue to go to Kingisbyres? It was obvious that he still detested her. Indeed he said so, and if he did not in so many words say the same about Catherine, that was, I supposed, out of regard for my feelings. As for Hero, I did not believe that he had any serious interest in her whatever. I was about to ask the question again, but stopped. Perhaps his reply to me had been not merely a piece of foolery, but a deliberate evasion. Suddenly I had a feeling about the whole matter, about the multiplicity and obscurity of motives, and this feeling grew and broke over me like a wave, so that I was left standing a little battered, still feeling the cold shock of human solitude. It would after all, be useless to ask Alastair this perfectly simple question, since he did not mean to give me the answer, and indeed perhaps did not even know it.

All through the long walk that Alastair and I took over the moors that day I was very happy. Of the things which made me happy my love for Catherine came first. It had become an obsession with me. In the time which had passed since I had met Catherine again at Kingisbyres we had spent some part of almost every day together, and often we were alone. The two images of Catherine, the one which I had formed in my mind during the term when I was separated from her, and the other made by the girl I saw every day, and which had during the first days of our reunion often slipped absurdly out of focus, were now reduced to a single image again.

It was this image which obsessed me then, and which fascinates me even now. Her vitality was electric, astonishing. If I close my eyes I can see a clear picture of her, walking, laughing, talking, running down a bank, throwing back her hair, putting her hand on my sleeve, smiling and holding up her lips to be kissed, and I used to think even then that she was the kind of person who dies young, and of whom people say that they cannot believe she is dead because she was so full of life. Her vitality showed itself, among other ways, simply in physical energy and endurance. Catherine could go on walking, cycling, playing tennis, swimming, ragging, dancing, for ever. Alastair and I, tough by nature and further toughened by the rigours of life at Nethervale, were often left behind. For Hero, also tough in her own way, the pace was sometimes too hot. On one day in particular we had all four met at Kingisbyres after lunch, played tennis for a couple of hours or so, gone swimming in the river—cold as liquid electricity, Catherine screaming like a madwoman—and afterwards been run by Alastair, in a car borrowed from the garage, into the local town, where we ate fish and chips and peas and vinegar and danced at the Palais for hours until I at least began to hear my own voice as, falling asleep, one hears voices in a railway compartment. But there was Catherine, her eyes shining, exhorting me to one last dance.

And there was her spontaneity. She said 'Let's explore the attics', and at once we were all four embarked upon a long dusty exploration of rooms which even I had never entered, rooms full of vast trunks, incredibly heavy dressing cases, bundles of shoe-trees, stacks of *Country Life*, sheaves of queer-shaped old tennis rackets. And there were photographs, school and regimental groups, cricket groups, farouche-looking moustachioed young men in hunting kit or steeplechasing silks, Edwardian women with parasols and vast hats. One was of a group of people—a shooting party, the men in breeches and spats and boots—drawn up on chairs and rugs in front of the house. It was dated 1905, and the names or initials had been written in below in a rusty ink: 'J.', 'Ly. M. Kinloch-Stuart', 'Self'.

'Oh God,' said Catherine, 'I do feel so frightfully common sometimes. It's so awful being called Harvey. Do you know'—and she looked at me with passionate gravity—'sometimes I'd give *anything* to spell it with two ees.'

Catherine had a way of saying whatever came into her head, and although this sometimes made her sound silly, the air of indifference to opinion, and of candour, which she had, gave her dignity. This was most marked in her relationship with her mother. I was always being astonished by the freedom which her mother permitted, and my astonishment was reinforced by Hero's, who, as she and I had been dancing at the Palais, had suddenly giggled and said: 'You know, when I get back to London Mummy will either send the car to meet me at King's Cross, or else her maid to escort me to Victoria. She'd have a *fit* if she knew about this.' Mrs Harvey, I am sure, would have been delighted to impose such a discipline upon Catherine, but Catherine, without ever having had a row about it, had made it impossible.

'How much,' I asked her once, 'does your mother know about us?'

The evening before, as Mrs Harvey had been present when Alastair and I had left, Catherine had kissed me in front of her. She had not kissed me as she would have done if we had been alone, or even as she would have done if only Alastair and Hero had been present; she had kissed me with casual affection, but still she had kissed me, and once again her openness, her lack of furtiveness and even shyness, had astonished me.

'*Most* of what there is to know,' said Catherine. 'She asked me, and I said I was in love with you, and you were in love with me. I told her I wouldn't do anything silly if she didn't try to stop me, but that if she *did* then anything might happen—I sort of couldn't answer for it.'

'And what did she say?'

'Well, she sort of sighed and said she didn't know what girls were coming to, but I said they were mostly the most frightful sticks, as they mostly always had been, but probably there had always been different ones and I didn't think it was girls like me that got into the worst messes and disgraced their families.'

There was another aspect of Catherine's character that I discovered accidentally one day. I was saying good night to her, and with the inquisitiveness of love I asked her what she would be doing in the evening.

'French,' she said.

'Do you have to work in the holidays?'

'I don't *have* to. I just do.' Her voice was indifferent, a little off-putting.

'Catherine,' said Hero, in her smooth, slightly mocking voice, 'is always stuffing French and German.'

'What—' Alastair's voice expressed a genuine surprise which he turned into a fake surprise. 'Are you a *clever* girl, Catherine?' The two of them were looking at one another, and I expected that Catherine would reply in the tone of conventionally friendly insult with which she usually replied to this kind of remark from Alastair. I was taken aback when she said, in the same indifferent voice:

'I'm not a fool.'

A day or two later, when we were alone, I asked her about her French.

'I'm good at languages,' she said. 'I like doing them, that's all.' And through the holidays, I found, she did quite a lot of French and German. It was an activity she carried on quite alone, with no particular encouragement from her parents, and while she didn't conceal it in any way, she never said much about it. It was simply there, an interest, a compartment of her life into which visitors were not invited.

On the day that Hero went home, I saw Catherine only very briefly, meeting her at a ruined cottage on the moors between Nethervale and Kingisbyres, which was one of our regular meeting places. After a time I asked politely whether Hero had departed according to plan.

'Oh yes, surrounded by copies of *The Field* and *Horse and Hound* and all that sort of thing. She sent you her love.'

'Me singular,' I said, 'or Alastair and me?'

'Oh Alastair too, I suppose.' She giggled, but that did not make me suppose that she was 'coming round to' Alastair.

'Tell me,' I said, 'do you really like Hero?' Catherine looked at me in astonishment.

'*Of course* I do. I'm very fond of her indeed, and you must be too. Aren't you?'

'I feel that she's not easy to get to know.'

'No.' Catherine spoke judgmatically. 'Perhaps she isn't. But she's terribly sweet you know. She's an awfully loyal person.' Not for the first time when Catherine was talking, a faint tremor of embarrassment ran through me. She had a way of making solemn pronouncements in words which seemed to me a little distasteful. I didn't understand at the time that in speaking in this way about Hero, for instance, Catherine was expressing what was not so much a wish as a hope; or, more generally, expressing a need which she felt for loyalty.

'You remember,' said Catherine a little later, as we were getting ready to part, 'that I'm going to play tennis at Allenlea tomorrow?' Allenlea was Crimond's house.

'Yes,' I said. 'Shall I see you afterwards?'

'Well, Charles said something to Mummy about how there would be some people there and we might have a sort of fork supper and dance afterwards. I don't expect to be back before midnight.'

'Oh,' I said.

'You don't *mind*, do you?' There was the faintest touch of impatience in Catherine's tone, and I realized that, after all, I couldn't expect to monopolize her, that I was very

lucky to see as much of her as I did, and that I owed my
luck to her strength of character. So I tried to respond.

'No,' I said, 'I don't mind. I only hope that Crimond gets
a hernia with that backhand of his.' Catherine laughed.

'You're awfully unfair about his tennis.'

'I'm not. He plays tennis nastily. All he's got is a kind
of brutal energy. It's an ugly sight.'

'Oh, don't be silly, Patrick.' Catherine leant down and
pulled her bicycle towards her from the low, mossy wall on
which she had leant it. She was still half-laughing, but she
was annoyed as well. 'One may or may not like Charles,
but he's really very good-looking, you know.'

'I've never noticed it,' I said. 'He always looks like the
butcher's boy to me.'

'I dare say you haven't noticed it,' said Catherine. She was
now pulling on her gloves, blue woollen gloves, which I knew
were part of her school uniform. 'But I can tell you that
Charles has the kind of good looks that appeal to a woman.'

I laughed, with a bitterness which was no doubt histri-
onic, and after searching for, and failing to find anything
witty to say, I said: 'You sound about forty.' I had bent
down to collect my own bicycle, and as my eyes were on a
level with Catherine's I saw her frowning, offended look.

'Sometimes,' she said, and as she spoke her face cleared
again, 'I *feel* about forty. I don't suppose I shall feel so very
much different when I *am* forty. Do you?' This time it did
not seem to me that there was any affectation either in her
voice or her words, and perhaps for the first time in my life I
had a glimpse of the adult condition, which I was supposed
to be already attaining, as something unified and coherent,
so that myself at forty might be quite recognizably the self
I now knew, and not some complete stranger to whom I
had yet to be introduced.

'No,' I said, 'perhaps I shan't.' We kissed one another
good night with the greatest affection.

How happy I was!—and how, near the centre of that
happiness, was Kingisbyres, which now, more than ever
before, appeared both as a house familiar and homely, and
as a place beautiful and romantic—because it sheltered
Catherine.

SEVEN

'WELL,' SAID MY FATHER, 'if it's what you really want
to do. . . .' He sighed and then looked out of the window
in silence for a few moments. 'I don't know anything
about such a career, of course. I shan't be able to give
you any advice.' There was another silence, and then he
added: 'And I'm not in a position to go on maintaining you
indefinitely.'

'That won't be necessary,' I said firmly, 'I'll get a job.'
But the very phrase in those days, at the beginning of the
'thirties, was ominous.

'Well, anyway,' my father said, 'you'd better see about
the necessary arrangements. I suppose there will be papers
to sign. And what about somewhere to stay? I take it you
and Alastair will dig together?'

'That was the idea,' I said.

'Alastair will have a great deal of work to do, you know.'
My father looked at me doubtfully, and for the first time
I was envious of Alastair's success and of his clear-cut
future.

'I shall not keep Alastair from working,' I said, and
although this was true—since no one could have kept
Alastair from working—it was not in any case what I
meant. If what I meant could have been put into words, the
words would have been something like: I'll show you yet.

On the day following this conversation I met Catherine
again, in the morning, at the ruined cottage. I was going
to have tea at Kingisbyres officially, so to speak, in the
afternoon, but this was an extra meeting. This cottage at
which we met was in a hollow on one of the high points
of the moors. A disused track ran from the naked road
for about sixty or seventy yards round a suddenly rising
shoulder, and beyond that there was a kind of dip, and the

walls of the cottage, completely broken down in one corner, but rising to about four feet at their highest. A stream ran past it, and because it was high and isolated I always was particularly conscious there of the three most characteristic noises of the moors, shallow water running over stones, the papery noise of the wind in whinny grass, and the calling of the curlews. This morning it was clear and grey, the wind came in sudden rushes, and one of these, as I waited for Catherine, brought a quick shower of rain. She arrived on the tail of it, with her face flushed and her eyes sparkling, with droplets of rain on her hair above her forehead where it had escaped from the scarf she had tied over it. She was wearing a blue raincoat and grey woollen stockings, which were both part of her school uniform, and as she arrived she looked almost embarrassingly schoolgirlish, so that instead of kissing her I made some lighthearted teasing remark. Obviously in high spirits, she replied in the same tone, and for a few moments we behaved rather like an affectionate if rather hearty brother and sister than the young lovers we purported to be.

'How did you get on at Allenlea?' I asked. Catherine, warm from her cycle ride, was pulling off her coat, and now threw it down on the wall.

'Oh it was marvellous,' she said, and my heart winced under a lash of jealousy. 'Charles had been to all kinds of pains and troubles to make everything just so.' She laughed, and my heart rose again, because it seemed to me she was laughing at Crimond. Perhaps she was, but she went on: 'I know you don't like him, but you know he's much nicer when he's in his own home. He's really an awfully good host!'

'Were there many people?' I was determined to take this occasion in my stride if that were possible.

'Quite a lot. Charles's sister Vera was being hostess, and there was her husband. And then the Cullens that I've met already, the ship-building people you know; Rosemary is my age and Dicky's at Cambridge, and there was a friend of his from Cambridge who's staying with them who's quite mad. And the Barbours, I hadn't met them before—they came over for the day. I thought he was

frightfully amusing.' This was a name I knew very well:
Major and Mrs Barbour of Balgirnie appeared frequently in
the papers. Rich, and rare amongst the indigenous county
magnates in being so, he was also known as a one-time
international polo player; he was one of those people about
whom there hangs an aura of raffishness, whose reputation
gives off an extra-special whiff of whisky, cigars, and the
Divorce Court. 'And one or two other people,' Catherine
concluded. 'Actually people Mummy and I knew already.'
I knew this conclusion meant that the party had been in a
way disappointing. Charles Crimond had not been able to
procure—if in fact he was quite on terms to do so—the
people that the Harveys really wanted to meet, the handful
of county neighbours who were Captain Keith's normal
callers. But I was not reassured. I detected in Catherine's
tone some satisfaction that made me anxious.

'What did you do all the time?'

'Well, there was the tennis, of course, and tea, and later
on drinks and dinner, and afterwards we played games like
"Murders" you know, and Archie Barbour went into the
gunroom once and'—Catherine giggled—'loaded a gun and
fired it out of the window when he was supposed to be the
murderer, and everyone nearly had a fit. Actually, I think
he was terribly drunk, people say he nearly always is, and
he tried to make everybody else drunk, and we played other
games like "Sardines". Not Mummy of course, she sat in
the drawing-room with Charles's uncle and aunt.'

'Did Barbour make an attempt on you?' I made my
voice light.

'Not more than one or two other people.' Catherine's
laugh was one of pleasure, not embarrassment. 'After all
it's what those sort of games are for.'

'And Crimond?'

'Yes, of course.' Catherine was looking at me with a look
I could not fathom. 'It was rather different.'

'Different?' I heard the pain in my voice.

'Yes. He was quite serious about it, and very nice. I like
him.' She continued to look at me, unsmiling.

'You mean you . . .' I hesitated, not quite knowing what I
wanted, what I dared, to ask. 'You liked his kissing you?'

'Yes, I did. . . . Does that upset you?'

'No,' I said. The blow was so numbing that I hardly knew what I was saying: I only had an instinct to hide my hurt. 'No, not really.'

'Patrick—' Catherine was sitting on her coat on the wall now, and I was sitting on another heap of stones facing her, and she put her hand on my sleeve and gave me a troubled, questioning look: 'Is that really true? I haven't hurt you terribly, have I?'

'I don't know—I mean I don't know what you're telling me. I mean, aren't you fond of me any more?' Catherine was obviously taken aback.

'But of *course* I am!' She clasped my hand. 'Why shouldn't I be? Just because I quite like Charles—and he's much nicer than you think—that doesn't mean I don't like you. Or don't want you to kiss me.' She smiled, and I responded to the invitation. But I had still a sensation of deep pain and anxiety, and after a moment I broke off and looked into Catherine's eyes.

'Do you—' I said, and I would have given a great deal not to have been driven to ask this question, not to appear humiliated and naked. 'Do you still prefer me to Charles?' She continued to look me in the eyes for a moment, and then nodded.

'Yes,' she said. 'And perhaps I always shall. But I don't think I'm ever going to be awfully good at being faithful, and now I'm too young to even try. Perhaps you are, so perhaps you blame me. Or do you understand a bit?' She looked into my eyes again. 'Do try and understand,' she said. 'I know it's a lot to ask.'

'I'll try,' I said, but I spoke very doubtfully. Yet it was only a few weeks since I had been telling myself that this affair could not last. And although at other times I had indulged in fantasies in which Catherine and I remained faithful to one another, got married, and lived happily ever afterwards, I knew they were fantasies. What had I expected?

'You're coming this afternoon, aren't you?' Catherine's voice, I thought, lacked enthusiasm, and although I half-felt that it was somehow my duty to go, that this was my chance to fight back against Charles Crimond, I felt also that I needed time to recover from the shock of what she had just told me, and that in the condition to which I had been reduced, I could not bear exposure to the radiations of Catherine's energy.

'Well,' I said, 'I was wondering—some things have turned up that I ought to do—perhaps we might meet tomorrow instead?' When I had begun to speak I had been afraid that my voice would break, but by the time I had said this my relief at the prospect of being alone with my pain, of being able to hide myself like a sick animal, was so great that I actually raised a smile.

'Patrick!'—I heard the relief—'you are really being most terrifically understanding. I was afraid you might be hurt.' She must still care for me quite a lot, I thought, and it was like a breath of anaesthetic. 'You wouldn't mind then, would you, if I went out with Charles this afternoon?'

This felt as though I had emerged from an anaesthetic in the middle of an operation. I could see Crimond, with his meaty good looks, with the touch of caddishness which never quite left him, and I could see Catherine in his arms. I wanted to protest, to beg for mercy and kindness and at the same time I knew it would be useless, that the only sensible course was to laugh and agree, even if, when Catherine left me, I had to roll about moaning on the grass.

'Frankly,' I said, 'I would rather you didn't.' I did not speak clearly, I did not look at Catherine; I think there were tears in my eyes.

'Oh Patrick!' Catherine perhaps spoke with kindness as well as impatience, but I heard only the impatience. 'I can't not ever go out with anybody but you. I'm too young.'

'You seem to be young only in patches,' I said, 'like mange.' I spoke bitterly, not in the least meaning to be entertaining, but Catherine suddenly laughed, a gurgling, rippling noise of amusement and pleasure.

'Oh Patrick—you are wonderful really! No one else can say things like you.' She paused. 'Look—I don't really want to go out with Charles terribly, but I feel I ought to. We shall be back quite early, and tomorrow I'll tell you all about it.' She smiled, and although I sensed her

determination to do exactly as she pleased, I was weak
enough to feel momentarily soothed. Catherine picked up
her bicycle, and for a moment again I saw her as a rather
sturdy schoolgirl in grey stockings.

'Will you go back a bit of the way with me?' She smiled,
and I was tempted—how tempted I was!—to go with her,
to speak to her, to try to persuade her to love me again. But
at last, mercifully, I was touched by a kind of exhaustion. I
couldn't bear any more of it.

'My brakes seem to have come apart,' I said. 'I must do
something about them.' I hoped she would offer to stay
while I did it.

'Well,' she said, 'I really must go, I'm afraid.' And in a
moment I felt the touch of her cold cheeks, and for just
an instant of her warm lips; a little stone flew from under
the rear wheel of her bicycle, and she had gone. Suddenly
I became conscious again of the running water, the wind
in the grass, and the calling curlews—these lonely noises.
I sat down on the low stone wall and put my head in my
hands. I may have sat there for some time; then I got
up, padlocked my bicycle and set off across the moors.
Fortunately I had taken it into my head to say to my
mother that I might not be back for lunch; I was free
to walk.

It must have been about twenty to one; I walked, almost
without stopping, until six o'clock. I walked along path-
ways and old tracks, but aimlessly, and after I had been
walking for an hour or two I began talking to myself,
composing speeches to be made to Catherine, speeches
sometimes cutting and sometimes sentimental, and at last,
after I had composed some really elaborate scenes in which
Catherine, bruised and battered by the world, returned to
me for protection, I recovered some equanimity. But it had
not been an easy process, and I was left shaken. Several
times when I had reached the haven of sentimentality, I
was swept out of it again into a dreadful feeling of dull
anguish, of unrelieved *suffering*, which frightened me. If
I could feel like this at seventeen, what could real *adult*
suffering be like? How relieved and perhaps incredulous
I should have been to learn that, looking back on that

afternoon, a good deal more than seventeen years later, I can still say that it was perhaps the most unhappy of my life.

I don't remember the evening; I must have been tired out. But the next morning I cycled over to see Alastair. Since I had last visited him the desk which the Captain had given him had been installed. It had replaced the rickety card-table, and had an expensive-looking green light upon it. It altered the appearance of the whole room.

'It's handsome,' I said. Alastair looked up at me then down at the table again. He was smiling his city-sacking smile, but discreetly.

'It is,' he said, 'isn't it?' Then he stopped smiling. 'Catherine was round here last night,' he said.

'Catherine?' I felt myself flush with surprise and embarrassment. Yet in one way I was not surprised, for I had a feeling about Catherine that it was natural for her to do unexpected, unpredictable things. 'What did she want? Did she—' I broke off. I was afraid that Catherine might have given Alastair an account of our meeting, and that, even if I had not perhaps looked foolish in such an account, offended my sense of reserve.

'She was a bit upset,' said Alastair, and my heart bounded with joy.

'About . . .?' I was going to say 'about me?' but fortunately that same sense of reserve stopped me.

'It seems she spent the afternoon with Charles Crimond?'

'Yes,' I said.

'Well'—Alastair was looking down his nose at the desk in front of him; it was covered with pages of mathematical formulae—'he seems to have thrown himself upon her just as she was leaving his house.'

'He didn't!'

'He did! Catherine told me all about it He—' Alastair gave a kind of snort. 'Oh God,' he said, 'I can't help it, it's so bloody *funny*,' and he began laughing, struggling against his laughter to make himself intelligible. 'He was g—was grunting—like a pig—and they tripped and fell on the floor and—and—she blacked his eye.' I giggled.

Amongst all my other feelings the thought of Catherine blacking Charles Crimond's eye was agreeable.

'But,' said Alastair, and although he was no longer laughing aloud his eyes were sparkling with pleasure, 'that's not all. *He's in love with her!*'

'What,' I said, 'you mean . . .'

'I mean he's seriously in love with her. Catherine told me all about it. She says he literally went down on his knees afterwards and begged her to forgive him and not to tell her mother. In fact he made just the kind of cloddish fool of himself that you'd expect.'

'Why did Catherine come here?'

'Because she thought she might find you.' For the second time in this conversation my spirits, already high because the afternoon for which Catherine had abandoned me had gone so badly, soared. 'She wanted to lay her head on your shoulder.' Alastair gave me a look that was perhaps faintly satirical; it made me see myself in a rather silly light, the light of a comfortable old sofa on which people might lie and gently weep away the sorrows and brutality of the real, harsh world.

'I hope,' I said, 'that you weren't what she calls Scotch and glum to her.'

'Scotch and glum—so that's how she finds me, the wee biscuit-making bitch.' Alastair laughed momentarily, and then answered quite seriously: 'No, I don't think I was. I tell you, she was upset. I think we like one another better now. Incidentally she told me about the row you'd had.'

'It wasn't exactly a row.'

'Well'—Alastair's voice was impatient yet good-humoured —'whatever it was then.'

'What did she say about it?'

'She said you were too good for her.'

'It's an illusion. Because she had a tussle with the chauffeur's nephew when she was fourteen, Catherine fancies herself as a Great Sinner.'

Alastair grinned. 'All the same, I wonder. Patrick—your paternal grandfather was a minister wasn't he?'

'Yes.'

'And the other grandfather was in the Navy?'

'Yes. Why?'

'Hang on a moment. What about your great-grand-parents?'

'My father's grandfather was a minister too. I don't know what my mother's was—something in India. Now tell me why you ask.'

'Oh—ancestry, you know. I was wondering if it counts. You're solid professional middle class. Your family clawed themselves out of the slums or the farm labourers' hovels a long time ago. But Cathy and Crimond still belong partly to the good old fornicating, gambling proletariat. And I belong there altogether unless I belong to the gambling, fornicating aristocracy.'

'This is a queer doctrine from you,' I said, and I probably sounded cold, because I hated to be cut off in this way from Catherine and Alastair, and especially cut off in the woeful dreariness of being middle class.

'I suppose it is.' Alastair picked up a pencil, seemed to weigh it on his finger a moment, and put it down again. 'But think of it—isn't it all these fervid ministers that made you such a golden-tongued bastard? Well, anyway, you didn't have a row with Cathy?'

'No. What was there to have a row about?'

'Very reasonable. Some people would have had a row, though, all the same. Some people would have beaten her.'

'For instance,' I said, 'Alastair Kerr, the Terror of the Gorbals.'

He laughed. 'You think that's all nonsense?'

'No. I can believe easily enough in Crimond's grunting like a pig. Anyway, I *do* believe in the Scotch being a violent people. It may have something to do with never having been conquered by the Romans.'

Alastair screwed up his face. 'That bunk!' he said.

'You mean history?'

'Oh all that stuff about national character and Hadrian's Wall and Bonny Prince Charlie.'

'But you don't think that bourgeois-proletariat stuff of yours is bunk?'

'As a matter of fact I do. I think it's utter nonsense.'

'We spit on Marx?'

'We spit on Marx.'

'Do we spit on Freud?'

'We spit on Freud. We spit on all foreign-Jewish scum.'

'Who else do we spit on?'

'We spit on Bonnie Prince Charlie and Flora Macdonald, on Rizzio's blood and Mary Queen of Scots and the Flowers o' the Forest and Archibald Bell-the-Cat.'

'The end of an auld sang?'

'We spit on great greeny-yellow gobs on the end of an auld sang.'

'What do we not spit on?'

In a liturgical voice he began: 'On the Treaty of Union, the Society of Sons of the Manse and the Maintenance of the Ministry Fund; of all company directors in the City of London and overseas who may be of Scottish origin we lick the shoes; all Scotsmen who have succeeded at the English Bar are remembered nightly in our orisons. Above all the sons of man we honour and revere the Right Honourable Ramsay MacDonald.'

'What nonsense—the big sumph that he is!' Miss Craig had opened the door and was regarding Alastair from the threshold with an expression of mild disapproval. 'Now,' she added, 'if you boys arenie' to be working you might as well be outside taking some exercise.'

'What exercise, for instance?' Alastair looked at her innocently.

'You could be sawing some logs for the fire.'

'Well, now, so we could.'

Alastair was too impatient to be good at sawing logs. He wasted energy, pushing the saw and swearing, so after a few minutes I took over sawing and Alastair split the logs with an axe. That was work that he liked; it was both violent and controlled. From the corner of my eye I saw the easy swing and the powerful stroke, and at each stroke a log was halved. For that matter, I got on with the sawing pretty quickly. How fit we must have been in those days! We worked with a kind of animal contentment, hardly conscious of the pleasure of breathing the cold, resinous air.

Catherine may have been standing there for some

moments before we saw her. She stood at the corner of
the house, at the end of the passage which led from the
front of it to the cramped little yard in which we were
working. When I saw her she seemed to be standing very
still, watching us. I saw the axe flash down again and heard
the crack. Then I said, 'Hello,' and Alastair also turned and
greeted her.

'I telephoned you,' Catherine said to me, 'and your
mother said you were here. You know I was looking for
you last night?'

'Yes. Alastair told me.'

'Did he tell you about how badly Charles Crimond
behaved?' She was very serious, using a shocked voice that
would have been suitable for an Edwardian chaperon.

'I heard he grunted like a pig, and you blacked his
eye.' Dropping her shocked tone, Catherine giggled, and
suddenly we all laughed.

'Oh dear,' she said, 'and now I've had such a letter from
him, absolutely grovelling and fearfully *solemn*. I shan't
know what on earth to say.'

'Say your father is calling on him with a horsewhip at
eleven o'clock tomorrow, and that if he will name his second
I shall be calling on *him* on behalf of Patrick.'

'Say you're giving a party and you want him to do animal
noises at it.'

'Or should Patrick and I send him a piece of steak?'

Catherine giggled again. Her eyes were snapping with the
pleasure of our fooling and at being the centre of attention.
As she giggled her underlip seemed in some way to turn
down a little, and this excited me. I wanted to see her alone,
but now that she seemed to look upon Crimond merely as a
joke there was plenty of time, and meanwhile I was pleased
that she and Alastair had dropped their hostility. I felt
wonderfully soothed and happy; yesterday's agonized tramp
over the moors seemed like a bad dream. What had happened—Crimond's having contrived to inspire Catherine
with both distaste and cruel amusement, and Catherine's
being, no doubt, about to ask my forgiveness—it was all
like one of my jealous fantasies, like any jealous lover's
fantasies, come true. So we stood round for a time, talking

and laughing about nothing, and Catherine tried to split a log, and then we laughed some more. Then she said she must go home, and asked me to cycle back with her. Alastair said that he was going to split a few more logs. We said goodbye, and Catherine and I were still fooling and laughing about nothing, simply frothing over with high spirits, as we led our bicycles out of the passage into the village street in front of the shop. Then, at that moment, Catherine said: 'Oh do hold this a moment—I've left my gloves.'

She spoke with the greatest naturalness, the greatest candour, and there was a moment's pause, a double-take, during which nothing seemed changed, and I was still happy. Then I turned, and looked at her, searchingly, painfully, and her eyes suddenly widened, and for the only time that I remember, she unmistakably, burningly blushed.

Part Three

A SENSE OF tranquillity, of sensual ease and mental freedom, of leisure, of fulfilment, of anticipation . . . a feeling
like a buoyant ship of falling, of rising . . . memories,
consciously dreamlike, exciting but not disturbing. . . .
Catherine's hand upon my arm, Kingisbyres in the snow.
. . . They came, and left me, and died in the down-soaring
trough of a wave, and returned; I entered this world again
and came out of it, passed through a lifetime of oblivion
and awoke to the sensation of eternity. But now I knew
where I was.

When I saw my face in the mirror I was smiling like
Buddha, I seemed to be walking on balloons, and as I set
about making my breakfast my movements still dreamt a
little. The fruit-juice out of the can had the savour of
something fresh-picked; it was inconceivably satisfying.
Afterwards I washed in cold water, splashing it over my
head, throwing it about as though I were washing at the
pump. It seemed abnormally crystalline and refreshing.
Then, slowly, I ate three fried eggs and bacon and sausages
and fried bread and olives and toast and marmalade. I drank
a good deal of rather black coffee.

By the time I had shaved and dressed I felt better than
normal—wonderfully rested. When I put my head out
of the drawing-room window the east wind seemed, not
brutal, but lively and challenging, the air fresh and clear.
It gave me a holiday feeling, and I wanted to go out for a
walk. But first I had to look at Alastair. In his bedroom
it was dark, but I heard his breathing, slow and heavy,
snoring a little, and when I pulled back one of the curtains
I saw that he was buried fathoms deep. He lay half on
his back, and his face was heavy and relaxed, his mouth
open, with the lower lip hanging a little. He looked almost

stupid, but the lines of strain had vanished, and the result was curiously youthful, especially with the ruffled hair and the open-necked, careless-looking pyjamas.

'Alastair!' My voice, addressing someone who was so obviously not there, sounded odd.

'Alastair!' I spoke more loudly, and putting my hand on his shoulder, shook it gently. There was no response whatever. I shook a little harder; the note of his breathing changed and he closed his mouth momentarily. That was all. I decided to wait.

In the street I walked quickly, gulping down the keen cold air. I walked up the High Street. As I remembered it, it had been a slum, smelling figuratively of history and literally of extreme poverty, a horrible smell like stale sweet biscuits. Old men, derelict and grey-faced, with cloth caps polished black by hard old fingers, had mooned and spat round the entries of the wynds, too well aware of the value of attention to give it openly, but following passers-by with the pupils of their eyes. And on Sunday morning the congregations of the local churches had picked their way round frozen pools of beery sick. It seemed different now; it had the mild Welfare State look.

I hardly realized where I was going until suddenly, as I turned a corner, I found I was near the digs where Alastair and I had lived during our stay in Edinburgh. They had belonged to an old acquaintance of Alastair's aunt, and because of this we had been looked after, 'mothered', in a way which often irritated me. Alastair had more sense; at least if he was irritated he hid it. Once, when he had kept me waiting, I flung into his room and found him changing his socks.

'Carrying out Nannie's orders?' I asked. I was in a stupid ill temper.

'Yes.' Alastair rolled the thick grey sock methodically over his large foot.

'We shall be hopelessly late.'

'Better than catching pneumonia.' He had been exactly what Catherine meant when she said 'Scotch and glum'.

This strain in Alastair, this calculating, cautious, hard-working strain, was very much in evidence in Edinburgh, particularly at first. His wildness was damped down, as though, now he was responsible for himself, the responsibility weighed on him. He attended lectures and tutorials, worked in one or other of the libraries, worked in his room at our digs, all according to a time-table which he kept in his diary, in a rather stodgy, routine-bound way, and without the pleasure in mathematics which he had discovered during his last year at Nethervale.

But as time went on he began to relax. He had got to grips with his mathematics again, and as he was enjoying the work he did not need to hold himself to it. He returned more to his natural pattern—the long spells of concentration, the sudden breaks. I became familiar with the gesture with which he swept his arm across the table, tumbling books and papers on to the floor. Then he would fumble in his pocket for a cigarette or the price of a drink, and ask me to go out with him. But the break was not because he was simply tired of working; it was the same sense of method which held him to his work when he wasn't enjoying it which made him break off when he had been working long enough. About this time too he began to play bridge, at first with a group of his fellow-mathematicians, but very soon with older people, and in time he was a regular visitor at several houses where high-class bridge players were always welcome. One of these, I noticed, was the house of a young professor who had been a Fellow of Trinity; in another he played with the family of a man who was the representative in Scotland of one of the great industrial combines. The first time I made a friendly-malicious comment on this, Alastair was evasive and ill-tempered; a few days later however I came in just as he was going out to play bridge at the professor's house, and he smiled cheerfully and said: 'You see before you one of the glories of an imperial race—a wee Scottie on the make.'

Yet in the event it was I who got 'settled in life' (as it turned out) before Alastair, and by using social contacts at that. It had come about in this way. At some time during my first year at Edinburgh I began to have doubts about my vocation as an artist. They entered my mind like a Fifth Column, and by the time I was aware of them they were formidably strong. In the course of the work I did at the Art College it was driven into me that I didn't have it in me to improve vastly on a talent which was quite genuine, even quite interesting, but not strong. I became disheartened, worried, and in the end frightened.

For what on earth was I to do? Suppose I continued in the Art College, what could I hope for? I knew now that I could never hope to live by painting pictures. When I say I knew it, I mean that after weeks and months of painful shilly-shallying I at last found courage first to renounce and later finally to murder this most cherished of illusions. There used to be a legal punishment in Scotland in which the victim's ear was nailed to a post and he, with his hands tied, had to summon up resolution to tear himself away. It was an experience rather like that. Renouncing the illusion suddenly left my immediate course strikingly clear, as though I had been subconsciously preparing for it. Perhaps I had.

First of all I sold my stamp collection. (How many gambles with fate, how many catastrophic follies must begin with nervous young men rushing out with stamp albums under their arm!) The next day, without telling anyone, I caught the Flying Scotsman, and the following day kept the appointment I had made with Mr Agmondisham. He received me in the almost ambassadorially gracious manner that I remembered, but he was balder, smaller, and heavier than I had thought. He was sitting at a big desk in the big room in his flat in which he showed his pictures and did business, a room on the whole much more like a private room than office or gallery, and yet with something about it which put me on my mettle by suggesting the harsh exhilaration of the life of careers and making money. I told him the whole story, using all the skill I had in presenting it—the double-bluff modesty, the deference-which-does-not-hide-an-inner assurance, the business-like directness, the *suppressio veri* and the *suggestio falsi*—and all the other tricks which even people much more honest than I use ruthlessly on such occasions. In the end I asked Mr Agmondisham to find me a job. His question took me by surprise.

'Can you type?'

'No,' I said.

'And I suppose you can't do shorthand?'

'No, I'm afraid not.'

'You see—' Mr Agmondisham, who had taken a step or two away from the desk, apparently cogitating, now returned, sat down, swung his chair round and gave me a brief explanation of the way he ran his business. His main asset, and his main interest, lay in knowing where to buy pictures. He was really a specialist in the contents of country houses, and his knowledge was in its origin social. 'I don't only know who owns paintings,' he said. 'It's my business to know who's going to inherit them. Sometimes it's in the nature of an actuarial speculation.' Mr Agmondisham's smile was extraordinarily bland. 'So you see, I hardly need an assistant. But I do employ a secretary. Look here,' he added, and his manner changed; he sounded very business-like indeed, almost curt, 'if I make a proposal to you, will you consider its disadvantages very carefully?' I said I would. The proposal was that I should first of all learn typing and shorthand. He would then employ me as secretary-cum-research assistant. It was, he said, a job with no discernible future, since it was hardly possible to set up as a dealer on one's own account without substantial capital. I was not discouraged by this—the future was too dim to worry me. I was more concerned by the smallness of my wages and the anti-climax of returning to Edinburgh. My idea had been a do-or-die one; either get a job in London or return to Edinburgh in despair. Instead I was returning to Edinburgh to take a shorthand-typing course. I was rather ashamed of this, and I kept quiet about the salary.

Even so, my getting a job at all upset Alastair. He began to do all over again the various bits of arithmetic with money and time which were intended to show how long it would be before he began to make money at the Bar. The results were discouraging; in fact I think it was at this time he realized that his ambition to go to the Bar was, after all, not the most effective or quickest way of exploiting his mathematical abilities. The worst phase of this impatience, this fretting about the long way he still had to go, came just

before his Cambridge scholarship examination. He sat this
at the end of the Christmas term—his second Christmas
term at Edinburgh—and even if he got a scholarship he
wouldn't be able to go up to the university in a bye-term;
he would have to wait until the following October, nearly
a year.

'A year of my earning life lost,' he said. 'That may mean
ten thousand pounds or more.' He was perfectly, even
grimly, serious. He held this note in everything connected
with the examination. His wildness and insouciance were
suppressed; he began once again working so dourly, so
rigidly to a time-table, that for the first time I began to
fear for his success; he acted like all the worthy plodders,
all the hard-working note-takers, burningly covetous of
pensionable jobs, who seemed to me to form the bulk of
the student body of Edinburgh University. On the day
before he left for Cambridge we went to see a revival of
'Duck Soup', but he didn't laugh very much.

The results of the examination were due on the Saturday,
a week after he came back from Cambridge. He had come
back to Edinburgh ostensibly to do some work, but really
I think, to avoid his aunt and the post-mortem which my
father would have held. He had been told the telegram
would arrive in the afternoon, and when I came in to
our digs about twelve o'clock he was out. I had been
infected by that wrought-up nervy feeling of waiting for
news, and when I was called to the telephone and found
that it was my father speaking I couldn't at first take
it in that he was telling me what we had been waiting
to hear.

'. . . I'm very glad,' he said. 'He deserved it. The
best pupil I ever taught. "Scholar of Trinity College,
Cambridge"—it always looks well in *Who's Who*. Tell
Alastair I said that.' This was the generous, encouraging
touch my father could produce for a pupil, and he
was truly delighted, yet I heard in his voice a faint
muted rasp of bitterness, the whisper of a sigh. Was
he thinking of the day when he himself had heard
this same news?—of the contrast between what he had
expected then and of what had happened to him since?

Or was he thinking of the contrast between Alastair's position and my own? For a moment, as so easily happened, I caught his depression; then an idea came to me which lifted it. I rushed out of the house, and before I had time to complete the calculations about paying my laundry bill, buying Christmas presents, and so on, which crowded into my mind, I was running back with a bottle of champagne. I put this on the table in my bed-sitter, and then went down to borrow glasses from our landlady. While she was wiping the glasses I told her the news and asked her to join us. Then I rushed upstairs again.

But when I entered my room Alastair was already there. He must have just gone in and seen the champagne bottle on the table, for as I walked through the open door with the glasses in my hand he looked at me and said 'Ah,' a noise gentle but full of meaning, like the noise made by some women when they are satisfied in love.

'My father telephoned,' I said; and I picked up the bottle and opened it clumsily, so that the wine frothed over on to the dark, worn, velveteen cover of my bedside table. We both finished our glasses at a draught, and as Alastair put his down he suddenly laughed with joy.

All this passed through my mind now as I walked, because it was in these streets that we had fought our way through the east wind, in those pubs that we had played darts, in those shops bought cigarettes. Now, after London, I was once again struck by the hardness, the *stoniness*, of the streets. And the pubs, I knew, were mostly bleak places, machines for getting drunk in. After London, too—the West End where I lived and worked—everything looked slightly proletarianized. This was the Scotland of the nineteenth century, the grim, competitive little country that exported successful men. Then, a few hundred yards further on, I turned into George Square, and at once moved back into that earlier Scotland with its special manifestations of grace and homeliness, elegance and dignity. I thought of Kingisbyres; and then, a little later, I thought of Catherine.

What had happened between Alastair and Catherine in those holidays in which they had first come together I had never exactly known. I knew that they had had a love affair, brief, adult, passionate, which had ended suddenly when Alastair had had an heroic row with Catherine's father. I saw them both occasionally, but between Alastair and myself there was a pact of silence, and as for Catherine she had a kind of troubled kindness which forbade her to speak of Alastair to me. I was never angry against Alastair. I knew that Catherine had left me of her own accord. She was like that. It had forced itself upon me, in bewilderment and pain, that she was insatiably inconstant. Who had she turned to after Alastair? I don't know. After the row with Mr Harvey neither I nor Alastair had seen Catherine for a very long time.

The recollections which had been set in train by the sight of our old digs petered out as I turned into the King's Park and walked up towards the Crags. From the top there was the usual view; it was astonishing how many different shades of smoke there were. I saw the Old Town which I associated with executions and the roll of drums, and the New Town which I associated with literary critics drinking claret. Then I thought of Alastair and of how exceedingly angry he would be if I were too late in carrying out his instructions. I began to hurry down, breaking away from the path and jumping down awkwardly over the rough grass. In the street I jumped on a tram which started with the usual mad jerk on the usual crazy flight.

When I got back Alastair was still asleep, but when I spoke to him he stirred, and when I spoke again he opened his eyes at once.

'How do you feel?' I said. He hesitated for a time, then smiled the smile, rather sly, which I had seen on my own face.

'I feel at one with God. Full of power. . . .' His voice was slurred, and I thought I would wait for a few moments before trying to get him up.

'Surely,' I said, 'it's love you should feel full of.'

'No, no. Power. I don't love. . . .' He yawned and seemed

to lose the thread. Then in a moment he said: 'Did I tell you that Harvey's selling Kingisbyres?'

'Yes, you told me.'

'Going to build bits on . . .' Alastair yawned again prodigiously. 'You know,' he said, and again in his slurred, inconsequent voice it seemed a new beginning. 'Harvey might get into trouble one day.'

'What kind of trouble?'

'Work done during the war at Kingisbyres without a licence. He's always . . . can't do without anything. . . .'

'I know,' I said. 'But I thought he was rather cautious as well.'

'He's clever enough. "Like rotten fish by night he stinks and shines." Who said that anyway?' Alastair still seemed not quite all there, but he suddenly threw the clothes back, got up, drank a draught of fruit juice, and made for the door. After a few minutes he came back, towelling his face and looking more awake. However, he went straight back to bed and refused coffee, food, and a cigarette.

'All my needs are satisfied,' he said, and he lay back and crossed his hands behind his head. 'I better have my dose, though. Two pills and a capsule.' I gave them to him and he swallowed them. 'Chum me down the road,' he said. It was the kind of Scotticism I had broken him of at Nethervale. I laughed and took one of the brilliant ultramarine capsules and one of the pills. After a moment or two I noticed the same slight smile back on Alastair's face. But it was some little time, perhaps two or perhaps ten minutes, before he spoke.

'We had some good times at Kingisbyres, hadn't we?' The naked sentimentality in his tone made me realize, with a slight shock, how much he was under the influence of the drugs.

'Yes,' I said.

'I don't think I've ever enjoyed swimming so much since.' His smile broadened. 'And Cathy and I in the High School. . . .'

'The High School?'

'That loft. Cathy called it that because she learned so much there. . . .' Alastair's eyelids dropped, but before I could move—I was leaning against the foot of the bed—he suddenly opened them again and in his normal, wide-awake voice said: 'What was I talking about? Cathy and me?'

'Yes.'

'I used to have feelings of guilt sometimes about stealing your girl.'

'Even then I knew she had stolen herself.' I had a curious feeling of impersonal melancholy; the feeling, I suppose, that women get from a good cry at the pictures. I realized with a small part of myself that I too was under the influence of the drugs.

'Yes,' said Alastair, 'she threw herself into my arms. Literally.' He had some difficulty with the word 'literally'. 'That night after the Crimond fiasco. My little pseudo-upper-class Jean Armour . . . y'know what Burns wrote about meeting Jean again?' Alastair's voice was wandering and drunken. ' "I took advantage of some dry horse-litter, and gave her . . ."—listen to this—"such a thundering scalade as electrified the very marrow of her bones." ' I had difficulty in making out what he said; then suddenly it penetrated.

'That very first night,' I said, and as Alastair's eyes closed I seized his shoulder, 'did you and Catherine—?' He looked at me owlishly.

'Electrified the very marr'—' he said, and then I knew he was asleep. My hand slipped off his shoulder, and quite suddenly I was crying with the tears running down my face, and my breath coming in sobbing gulps.

'Oh God,' I said, and I heard my own stricken voice. 'That same night . . . my darling, how *could* you? Oh my darling. . . .' An appalling misery weighed me down, a misery of lost loves, lost causes, lost Kingisbyres. I was young again; I had lost my middle-aged callousness, and for a long, terrible, piercing moment, I suffered.

Then, equally suddenly, the tiny remote part of myself which had been watching came back to me and filled my consciousness again. I wiped my tears. What had I been weeping about? I hardly remembered. I too was beginning to feel sleepy.

I got up, and undressed, carelessly, dropping my shirt

at my feet, and washed and brushed my teeth, remembered how Alastair had told me Mr Harvey had bought Kingisbyres, and added: 'But it won't do them any good of course. I put them under a curse, you remember.' Alastair had been rather drunk at the time. I thought of the curse again now. It seemed to be working; the Harveys were selling Kingisbyres. I was suddenly even more sleepy, drifting and confused. I remembered the curse again, and Kingisbyres; but now it was a different thing, for I was at Kingisbyres and it was not a curse I was drinking, but a toast. I was drinking the health of the bride, and it was Alastair who was going to reply. For Alastair had married Catherine.

Part Four

IT WAS AT Dunkirk-time that Alastair married Catherine, and it didn't seem enormously surprising because nothing was enormously surprising just then. Yet if I had been told it a year earlier I should have found it as hard to believe in this marriage as in the fall of France, and I have thought of it since as historians do about an historical event—puzzling, weighing evidence, brooding. Should I have foreseen such a possibility? Was there some clue? What evidence did I in fact have?

Let me go back—back to the quarrel with Mr Harvey. It took place during our first vacation from Edinburgh, the Christmas vacation following upon the summer when Alastair had first made love to Catherine. Their love affair had begun again, I knew, as soon as Catherine had come home from Berkshire. Still neither spoke about it to me; still I saw both of them. The row happened in the local county town. Alastair and I had driven in, as usual in a borrowed car, to collect some books he had ordered. We had one or two commissions to carry out, including one for Catherine, to look at the progress of some restoration work on a satinwood table, which, on my advice, her mother had bought for her at a local auction, and, again on my advice, was having treated by a little man I had discovered. I spent a long time over this. When we got into the car in the lane where the shop stood Alastair muttered something impatient and let in the clutch with a bang. We were almost on a blind corner, and as Alastair made to take this he had to pull up sharply, nose to nose with Mr Harvey's big Daimler. It was a near-miss, not alarming, but slightly jarring to the nerves. The blame for it was I think, shared equally. After he backed, the chauffeur got out and, with ostentation, looked to see if his car had been damaged, which it obviously hadn't. There was something insolent and offensive in the way he did it, and I felt rather than saw that it enraged Alastair. He gave a blast on the horn, and the chauffeur, still only a few feet away, started angrily. He had already turned towards us when Mr Harvey put his head out of the door and said: 'Oh come on man—he didn't hit us.' I heard his voice very distinctly, impatient, yet somehow with its Glasgow sing-song, complacent. As he looked out he must have recognized me, because he got out of the car and came over. I'm sure he didn't recognize Alastair until he was beside us.

'Well, well,' he said, 'these things will happen!' Although he was annoyed he made a surprising effort not to be disagreeable. In order to meet him in this I got out of the car, laughed, and made some remark in the same spirit. Alastair got out too, but only nodded, and stood on the other side of the car from us. Harvey, in fact, was behaving better than he was, and no doubt they both realized this.

'I was just going to call on Sandilands to see how they're getting on with some work they're doing for me.' Mr Harvey pulled off his gloves and put them in his overcoat pocket. The overcoat was soft and rich-looking.

'We've just been there,' I said. 'Catherine asked us to report to her about the progress with her table.'

'Did she now? It seems my family can't get on at all without the help of you two young men!' At the best it was an ambiguous remark; it could have been interpreted as a hint to get out from under his feet. As he spoke he smiled his pursy smile, and although there was something slightly absurd about him, there was also something formidable, and if Alastair hadn't been there I would have set to to pacify and please him. But with the sense of Alastair's hostility smouldering dangerously on the other side of the car I hesitated, and Mr Harvey, supposing no doubt that he had subdued both of us, and seeking to finish the job, turned and addressed Alastair.

'If you go on driving like that, you know'—his tone was the affectedly light one that conveys a serious rebuke— 'you'll need all your skill as a famous King's Counsel for yourself one day.' He smiled the same patronizing little smile, perhaps trying to reduce the effect of his words, but in the brief silence I knew it was too late.

'By that time,' said Alastair, 'I'll have a chauffeur to do my careless driving for me.' His voice was cold, without anything in it to tone down its deliberate offensiveness. They looked at one another across the bonnet of the car, declaring open war.

'That's hardly a tone to adopt to me, young man.' The words were pompous, but Harvey was not unimpressive; I suppose board-room rows had taught him to keep his temper and score his point. My stomach sank a little.

'I'm sorry that I should be forced to use it.' Alastair's coolness was undoubtedly provoking, and it provoked.

'You're an insolent young pup,' said Mr Harvey. He had now lost his temper. 'I've thought so for some time. You think you're a big man, don't you? But you're just a silly wee laddie that's going to have to do as he's told. Let me tell you that this hanging around my daughter has got to stop.' He ought to have stopped there, since this was something about which he was in a position to give orders and see they were carried out. But his rage had got the better of him. 'Do you understand?' he added.

'Man,' said Alastair, and suddenly he used the voice and manner he used in the village, slow, sardonic and Scotch, 'Ah cannae help but understand you. It's like smelling a midden.'

Mr Harvey, whose face was normally pale—even white—but who had slowly been turning red, flushed darkly.

'You—wee twerp'—he was almost squealing—'I'll make you pay for this!' He was raving, now, and the clichés of rage poured from him. I saw the chauffeur standing beside the Daimler with a contented, insolent expression. 'I'll serve you out for this—see if I don't!'

'Are you threatening me?' said Alastair: the words burst from him, for he too, was raging now; I saw his chest rising and falling. Perhaps Harvey did, too, for he calmed down.

'I wouldn't threaten a nyaff like you,' he said; he was obviously struggling to master his temper. 'But mind what I told you.' Like Alastair's, but probably unconsciously, his voice had become very Scotch.

'I shan't forget it,' said Alastair. His voice was low, and Harvey, who had half-turned away, seemed to pause to hear it. I noticed again how Alastair had power to make people listen. 'Don't imagine I shall.' Now, twenty years later, I can still hear the very tone in which he spoke. Harvey looked at him, taken aback, freshly indignant and perhaps freshly uneasy. Perhaps he meant to speak, but in the end he only gave a kind of grunt, and walked rapidly over to his car—a smallish, upright, springy figure in citified clothes—and an instant later the car swung past us with the chauffeur very upright, looking straight ahead.

The row with Mr Harvey had only precipitated a break with Catherine which, since Alastair and I were due to return to Edinburgh, would have occurred anyway. The summer after that Alastair and I both got vacation jobs abroad, and during the brief period we were at home Catherine was staying with friends in England. In September she went to stay with a French family, and in the following spring moved to an Italian one. She wrote to me occasionally. The staying with families was a compromise; she herself had had an idea of staying at school until she was the appropriate age and then going to Oxford and studying modern languages there. But her mother wouldn't hear of this. She thought Oxford dowdy for women. *Her* idea was a finishing school in Lausanne run by a titled Englishwoman. But Catherine still wanted to go on with her languages; hence the families. She did not appear to have any special interest in the culture of the countries concerned; it was simply that their languages offered a kind of intellectual task which she had learned to enjoy. It might have been chess. I was a little surprised that she wrote to me. I thought that perhaps, with the family loyalty which was a curiously strong trait, she would break completely with Alastair, but in the first letter she wrote she was angry with *me*, for not stopping 'that idiotic row'. There was in fact a note of 'men are such great big sillies' in her letter that slightly embarrassed me, as Catherine often did embarrass me by some attitude I thought affected or naïve. It was in fact two years before I saw her again.

This was in London. It was quite unexpected. I was working as usual in Mr Agmondisham's flat one day—he himself being abroad—when the telephone rang, and it was Catherine. She was passing through London, she said, on her way to Kingisbyres, and I might, if I cared, take her out to dinner. I said I should be delighted, although even as I spoke I was doing sums in my head. But whatever scraping and borrowing I had to do I would have said yes in any case, and would have entertained Catherine in the style to which she made it clear she was accustomed. I was agitated all day after the telephone call, and as I changed in the evening I noticed that my hands were shaking. Yet I was no longer in love with Catherine. This agitation was something that was left over, an emotional relic.

We dined at a smart new restaurant and Catherine was very pleased. She told me she approved of me. She said I was less nervous, more assured. She was elegant, seeming older than her eighteen years, and foreign looking. She was very tanned, and wore a purple lipstick and beautiful exotic Italian sandals. She was on her way home from Venice to spend Christmas at Kingisbyres. She gave me an enthusiastic account of her eight months in Italy—picnics, yachting, dancing, a love affair.

'Mummy wanted me to have a season here, you know, but I knew I would have more fun in Venice.' Catherine took a sip of hock, and then quite suddenly, the hard social manner melted. 'Anyway'—she looked at me, and her face lighted up with amusement—'the fact is that Mummy just doesn't know quite enough people.' In that moment we came very near to one another again.

Later, when we were dancing, she asked about Alastair.

'He's at Cambridge, of course,' I said, 'working hard. Don't you ever hear from him?' Catherine shook her head.

'We broke up completely,' she said. We danced in silence for a moment, but the band was playing the kind of slow foxtrot which makes people romantic and confidential. 'Alastair scared me,' said Catherine. 'I never knew what he might do.'

'I know the feeling.'

'It's funny, but he could give you the most extraordinary

feeling of security, of being guarded and looked after, and at the same time a feeling almost of being in danger.'

'Rather like being Henry VIII's wife,' I said.

'Yes.' Catherine looked up at me. 'You know that's it exactly. You always say such good things, Patrick.' She rolled her eyes at me a little, I suppose out of habit, and pressed my hand appreciatively. But she at once took up the tack again. 'Sometimes he seems so set on this career of his he seems absolutely stodgy, and then suddenly he makes you feel he might throw the whole thing overboard. I've got a reckless streak myself, but Alastair is too much for me. I think that deep down I must just be a canny wee Scotch lassie.'

'Alastair,' I said, 'is the most Scotch person I've ever known or ever expect to know.'

'Well, I think it's all very absurd; I mean now, in modern times. It's all very well for Americans to be brash and Russians melancholy and Italians talkative, but it seems absurd for *little* countries to go on being frightfully something or other. It's just an out-of-date thing for the human species.'

'Like going to the lavatory?' Catherine's giggle attracted the attention of several couples near us.

'All the same,' she said a moment later, 'I wish I had had enough nerve to go on with Alastair. He made me live all the way through to my finger-nails.' She was silent for a moment, serious. Then she said: 'Of course, I have a lot of fun this way too.'

That was the Christmas of 1935. I didn't go home and so I didn't see Alastair until he came to London a few days before the end of the vacation. I told him about my meeting with Catherine. When I mentioned her name he smiled.

'Cathy,' he said. 'So you saw Cathy.' He didn't ask how she was.

'Yes. We talked about you.'

'And what did my two old friends say about me?'

'Catherine said you scared her.'

'Cathy's trouble,' said Alastair, 'is that she's too damned respectable.'

It never crossed my mind then, and it is no more than a hazarded suspicion now, that he had been seeing Catherine over Christmas.

During the next two years or so I saw Alastair every vacation, and visited him once at Trinity. I also saw Catherine several times, when she was visiting London. But the three of us never met, and even if we had all been in London at the same time it wouldn't have occurred to me to arrange a meeting. I thought of them as people who had had an affair and finished with one another. There wouldn't have been anything embarrassing about their meeting, but there wouldn't have been any point in it. That was how it seemed to me. Neither mentioned the other to me. Catherine had always both a current affair and a current project. For a few months she had a job in the export department of a Clyde shipbuilding firm, but she was always going abroad, to Cortina and Juan-les-Pins and similar places where the set of people she had got to know in Venice used to go, and she quit the job. Her mother, she said, was worried about her, but her father was getting richer and richer by making biscuits cheaper than anyone else. It was the unemployed, she said, who ate them.

In 1938 Alastair went to Princeton. I was sorry to see him go. We had always seen enough of each other to avoid drifting apart; I certainly thought of Alastair as my closest friend. I am sure he considered me in the same light. But we were not seeing one another daily; we each had our own preoccupations, our own separated lives. And for more than a year before the outbreak of war I was abroad. And the last time I saw Catherine before the war was when she came back from Switzerland in February 1938.

In September 1939 Mr Agmondisham was called up, and I was given a temporary job in the Foreign Office. In the spring of that year he and I had had a certain amount of success with a book in which we had collaborated, called *The English Gentleman and the Grand Tour*, and it was because one of the senior people in the Foreign Office had read this book that I got a job there. The book had in fact given Mr Agmondisham—I continued to think of him in this way long after we were on Christian-name terms—a considerable reputation. Even I, as the junior partner, had come to be known in circles where people are interested in this kind of subject.

Alastair stayed on for a time at Princeton. He had been from the beginning extraordinarily happy. 'I feel more at home here,' he had written, 'in a way, than I do at Cambridge. Nice people, the English, but I've never really got over my good old Scotch hostility. Yet again, like the good wee Scotty I am, I've been conditioned to feel that success is genuine only when it's been registered in London.' Then his letters became fewer. When he did write he almost always mentioned that he was working hard. As war came obviously nearer he asked me how near people in London thought it was. 'I shall want to get back and get into it, I suppose, but I must get my thesis finished first. I have some views about investment in under-developed areas which will be valuable when Europe is in ruins and you and I are under them. Anyway I want to look at Europe first and maybe the War Office will fix it. Then I'll write a book called *The Scotch-American Bum and the Grand Tour*.'

When war actually broke out he sent me a note beginning, 'It turns out those orchids I sent to Mrs Chamberlain were a complete waste,' and saying he would be home soon, but at Christmas I had heard nothing.

One evening in January, when I was working late and alone in my room, the door opened and a woman's head appeared round it. I was working by a desk-light, and everything beyond the borders of this was obscure. The head said, 'Hello,' and I knew from this that it was a social and not a business call.

'Hello,' I said. 'Would you mind turning on the light so that I can see you?' The central light came on and I saw a blonde girl in FANY uniform; she had the FANY appearance too, the highly tailored assured look of one who could afford to serve her country without pay.

'You've forgotten me completely, haven't you?' The smile on the smooth high-cheekboned face became broader; some people seem to derive more assurance even from being forgotten. I gave one of those guilty and doubtful mutters which people in this position do. Then something, some angle of the cheek, some movement, brought it back.

'You're Hero,' I said, 'Hero?'

'Prime-Challis.'

'Of course. Do come in and sit down.'

I was surprised; not so much at running into her (for already, even in the phoney war, I had learned that in war one was always running into people), but that she should have troubled to look me up. I remembered her aloofness.

'I saw your name on a board downstairs,' she said. 'The General I drive is at a conference here. I thought it must be you.' She smiled again. She seemed not only nicer, but possessed of more character than when I had seen her last.

'Who is your General?' I asked, and she told me, and I knew his name, and we talked a bit about people in her office and mine. Then:

'Have you seen Catherine recently?'

'No,' I said. 'I haven't heard from her for about a year. Is she still in Scotland?' Catherine had given me to understand, in the last letter I had had from her, that if war broke out she was going to do some job of epic importance and incredible secrecy in Scotland.

'Why, no. She's here. She's a Wren, in the Admiralty.'

As Hero said this and Catherine was revealed as being in London, I was suddenly anxious to see her again. During those months when I was waiting to be called up I had for the first time the sense of having grown older, of having had a part of my life slip into something which was no longer continuous with the present, but had become 'the past'. It may have been that my interest in seeing Catherine again was an interest in seeing myself in this new mirror. Whatever it was, it was sharp and real.

'I must look her up,' I said.

'I shall be seeing her tonight.' Hero looked at me more directly, and I noticed that her make-up, although 'discreet', was very careful and beautiful. 'At a party. If you were free you could escort me.'

'I should be delighted to.'

'Good. It will be a reunion. It only lacks Alastair. Catherine tells me he's still in America?'

'Yes. He's expected back any day.'

'What's he going to do?'

'Go into the army, I suppose. At least that's what he's coming back for.'

'He really was a most extraordinary person. He puzzled me very much.' She laughed and got up.

When I called for Hero later that evening I was feeling pleased to be taking her to the party, for although her good looks and her style were rather a standard product, their standardization was somehow itself an attraction—it was like taking out an essence of all the expensive prettily enamelled young female officers in London. But my feelings about that, although lively, were less strong than my feelings about seeing Catherine again. When, at the party, I saw her, she was speaking to someone, but she broke off at once.

'Patrick!' Her scream had the exaggerated, almost hysterical note that I remembered, and she put her arms round me and kissed me full on the lips in a way that took me back to the way she had used to behave at Kingisbyres. Several people glanced at her. And she stood there holding both my hands and babbling and laughing with a joy which I suddenly shared. Yet she had changed. I was surprised to find that she was slender and rather small. She was not pretty but she had her dark style and vividness, and she gleamed with the phosphorescence of sexuality. Altogether it seemed much longer than two years since we had met.

We had a rapid re-establishing conversation. Always businesslike, Catherine asked me a series of questions about my job in the Foreign Office, my salary there, and whether I knew Giles Waterhouse. As it happened, I did know him by reputation; he was a broken-down old peer who had been given a low-grade clerk's job and was widely believed to be a kleptomaniac.

'Intimately,' I said. 'Though as a matter of fact I spend more time with Harry Lanarkshire.'

'Oh? I don't think I know him, do I? Is he young?'

Hot on the scent, Catherine was almost quivering with concentration.

'Very,' I said. 'He was born only a moment ago.'

'Patrick—you are mean!' She was annoyed, then laughed. 'Isn't it funny how we do the same things again as soon as we meet? The first time I ever saw you you told me your father was an unemployed lavatory attendant.'

'So I did.'

Hero, who had been standing beside us, laughed.

'I was saying to Patrick that when Alastair gets back we must have a reunion.'

'Why yes.' Catherine sketched a motion of clapping her hands. 'Will you two take us girls out dancing?' This again—the eagerness for pleasure—was familiar.

'We should be delighted.' And indeed it seemed to me a good idea. The war, which had given me an interest in 'the past', I suppose had done the same thing for everybody. And conversely it had given people the idea of starting afresh, getting rid of old animosities, old embarrassments, old feelings—luggage which it had become tiresome to lug about. In my case it was a growth of indifference I had got rid of. I was almost surprisingly happy to be talking to Catherine. I had remained fond of her, and she of me, and her vitality perhaps made her affection seem even warmer than it was.

'What are you doing in the Admiralty? Are you using your languages?'

'Curiously enough, I am.' As always when this ability of hers came into the picture, Catherine seemed at once a little different. There was nothing at all dramatic about it; merely that she somehow gave the sense that this was a private world.

'Do you like it?'

'Yes I do rather.' She did not say any more. Nor did she ask about my book. Probably she had never heard of it; but now, when I had ceased to be in love with her, I knew that, even if she had, it was quite likely that she had forgotten all about it, or that it simply didn't enter her mind during our conversation. She had the self-centredness of people whose dynamo hums so loudly that they can hear nothing else.

Quite early in our conversation a Naval commander, very much older than Catherine, had come up to her, and I had been introduced to him as a 'very old friend'. He looked at me without favour, and ogled Catherine.

'That's my tonight's date.' Catherine hardly waited for him to leave us to give me this information. 'Do you think he's handsome?'

'I can detect some trim lines yet in the battered hulk. Why? Are you contemplating anything?'

'I'm really involved already. Not emotionally, exactly.'

'Oh?'

'You see William is awfully lonely. He's been separated from his wife for ages, but it's one of those awfully tragic cases where the wife is a Catholic.' Catherine, whose expression had become preternaturally pious, looked down at the drink in her hand as though this subject were too sacred and too painful to be discussed face to face.

'How dreadful,' I said. 'A man in that position must need a great deal of sympathy and understanding.' Catherine gave me a suspicious look, against which my impassive expression was not proof; and her own changed, by way of a curious, comic slyness, to a kind of shamefaced amusement.

'Oh dear,' she said, 'I wish I hadn't promised to let him take me home tonight. Then you could have.'

'Well, I brought Hero, you know.'

'Well, Hero could have got someone else.'

'Perhaps Hero doesn't want anyone else.' I spoke idly, meaning no more than some quite general and playful reflection upon Catherine's assumption, made more bluntly now than formerly, that everything could be rearranged for her convenience. But Catherine could not accept idleness about this subject.

'You and Hero haven't got a thing for one another have you?'

'That,' I said, 'I shall have to leave you to find out.' At this point I broke up the tête-à-tête, but before the party came to an end I had arranged to take Catherine out a few nights later.

As Hero and I were walking across the hall of the block

of flats where the party had been held—a hall which was very dimly lit because of the blackout—she tripped slightly, and when we got into the street, I said: 'You didn't hurt yourself, did you? I thought you were limping a little?'

'I am limping a little,' she said, 'but not because of that. I had an accident about two years ago. A horse rolled on my knee.' She spoke in a voice so negative that I knew the information was important.

'And your riding?'

'I can sit on a horse. That's about all.' I was about to make some conventional remark, but I didn't.

'Does it make you unhappy?' I said.

'It was distressing at the time. It's tolerable now. How brave of you to ask me.'

'I'm sorry if I appeared intrusive.' I heard my voice chilling to the rebuff. We were walking loosely, arm-in-arm for convenience in the blackout, and suddenly Hero stopped and clasped my hand.

'No,' she said. '*I'm* sorry. I try to avoid that kind of bitterness. What I said slipped out—as the truth does sometimes.'

'I know those feelings,' I said. 'I was going to be a painter, do you remember, and then I found out I wasn't good enough.' Again I had an impulse to turn the edge of our feelings by some ironical remark, but I resisted it, and we continued to tolerate these adult emotions. 'I thought you had changed,' I said. 'I don't think Catherine has. I don't think she's yet lost the illusion that life is illimitable.' We had still not seen a taxi, and were walking along in that blackout to which we were even then not wholly accustomed; it was an intimate situation, in which I could say things which I perhaps would not have said if we had been, say, in a lighted room.

'Has Alastair?'

'I haven't seen him for some time,' I said, 'but I don't think he has.'

The telephone call came through when I had just got back to my room from a conference and was feeling very pompous and Foreign Office.

'Do speak up,' I said, 'I can't *hear* you.' There was a crackling noise on the line and then suddenly a voice in my ear.

'Hold the thing closer to your ear then, you silly sod.'

'Oh it's you,' I said. 'Where are you speaking from?'

'The Black Watch Depot at Perth.'

'What are you doing there?'

'Racketeering. Can you hear me now?'

'Perfectly.'

'Then fix me a bed in London for ten days. Can I stay with you?'

'Yes.'

'Can I bring a woman into the house?'

'Yes. Have you got one?'

'No. But I hear women are very easy to make in a war. Is it true? I only landed yesterday. I hope . . .' The line crackled and the voice faded out. I flashed, and the operator came on, but since I hadn't made the call I couldn't renew it. Nothing more happened.

But I guessed that Alastair would arrive in London the following evening and I bought the bottle of champagne which had become traditional. (It was a tradition to which a number of sacrifices had been made, but in those days my royalties had given me a feeling of being quite rich.) When a ring came on the bell at the right time I chanced it, opened the bottle, and went to the door with a glass in each hand. Alastair was standing with a bag and when he saw me he put down the bag and took the glass without a word. Then:

'The good old cause,' he said.

'The good old cause,' I echoed, and we both drained our glasses. He wore one of those light American raincoats, and there was a careless, informal look about his clothes which might have been called undergraduate, although in his Cambridge days Alastair had in fact dressed quite formally. At Cambridge, too, he had acquired something academic in his manner, a tendency to frosty irony, a biting quality that had made him seem older. Now he seemed younger again. I had never seen him more full of life, spilling himself and his belongings over the flat,

talking and laughing about his life at Princeton, and the
voyage across with its submarine scares, and my being in
the Foreign Office, and the success of what he called 'The
English Gent', and his own future in the Army where
he had some graft that enabled him to go straight to an
OCTU.

He had come to London, he said, mainly to see a friend
of his, an economist who had taught him at Cambridge and
was now in the Ministry of Economic Warfare. He told me
something about this man and then began to lecture me on
how the war should be financed. This surprised me, for in
his Cambridge days Alastair had adopted a slightly ironical
tone about economics, as though it were a hobby in which
he could not expect non-enthusiasts to be interested. But
now it was different.

'How long is a piece of string?' He let *The Times* drop
on the floor after concentrating on it. 'That's the great
economic question of this war. That's what the Government
keeps asking itself, anyway. Only Keynes has an idea of
measuring it. He had some articles in this a couple of
weeks back.' Alastair nodded at the paper on the floor,
then fixed me with a donnish glare. 'Do you know what
the gross national income is?'

'Not to the nearest thousand million.' I had some feeble
idea of making a joke. But Alastair was very serious.

'Nor does anyone else,' he said. 'But I didn't mean the
figure. I meant the conception.'

'No.'

'It's an exceedingly important conception. You'll be
meeting it again. The gross national income means . . .'
Alastair gave me an exposition, no doubt as clear as it
could be made, of an economic technique which is now
familiar but was then new. In the course of this it appeared
that he had ideas which he was arranging to pass on to a
number of influential people of various kinds with whom
he had appointments. 'I wrote to old Clandillon,' he said,
'and he asked me to go and see him. But I gather he's been
ill, and out of things. I'm not going to try and argue with
him, of course, but I thought he might tell me some things
nobody else could tell me. I wonder—' He broke off and

sat in silence with a slight, moody frown. Then suddenly, when he came to the end of his cigar, he laughed.

'For a private soldier,' he said, 'I shoot off my mouth pretty goddam freely. Now tell me the news.'

'I saw Catherine,' I said.

'Dear little Cathy. You know what, Patrick—after a lot more experience I still think of Cathy as my favourite nymphomaniac.'

'And I saw Hero.'

'Not little Miss Surcingle!'

'Not any more,' I said. I told him about Hero.

'Oh well,' he said, 'worse things happen in war. And these girls are both in London?'

'Yes. We're to have a party with them.'

'Good. I want to see some English girls like Hero again. You know, American girls are more like Scotch girls—they don't have that wonderful upper-class remoteness that makes it a profound sexual experience just to help a girl like Hero to take off her coat.' Alastair rubbed his hands. 'Now. Let's go out and get stewed,' he said.

The party took place two nights later. At Alastair's suggestion we called for Hero first. We waited together in a hall while she came downstairs, and she greeted Alastair very warmly and kindly, and so that I felt she was pleased to see him, although what the difference in that controlled social manner would have been if she had been indifferent, it was hard to imagine. On his side Alastair laid himself out to please her from the first moment, and by the time we called for Catherine, only a couple of minutes in the taxi, it seemed to have been arranged that it was Hero who was Alastair's partner. I realized that he had always sensed her frigidity and felt it as a challenge. Catherine greeted Alastair tumultuously, as she had done me, but even more so, since we were not in public. She kissed him several times, and bubbled over with questions and comments, and laughed almost hysterically. Yet almost at once she began to tease him, all in the friendliest way, but somehow chiming in with the idea that she was my partner rather than his.

'Why,' she said, 'you even *look* American!' We had

collected in the bar of a restaurant after taking our things off, and it was true that the cut of Alastair's suit, the pattern of his tie, the plain white collar-attached shirt, were slightly un-English. 'And you know your accent's getting terribly confusing. It was Cambridge with a bit of Scotch left and now there's American.' Alastair smiled.

'It's the accent of the future. Standard Princeton-Anglo-American, clear, articulate and amiable. Readily understood by subject races. Doesn't rouse the worst instincts of the lower orders like Standard Mayfair County-and-Peerage, which will only be spoken after the war by a few Wykehamist Labour politicoes. The Conservative Party will ban it for members—if they've any sense. You'll have to learn to speak Scotch again, like your grandpa.'

'Oh *no*!' Catherine gave a wail of horror, which was only half-affected.

'Unless of course we're all compulsorily learning German.'

'You don't think we're going to *lose the war*, do you?' Catherine's horror this time was not at all affected; it was perhaps the first time that the possibility had ever presented itself to her imagination.

'Well, there are only two sides, and one of them must.' Alastair smiled again, a smile which was perhaps a trifle sinister.

'Answer the question, Alastair.' I was surprised by Hero's voice, lightly conversational, faintly mocking, and yet not at all to be ignored. I saw Alastair glance at her appraisingly.

'No.' he said. 'Considering America committed, as I do, it wouldn't be true to say that I think we shall lose.'

'Well, thank goodness for that!' Catherine apparently held the view, widespread at this time, that belief in victory was a matter not of judgment but of will-power. This moment of seriousness had the effect of stirring everyone up; the evening began to go extraordinarily well. At dinner we were all very gay, and after dinner we went on to another place and danced. Here I was thrown together with Catherine again; she had always been passionately fond of dancing, and I liked it; Alastair disliked it, and Hero, although she told me her knee didn't trouble her in dancing, sat out most of the time. As Catherine and I danced she talked a lot, as she always did, about anything that came into her head. She said Alastair was looking well and that she had never known anyone so improved as he had been by Cambridge and America.

'Honestly, when I remember him at first at Kingisbyres, he was a ploughboy, you know, really he was, and there you were radiating charm like an ambassador at a Court Ball—'

'Then it must have been the court of Marie Antoinette,' I said, 'and the Queen went dairy-maiding. Or had you forgotten that?' I was really curious to know how much of her own past Catherine had forgotten: I was sure she had a great capacity for forgetting.

'No,' she said. 'I hadn't forgotten.' We danced in silence for a moment, and I thought Catherine had said all she was going to on this subject. But apparently she had been thinking, because she added: 'I suppose it was fun for Marie Antoinette because it was a wonderful game of "let's pretend". But if her grandmother had been a real dairymaid it might have been a wonderful game of "let's *not* pretend".'

'Very well put,' I said.

'You ought to tell me not to bother my pretty little head with such difficult thoughts.' She laughed delightedly, and we went back to our table.

'Let's go on!' she said. 'Let's go to Candy's!' It was an hour later; Catherine still possessed her illimitable appetite for pleasure. Alastair and Hero were not anxious to go on, so what happened was that I took Catherine to Candy's Club and Alastair took Hero home. In the taxi I put my arm round Catherine and kissed her, and she responded with the spontaneity, the lack of nonsense, which had always charmed me. When we were dancing, she said:

'You don't care for me at all now—seriously, I mean?'

'No.'

'But you like me?'

'Yes,' I said, and I slightly tightened my arm round her waist.

'Good,' she said. I felt wonderfully at ease; I suppose we were both a little drunk.

'Is it possible for me to sleep with you tonight?'

'Yes,' Catherine said, 'of course. That would be lovely.'

And indeed it was lovely, an experience of sensual pleasure and pleasurable sentimentality. There were no surprises. Catherine was amorous rather than passionate, with me companionable rather than like a lover, but uninhibited, gracious and full of sweetness. She had— although this only occurred to me afterwards—the qualities, in fact, of a very high-class tart.

When I got back to the flat Alastair was having breakfast, sitting in a dressing-gown of mine that was short in the sleeves, and attacking a very large plateful of miscellaneous fried things. He was surrounded by daily papers.

'Good morning,' he said, and then he looked at me closely. 'I see she was able to let you have a razor,' he added.

'Yes,' I said, and against my will there crept on to my face that pleased hangdog smile which men wear when taxed by their friends with raffish behaviour.

'I met a girl at a party at Princeton once,' said Alastair, 'and . . .' He told me the story while I began to get my breakfast; it was indecent and funny. By the time I sat down, though, he had already got down to giving me his views on a statement by the Chancellor of the Exchequer that was in the papers. During the next few days I saw Alastair only at breakfast or, once, late at night. He was seeing a lot of economists and politicians. He had also paid his proposed visit to Lord Clandillon at his house near London, and had been given two introductions to men who would have been inaccessible without them. But he was disappointed in that visit.

'I did argue with him, after all,' he said. 'It was a mistake. He's getting old, and he thinks of me as a schoolboy. He was civil, but quite impenetrable. I should only have asked questions—questions that he might have asked himself again when I'd gone. These introductions—he didn't give them to me because he thought I'd got anything worth hearing—he gave them to me because he's got the habit of patronage. Still'—he grinned, looking suddenly young and mischievous—'*they* don't know that.' Despite the greater youthfulness of his manner Alastair was far more serious than he had ever been. Once, when I had just gone to bed, he brought two men back with him, and about three in the morning I woke up and heard them still talking in the sitting-room, with Alastair speaking for a long time in an even, quiet, yet contentious voice which impressed me. Once, however, I found his bed had not been slept in and he came in just as I was going out, looking rather hungover, and *not* shaved.

'My turn,' he said. It didn't occur to me then, nor for a long time afterwards, that he meant he had spent the night with Catherine, nor do I know to this day whether he had done so. I know that he did take her out once, but that was to meet an important industrialist who was a friend of her father's and sat on some Government committee.

Then suddenly, in the middle of a busy week, it was time for him to go. I meant to see him off, but didn't get there; his departure was inconsequential and mismanaged. A few days later I had a postcard giving his Army number and address; that was all. Looking back on it I can see that was the real beginning of the war for me. Afterwards everything else was inconsequential and mismanaged and happened at once, but without the full impact of peace-time life. I rang Catherine at the Admiralty, but they told me she had moved to another job, and when I rang her flat she was out. And I rang Hero and she had a bad cold. And then I got my calling-up papers, and for several days after that was insanely busy on an endless series of questions about what would happen if Venezuela invaded Tibet or something. In the end I left London, in the old clothes which the calling-up papers paternally yet somehow grimly recommended, carrying a fibre suitcase done up with rope, in the middle of the blackout, without having telephoned anybody or done any of the things which a few days before had seemed important, but which, as uniformed men moved about me in the darkness carrying kit and mugs of tea, seemed already to belong to another world.

When, some three months later, the German attack on France began, the old world had still not caught up on

me. I was at an OCTU, an anxious hurrying figure
amongst a horde of anxious-hurrying figures, with shiny
boots and an air of super-saturated soldierliness. I had
been moved about a good deal, and letters caught up with
me erratically, a note from Catherine full of allusions to an
earlier letter I hadn't received, one from Hero, nice but
impersonal, and two very brief ones from Alastair, the first
saying he had almost been RTU for insubordination but had
now passed out first in his course and was rejoining the
Black Watch, and a second saying he was going on a course
in Surrey. This last I had the day the Germans invaded
Holland.

The training course I was on, which I wasn't finding
especially easy anyway, was speeded up to Stakhanovite
levels of intellectual toil, and a course was fitted in behind
us, so that the huts and barracks in which we lived became
chaotic. For the last week of the course I and most of
the people on it were pretty chaotic too; we passed out
of it—most of us—and came to realizing that the British
Expeditionary Force was trapped in France and invasion
was in prospect. I had orders to report to a unit which, I
was told, was being put together with sticky paper on the
Dorset coast.

On my last day, just before leaving for the station, I
called on a man I had known in London, who was in
the course behind mine. As it happened he was in a building I had been in myself earlier on, and as I was leaving
he looked for his letters in a nest of pigeon-holes by the
door.

'Good God,' he said, 'I wonder if this could be for you?'
It was a telegram, addressed to 'O/Cdt. P. Shay'. I opened
it and read: 'Cathy and I being married eleven tomorrow
Caxton Hall suppose you could not possibly make it query.'
The telegram was several days old.

It didn't make a tremendous impression on me; I registered it, but I was really thinking about the train I had
to catch. And even when I had caught it I didn't manage to raise any surprise. The Germans, of course, didn't
invade, but at that time it appeared almost certain that
they would. It seems silly now, although I hardly know

why it should, but on that journey, and for a fair time afterwards, I thought it likely that before long I would be dead. I hadn't reached the stage of being actively alarmed about the prospect, but it made things in which I would ordinarily have been interested seem irrelevant.

Part Five

AFTER DUNKIRK-TIME I didn't see Alastair, Catherine, or for that matter any of my old friends, for nearly two years. I went abroad a few months later, and from then until early 1943 I was in the Middle East. I was invalided home, not because of wounds, but because I had developed one of those mysterious illnesses which doctors like to show to other doctors, and I was flown to a hospital near London as a kind of gift from one military brigadier to another. This second brigadier was a famous expert, and cured me very quickly with a new drug. Thereafter he kept me about for several weeks, feeding me up and taking samples of my blood about every third day. I lived in what was called the Observation Ward, a small, early-Victorian villa amongst trees, remote, miniature, and idyllic. This turned out to be the second turning point of the war for me, the hinge of my personal fate. Up to then I had been on the whole overworked, anxious, bored, and kicked around; from now on I was leisured, had no responsibility that I didn't want, and was my own master to a degree which— to a man without private means—is only possible in some colossal organization like the Army, where an individual can disappear like a mouse in the wainscot.

I had been so interesting a case, and responded so quickly to his new treatment that, if he could, the brigadier would have given me the Military Cross. Instead, at my request, he recommended that I should not be re-exposed to infection, but should be employed in England for several months. He also arranged for a long convalescent leave. So it happened that I found myself in the last week in March leaving St Pancras for Glasgow on my way back to Nethervale.

During these two years I had been very much cut off from everyone. I had written to Alastair and Catherine,

163

but it was months before I heard from Alastair in reply, and then his letter had been brief, with a promise of a longer one to follow. The main item of news had been that Catherine was pregnant, but the longer letter never followed, and in the only letter I had from Catherine she said she had miscarried, and sounded depressed. I heard once or twice from Hero, but she was out of touch with Alastair and Catherine, and for news I had relied mainly upon the long letters which, unfailingly, my mother wrote to me every week. It was mostly because of these letters I had an outline of what had been happening.

When Alastair had married Catherine—and no one had any warning of this whatever—he had been on his way to France, among the last British forces to be sent there. He had been involved briefly in action, evacuated from Dunkirk, and then been training in Scotland for several months. Then he had been in England, then back to Scotland, then in India. For the last year or more Catherine had been living at Kingisbyres with her mother, although when I travelled up I didn't know if she was still there. The house itself had been requisitioned in 1940 as a headquarters for the Polish Army, and the two women had lived in a sealed-off flat in what had been the servants' quarters. Mr Harvey was seldom there. His firm were carrying out Government contracts in some new factory near Edinburgh, and he spent a lot of time there and in London, where he was adviser on something to the Ministry of Food. It was understood that he had patched up his old quarrel with Alastair and that Alastair was at least not disowned as a son-in-law. The Captain was still living in the Grouse Lodge on the Clandillons' estate, Lammermuir, looked after by Henstridge.

All this was what my mother stated directly in her letters. But there were other things which were not directly stated. Torn between her horror of repeating gossip which might be malicious and her fear of concealing from me anything which might be of importance to me in friendships which she knew I valued, my mother had tantalized me with hints and suggestions, sometimes imagining that I knew more than I did, and when I asked for explanations retreating into ambiguities and even incoherence.

'I expect,' she wrote on one occasion, 'that Alastair will have written to you about the incident with his Polish friend, which I believe Catherine and her mother were most anxious about at the time. These Poles are of course a wild lot. As you know I don't greatly care for them—and to be candid this particular friend of Alastair's and Catherine's is one of the worst. Alas I can't either pronounce or write his name!—but you will know whom I mean.'

I begged my mother for a full explanation, saying that I had heard nothing and wasn't likely to, and in reply she wrote:

'I do hope that in writing about the incident at all I haven't been indiscreet. . . . The story is that Alastair and his friend took some Army car without permission and had a slight accident. So that the friend was absent without leave the following morning and went to some other work soon afterwards—sent away in disgrace, so people said. It is said they were both drunk which I hope is not true. But apparently Catherine was very upset about it all.' This explanation at first satisfied my curiosity and quietened the uneasiness which, somehow or other, the earlier letter had caused. The incident was almost painfully normal; people like Alastair could be expected to do something like that about once a year. On second thoughts I was less happy. Although Alastair was so reckless in some ways, he had always been careful about driving after drinking, or even driving with someone who had been drinking. I felt that there was more to it than appeared, and when I remembered about it I was still uneasy.

Another mystery was about the Captain.

'I was able the other day to call on Captain Keith. I can't do so very often—transport is so difficult now. He is still at the Grouse Lodge, and is physically well. And it is a mercy that the faithful manservant is spared. Both Captain Keith and he asked after you very warmly. I'm afraid things must be sad and lonely for him, for naturally enough many people don't go to see him who might do so. From all you have said about his odd eccentric views I should be inclined to believe that there has never been more in it than that; perhaps he has always been more unbalanced than I thought. Do write to him—he was so very kind to you.' As a matter of fact

I had written to the Captain once, and had no reply for a very long time; then:

MY DEAR PATRICK,

It is good of you to remember an old fellow like me. When I was young I never wrote to anybody so I don't deserve such kind treatment now. I am glad you have found some interests. My own experiences of soldiering were unfortunate. In peacetime I found it rather boring and the war we fought in the trenches was a scunner. Do you know what that means? It means it was sickening. Perhaps it would have been better if I had had more faith that the war we were fighting was going to do anyone the slightest good. The one in which we are now engaged is of course quite different—it is doing a great deal of good to Stalin and Co. But I know you don't share my views. Henstridge will post this letter in Glasgow.

Believe me, my dear Patrick,

Ever yours very sincerely,

CHARLES KEITH

PS—I am told that imbecile slanders are being circulated about the King of the Belgians. All rot! Don't believe it. What else could he do?

I couldn't make out what my mother's hints were all about. And why was Henstridge to post the letter in Glasgow? The two small mysteries were in my mind as I travelled north.

When I got out of the station at Glasgow there was the familiar thin drizzle and the familiar weird accent in voices full of character—familiar, and yet, even then, already slightly foreign and 'interesting'. By the time I got aboard the smoke-reeking, uniform-packed bus, however, the strangeness had worn off, and as I walked up the path to my parents' home I had that odd feeling of never having been away. It was my mother who opened the door to me; she looked older, whiter-haired, but her air of gentle dignity, her touch of arrogance, had grown if anything stronger. And her unobtrusive will-power, I soon found, was as strong as ever. By this time I was quite well, disgracefully fat on the steaks, butter, eggs, and cream of the 'Observation Ward' as well as ruddy with compulsory open-air exercise. But my mother characteristically decided that I was tired, and almost as soon as I was inside the door a familiar feeling came over me: I was being willed to go to bed early and I knew that, against my will, I would go.

My father was in the drawing-room. When he rose to greet me I saw that he was stiff, which I never remembered him to have been, and he too was older and whiter-haired. Yet the purple veins in his face and the lacework of red at the corners of his eyes had grown fainter, and I guessed at once that he must be drinking less. He looked, now, much as he might have looked if he had never taken to drink; if he had had the career he and my mother wanted for him. Yet he had a slightly bleached look too. I saw that all through my lifetime my mother and he had been growing more like one another, with my mother winning.

'Well,' he said. 'Well Patrick.' And we shook hands and I asked him how he was. Then he began asking me questions about the Army and whether it was fit to take on the German Army on the mainland of Europe—he was sure it wasn't—and my mother began asking me about my illness. After a time she went out to prepare supper, and a few minutes later the conversation between my father and myself petered out. My father was looking into the fire; after a moment he looked up and said:

'Supposing we *should* win this war—do you mean to carry on as Agmondisham's assistant?'

'I really don't know,' I said. 'I think it's something to be considered when the time comes.' In fact the question often worried me. I had really gone as far as the job would take me in 1939.

'It hardly offers a career, does it?' At this question chiming in with my own thoughts I moved uneasily. In spirit I was back on the Embankment bench again. I am sure my father sensed this; he had been reluctant to make the remark at all; in a sense it had been forced out of him. 'And do you know what Alastair is going to do?' he added. Again he did not mean to point the contrast between Alastair, who would certainly have a choice of interesting and lucrative jobs, and myself; but it made itself.

'No.' I said, and from the sound of my own voice I knew that, if my father should now suggest that I seek a job with a pension, we should quarrel. But he said something quite different.

'Tell me, Patrick—have you ever seen any evidence that Alastair'—he hesitated—'drinks? I wouldn't like it if he developed that way. I know . . .' Instead of finishing the sentence he made a wry face. It was the first time he had ever overtly referred to his drinking to me. I was taken aback—almost alarmed—for I was sure he could not have brought himself to it easily.

'No,' I said, 'I never have. Alastair gets pretty tight occasionally but he doesn't drink in that sense. And I'm as sure as it's possible to be that he never will.' My father nodded. He seemed relieved.

'Why do you ask?' I added. My father made a vague gesture, a sign of concern.

'Your mother told you about the business with the car?'

'And the Pole?' I said. 'Yes, Mother told me something. Did they do a lot of damage to the car?'

'Oh no.' My father looked surprised. 'I don't know that they damaged the car at all.'

'Well,' I said, 'what *did* happen? What was all the fuss about? People do things of that kind. You know what it's like in the Army. They go to a party and get a bit high and they use the transport to take the girls home—well, Alastair wouldn't be doing that, I suppose, but he likes driving about. Or maybe it was the other chap.'

'This friend of his,' said my father petulantly, 'was a thorough bad hat. I saw quite a bit of the Poles over Civil Defence, and I've nothing against them. There's some prejudice you know. But Little Willy—some people called him that because he was like the Kaiser's son—he was a nasty piece of work. He had a very bad reputation with women, he borrowed money and wouldn't pay it back, and I was told the other Poles wouldn't play cards with him. I understand he had a title and was very highly connected, but his manner—well, it was the manner of a gigolo in a low continental resort.' (My father had never visited a continental resort, low or high, and had never, I am sure, seen a gigolo.) 'He spent a great deal of time with those people Barbour,' he added in culmination.

'And was this chap a close friend of Alastair's?'

'Apparently.'

'It doesn't sound like Alastair. What's happened to him now?—Little Willy, I mean?'

'Well, the Poles have all gone, of course, but only last week I heard Little Willy had been court-martialled—I didn't learn what for.' I thought it over for a moment.

'I shouldn't worry about Alastair,' I said. 'Even if this Pole was as black as he was painted, and even if Alastair were really such a close friend of his, I don't think it means anything. Alastair isn't going to the dogs. For one thing he's too ambitious.' My father nodded.

'I expect you're right,' he said. 'Only there were rumours—an atmosphere I couldn't account for. But Alastair simply isn't like that.' He spoke with assurance now, like a good schoolmaster who knew his boys.

It was not until the following day that I had any special conversation with my mother. I asked her about the Captain.

'I didn't like to tell you in my letter, because it's all very hush-hush, I believe; but apparently Captain Keith was almost arrested under Regulation 18B, but they didn't arrest him in the end on condition that Lord Clandillon was responsible for him and he never left Lammermuir.' My mother spoke in a tone of business-like solemnity, as though she were giving evidence in court, and this tone, added to the sinister effect of '18B', gave me something of a shock.

'But that's all nonsense,' I said. 'Really—these security people must be crazier than the Captain himself. I mean, he *is* a bit crazy.' My mother seemed hesitant.

'Well—?' I asked.

'Lady Clandillon spoke to me about it, and—'

'I didn't know you knew Lady Clandillon.'

'I met her,' said my mother vaguely. 'I thought perhaps I must have told you about it, since you know her. She spoke so kindly of you. And then she spoke to me about Captain Keith.'

'What did she say?'

'She said he knew some very sinister people.'

'He knew all the crackpot Legitimists in Europe. I imagine many of them were rather anti-Fascist.'

'And he once had a prominent Nazi to stay at Kingisbyres—he was one of the Kaiser's nephews or something.'

'All that proves nothing,' I said.

'But dear'—my mother spoke gently, yet firmly, since if loyalty was to be respected, facts were sacred—'surely that is the point of this Regulation 18B, that it doesn't require proof?'

'Yes,' I said. 'It is. I think I shall call on the Captain.'

'That would be very nice,' said my mother, and I felt that she had been leading me. She continued to do so.

'And I expect you'll be going to see Catherine.'

'Is she still at Kingisbyres?'

'Yes. Didn't you expect her to be?'

'No. I didn't somehow. I never expect her to be in any one place for very long. Anyway I thought she would have had to join the Wrens again.'

'She wasn't very well after she lost the baby. Perhaps it upset her very much. I have the impression she's rather changed recently. It may be just a fancy.'

'Changed in what way?'

'I don't quite know.' My mother spoke slowly, but she did not appear to be evading the question, rather trying to answer it more correctly. 'Older, perhaps. More grown-up.'

'You don't make it sound altogether an improvement.'

'Catherine had the charm of youth so strongly.' My mother smiled. She had enjoyed Catherine's irruptions into our house. 'Perhaps such gaiety goes with lack of responsibility.'

The war had made no impression upon the moors. No aeroplane could take off here, no glider could land. There were no tank-traps, no Nissen huts, no troops; only, sometimes, meandering up a hill-side, a line of butts from which rich Englishmen had made war on grouse. I wondered if they would ever do so again. Would there be enough Englishmen

rich enough? Or had these loud-voiced stockbrokers with
the glittering cars simply been a roll of the fat that England
was losing in the war? Cycling over the empty moors in
the pale sunshine, hunched against the untiring wind, I
suddenly felt Scotch again and smiled a malicious smile at
the thought of England losing her fat.

I was going to see the Captain. I had spoken to him on the
telephone, and been surprised by his robust, familiar voice.
I was so accustomed to the war's having changed things that
I expected it to have changed everything. He had told me
to come to luncheon any day. 'Any day Patrick. Take what
you get—you won't mind that. We'll have a good crack.
You know what that means? It means a gossip you know.
I want to hear all you've been doing.' His manner, so kind
and urgent and easy, was warming.

Speaking to Mrs Harvey, and even to Catherine, had
been something of a contrast. I had spoken to Mrs Harvey
because it was she who had answered the telephone, and
her manner had been, as always, very social and civil; it
reminded me of occasions when I had gone to cocktail
parties in London as a girl's escort and the hostess didn't
know me from Adam and never expected to see me again.
Catherine had been welcoming—she said I had arrived just
in time to prevent her from dying of boredom—but when I
remembered the ebullience with which she had been used to
greet old friends, I fancied I knew what my mother meant.
And the Harveys had not asked me to luncheon any day.
Far from it.

'You must come and see me,' Catherine had said, 'the
sooner the better. Come and eat. We'll reconstitute an
egg or something. Just a moment and I'll ask Mummy.'
Through the receiver I could hear aviary noises that went
on for some time. 'Look here,' Catherine said, 'could you
make it Thursday? It seems we can't even reconstitute an
egg till then.'

'Yes,' I said, 'Thursday would be splendid.' It had then
been Monday. I felt a little chilled. I had expected Catherine
to demand my presence the following day. After all they
could have asked me to tea. Presumably they could get
biscuits.

The Grouse Lodge was a mean-looking, gaunt building, with no trees about it other than a painfully regular belt of Douglas firs which acted as a wind-break. But as soon as Henstridge opened the door, none of that mattered. He too showed the years that had passed, mainly in the way his Adam's apple stuck out.

'Mr Patrick,' he said. 'Come in! I'm properly glad to see you.' His cockney accent, which had once seemed to be so strong, now when I was used to English troops made no particular impression on me. We inquired about one another's health, and when he heard I had been ill, he looked at me carefully and said: 'You don't look bad, considerin'.'

'You don't look too bad yourself,' I said. 'And how's the Captain?'

'You'll find he looks much the same too.' Henstridge gave me a peculiar, questioning look, and suddenly I realized that, after all, he did look older. Curiously enough he looked bigger, gaunter, but also feebler, and his eyes were faded and wet-looking. 'But,' he added, 'you'll find him changed.'

'In what way?' I said, but even before I had finished speaking I heard the Captain's voice somewhere above us, and in a moment he was standing at the head of the stairs, welcoming me. I went up and he shook me warmly by the hand. It was true that he looked almost the same, the same grizzled, active-looking squirearchical personage that I remembered; he even wore what looked like the same strongly checked suit and glowing dark-brown nailed shoes. He and Henstridge both fussed over me for a moment or two, giving me sherry and a cigarette, and a spaniel appeared from behind the desk and ambled towards me; it was very old, but not fat like many old dogs.

'It can't be Scout?' I said. The Captain shook his head. 'No. A son. We call it Spy, but Spy's getting past exercise. I must shoot him. It's a false kindness to keep them on. Anyway, he's gey near his latter end noo, as the old lady said of herself.' The atrocious Etonian Scotch was unchanged. 'Like his master,' he added.

'You don't look any older,' I said. 'You've changed less than anyone.' The Captain, who was filling my glass—Henstridge had left us—looked at me.

'I don't always feel myself, these days. Henstridge tells me I wander a bit. In my mind, you know.' His look was strained, and also—I saw it with horror—a little wild.

'What of it?' I said. 'I'm getting pretty absent-minded myself. Why only a day or two ago . . .' Rapidly I improvised a mildly entertaining story, and I saw the slightly flushed, odd look die away. The Captain laughed.

'Absent-minded,' he said. 'I suppose that's it. Perhaps Henstridge exaggerates. He's an annoying fellow sometimes. But a good one.' He began to tell me stories about ways which Henstridge had found of making himself and his master more comfortable under war conditions. In a moment we were both laughing. His manner was quite normal. Henstridge entered.

'Luncheon is served, sir.' His announcement rang out with a fine formality. 'But God strike me,' he added conversationally, 'I forgot to get the claret up.' He went out, and the Captain smiled as he rose to his feet.

'If I am a bit glaiket—you know what that means?—it means wandering in one's mind,' he said, 'I'm not the only one. But I'm not getting any younger.'

'We none of us are,' I said.

'I'm afraid that when the King comes to muck out his byres I shan't be there.'

For a moment I thought it was a joke, and smiled, and then, when I looked at the Captain and saw that the same troubled wandering look was back again I went over to him, and shook his arm, and said, 'Come, let's go through.' He came round.

'Yes,' he said. 'Yes. Let's go through.'

At lunch he was quite all right, so long as Henstridge was there. That's to say he talked most of the time about how we were fighting the wrong war, that we should let the Germans fight the Russians, and so on, all of which sounded very shocking at that period, but his manner was quite sensible. But as soon as Henstridge had left us the Captain leant across to me and said:

'I wonder if you would post a letter for me?'

'Why certainly.'

'Not near here—as far away as possible. You see'—he lowered his voice—'the Russians have no end of spies over here. They've influenced the Government against me, and they stop my letters. They've even turned Henstridge against me. I know he doesn't post my letters—my important letters.' He was becoming very agitated. 'This one is to Churchill. I write to Eden too. I don't trust Churchill. Never have. . . .'

Henstridge came in again, as on a signal—I suppose he had been listening outside the door—and went straight up to the old man. 'Now sir,' he said, 'don't excite yourself. I've put coffee and whisky in the other room. Why don't you tell Mr Patrick about the new road and how you persuaded the Army to lay it past the Creamery?'

There was a moment's pause.

'Yes,' said the Captain. 'That was rather amusing.' His manner changed quite quickly as he told me how he had persuaded some general that he knew to construct a road in such a way that it would be useful to the village of Kingisbyres after the war. As he was going out Henstridge contrived to drop a piece of paper at my feet in such a way that it was hidden from the Captain. On it was written in pencil 'your visit is exciting him keep him off politics respectfully Henstridge.' And in fact I did everything I could to keep the Captain calm, and succeeded pretty well until I got up to take my leave—as quickly as possible, since I took Henstridge's note as a hint. When I did so the Captain took a letter from his pocket. It was fat and heavily sealed.

'Now you won't forget,' said the Captain. 'As far away as possible.'

'I won't forget,' I said.

'You must have a drink before you go.' I didn't want one, frankly I wanted to get away; but I accepted. The Captain poured out two glasses of whisky and added water. Then he turned and handed one to me.

'The King,' he said, and as he spoke he passed his glass over the jug of water which stood on the table. As he looked at me I realized beyond any doubt that he was irreparably mad—senile.

'The King,' I said, and made the same gesture. I no longer felt embarrassed; only distressed, and sad.

'As long as I do that,' said the Captain. 'I'm safe. They can't get me, you know.'

'That's fine,' I said.

'No. Cunning as they are, they can't do anything . . . we'll win in the end you know. The King will come into his own again. And when he does, there will be a Keith at Kingisbyres to welcome him.' The Captain pulled out a large white handkerchief and wiped the palms of his hands and his forehead. He looked very feverish. 'I shan't be there, but—you will, Alastair. I've arranged all that. . . .'

I went over and rang for Henstridge.

That night I wrote a full account of all that had occurred to Alastair.

When I reached Kingisbyres it seemed that time had retreated. In the half-circle of gravel which set the gates back from the road, the weeds had come back like the jungle; the drive was overgrown and the fences sagged: all was as it had been in the Captain's time. But when I emerged from the trees and caught sight of the house it was even worse. What had been the lawns were like fields of muddy, wintry grass; on the part nearest to me there were what looked like abandoned allotments. Nearer the house were two Nissen huts; from the broken window of one a piece of blackout cloth moved repetitively in the wind. The windows of the house were empty and blind-looking. Yet Kingisbyres seemed to me still to be itself, although dressed like a beggar, it was not demeaned, but had a quality unaffected by dress. How graceful, how domestic, yet how proud it looked! Again now, looking at it, there came to me like a passion the wish that I had been born to own it. I had got off my bicycle and paused for a moment, but I was soon forced to move on. It was exceedingly cold and beginning to snow.

It was Catherine who opened the door to me. (I had expected this; Mrs Harvey was not the kind of employer who could keep servants in competition with the munitions factories.) She welcomed me more vociferously than she had done on the telephone, and we kissed warmly. I told her that she looked well, and this was true; the climate of the moors made everyone red-cheeked and clear-eyed, if they survived. Yet there was something, I thought, not right. Catherine was dressed in the orthodox way in a tweed skirt, sweater and cardigan. Good taste permitted, almost demanded that these should be well-worn; but I was surprised to note one or two stains on them. These set me looking at her again and now I saw that her brogues were not polished and that her hair had not been recently done.

'You're looking well too Patrick,' she said. 'Really fat. Did they do you well in Hospital?'

'Very,' I said. I told her something about it.

'Oh you are *lucky*,' she said. 'You would get yourself into a place like that and be surrounded by interesting people, while I'm mouldering up here.' The implication that I had in any way 'done well out of the war' was at that time quite untrue, and although I knew that Catherine was apt to make remarks of that kind, I was slightly nettled.

'If you're bored,' I said, 'you could always rejoin and seek a hero's death.'

'Oh God,' said Catherine. 'I've been thinking about it. I don't know if I could bear it again. . . . I thought I might go into Daddy's office.' She sounded vague and uninterested. 'Do come through,' she added, and she led me into a room I remembered as the main kitchen. It had been done over with a taste which surprised me. There was some of the original furniture; a row of huge copper pots stood where they had always done above what had been the range and was now an open hearth with a basket-fire blazing with logs; there were rugs on the stone flags and some agreeable prints and a Dutch still-life of vegetables. I said that it was nice.

'Do you like it?' Catherine asked. She seemed surprised.

'Very much. Did your mother do it?'

'Daddy mostly.' I had known for a very long time that there were depths in Mr Harvey. Among them existed the ability—the restraint—to let Kingisbyres speak for itself, as it had done in this room.

'Well Patrick'—Mrs Harvey entered, a little scrawnier, thinner, greyer—'you see what people are reduced to in the defence of democracy—living in the kitchen.' She spoke as though this might be the first intimation I had had of social changes. We exchanged civilities until she went through to dish up the meal. It was inferior to the meals which my mother produced every day. Mrs Harvey was no cook, and in any case the materials were all the most dreadful kind of war-time substitutes.

'You may think we're priggish,' said Mrs Harvey, 'but I make a point of never trying to beat rationing in any detail. With William advising the Ministry of Food it would hardly be the thing.' (Mrs Harvey, alone in the world, called her husband 'William.') The two women ate very little. They were both thin. Having noticed this I saw that Catherine was really very thin indeed. All through the meal an impression about Catherine was growing on me. Even without my mother's pointer I should have noticed it. Sometimes she was her old self; the vitality blazed out. But for the rest she appeared sometimes listless and sometimes nervously irritable, snapping at her mother in a way that was a little embarrassing. Her mother was extraordinarily kind and forbearing, as indeed she had always been to Catherine. Whatever the nature of the bond between them, it was strong.

After the meal I helped to wash up. The kitchen was Henstridge's old pantry, unrecognizable in white tiles and gleaming electrical equipment. I made an admiring remark—for kitchens seemed to me the right place for this kind of lavishness—and Mrs Harvey said something about the authorities having been generous with licences for alterations when the house was requisitioned.

'I hope,' I said, 'that the Poles left the place in decent condition. They have a bit of a reputation for swinging on the chandeliers.' I spoke out of my real interest in the house and from my knowledge of the Poles' reputation. For the moment I had quite forgotten the story about Alastair and Little Willy. I was reminded of it.

'They have made a bit of a mess. It's very tiresome.' Mrs

Harvey paused and drew breath—social breath, at any rate. 'And now,' she began again, 'I'm afraid I must leave you. I have a dreadful committee meeting.' She began to make arrangements with Catherine. The changing of the subject had been marked.

'Shall I say you'll be there on Saturday?' The question was addressed to Catherine; I hadn't taken in what had gone before.

'No,' said Catherine. 'At least you can say what you like, but I shan't go.'

'Oh darling—don't you think you ought to?' Mrs Harvey's voice was uneasy, expostulatory; I felt she was going over old ground.

'Mummy, don't nag!' Again that sharp, nervy note.

'I'm not nagging dear,' said Mrs Harvey mildly. 'I was just wondering—'

'Well don't wonder then.' Catherine now laughed; but her sharpness had been genuine. Mrs Harvey left, and a few moments later I heard her car. Now that she was alone with me Catherine became more as I remembered her, gossiping about neighbours—with a slight emphasis on county neighbours with whom she was intimate—and films and plays and books. We may have passed ten minutes like this, then I said:

'I lunched with Captain Keith the other day.'

'I hear he's going ga-ga.' There was a callousness in Catherine's tone which was familiar and which I had always disliked. I had meant to tell her what had happened, but I decided to take a sounding first.

'He asked after Alastair very warmly. He's very fond of Alastair, isn't he?'

'I suppose so.' She spoke indifferently, and I realized that Alastair had never mentioned to her his suspicions of his relationship to the Captain. I had been saved from an indiscretion. I decided to change the subject.

'Catherine,' I said, 'what's this story about Alastair and a Pole called Little Willy?' Catherine, who was brushing the hearth, suddenly stopped what she was doing, but did not for a moment look up at me. When she did her face had a look on it like disgust.

'Does everyone know about it?' she asked.

'Catherine,' I said, 'what on earth happened? You sound overcome.' Awkwardly I got down on my knees and took her hands. But she would not look at me again, and in the same flat voice said: 'What did you hear?'

'That Alastair and this friend of his took a Polish car without authority and damaged it and there was some trouble.'

'What?' Catherine was looking at me now; she was staring at me in astonishment so complete that it was quite theatrical. 'Is that true?' she said.

'It's what I heard from my parents. My father seemed to think Alastair was tight—which I suppose he was?' Catherine shook her head.

'No,' she said.

'He wasn't?'

'The story is all nonsense. At least there's a kind of dotty connection between it and what happened. But that only makes it worse.'

'Look here,' I said, 'I thought what had happened was the sort of thing people round here might make heavy weather of, but Alastair and you and I wouldn't give a damn about. If it's something else, I don't want to force your confidence.'

'Patrick don't be silly.' Catherine now sounded cross and normal. 'As though I minded you knowing. But I was beginning to wonder if everyone knew. Let's sit down and have a cigarette, and I'll tell you.' What Catherine told in her own words was confused and repetitive. The sense of it was this.

The headquarters staff of the —th Polish Cavalry Division seems to have been a cross between a Prussian Guard Regiment and the Hellfire Club. From ancient manor-houses on desolate plains, from mountain fastnesses of Andean remoteness, noblemen bearing some of the proudest and least pronounceable names in the Almanach de Gotha had come to Kingisbyres to polish their monocles and dream of revenge. The house had entered into a dream of the past before the serfs were freed, when ladies' hands were kissed and the candles on the table had been shot out with pistols. The Poles had included some men of almost simple-minded gentleness and the most fantastic gallantry; others had a streak of blackguardism of a purity not often seen. Amongst a large number of men with strange manners in foreign uniform it was not easy, at first, to distinguish. They had all spoken French, but Prince Henryk Skrzetuski—that was his real name—in effect *was* French, for one branch of his family had lived in France for several generations, and he had been brought up there. I imagine that both his descent from one of the Polish ruling houses, and his perfect French, had played a part in what happened. He had made advances to Catherine at once when he met her, and he was both insinuating and determined.

'I tried to avoid him, Patrick, truly I did, and to resist him.' Catherine smiled a little wanly. 'Perhaps it was rather funny, me as Lucretia. Anyway I didn't make much of a go of it. We were living in the same house, after all.'

When, in the end, she had succumbed, it was because Little Willy had told her first that he was being posted the following week; and secondly that since his wife had been killed by the Germans, he was determined not to survive the war. (Later he said his posting had been cancelled.) All the time he was pursuing Catherine he was gambling heavily, not with his fellow-officers, but with people like the Barbours, whom he had met locally, and some of their rich Glasgow business friends. Catherine learned that he was heavily in debt, received a discreet warning about him from another officer, and was subjected to his first attempt at blackmail, all within twenty-four hours.

'He was so downright about it,' said Catherine, 'that it frightened me. I mean he didn't just ask me to lend him money or drop hints. He simply told me he needed a hundred pounds and that if I didn't give it to him he would send Alastair the photograph.'

This photograph was one of herself which Catherine had given Little Willy—at urgent, romantic request—while she still believed that he was being posted, and had lost his wife, and so on. She had inscribed it on the back in terms suggested by Little Willy and designed, as she later realized, to suggest that her unfaithfulness was calculated and cynical.

'He was awfully clever about things like that,' Catherine said. She had refused to pay, although she might have done before long, but that Little Willy started winning at cards again and slackened the pressure. Then Alastair came home on leave.

'Why didn't you tell him then?' I asked.

Catherine inhaled deeply from the cigarette she was smoking and allowed the smoke to drift slowly from her mouth before she answered.

'Why doesn't one do sensible things?' she asked. But at once, in a brisker tone, she added: 'I was scared of what might happen. Henryk frightened me—I was getting so I was shaking with nerves whenever I spoke to him. And I didn't know what Alastair might do.' Catherine looked at me. 'I expect you've noticed,' she said, 'that Alastair's a bit unpredictable when his foot is on his native heath.'

'Yes,' I said.

'I was afraid of what might happen.'

I knew what she meant. I should have been afraid myself.

Little Willy had the idea that as Alastair was a son-in-law of the Harveys, who were obviously rich, he must be rich too, and decided to draw him into his card-playing circle. And so he did, but Alastair had won heavily from him. On the following day Little Willy, apparently more from mortification than from need, had renewed his blackmailing approaches to Catherine.

'He was raving,' said Catherine. 'I thought he'd gone quite mad. And he'd been drinking too. I promised him the money to keep him quiet, and then I told the story to Alastair.' The silence lengthened. Catherine seemed to have forgotten what she was saying.

'How did he take it?' I asked.

'You know what he's like sometimes when he's angry— quiet, and as though he were making fun of something. As soon as I'd finished he got up. I asked him what he was going to do, and—you know how he goes all Scotch when he's angry?' I nodded.

'He said: "Me and Little Willy's going to have a wee talk." Then he went out.'

Catherine didn't know what exactly happened after that, but apparently Little Willy had learned that Alastair was looking for him, and had taken a car and driven off. Alastair had taken another car and gone after him. There was a chase across the moors. Then he had to swerve to avoid a sheep and he ran into a ditch. Neither he nor the car was seriously damaged, but Little Willy had to be laid out on the heather to recover, and Alastair took the precaution of tying his feet and hands. Then he went through his pockets for the photograph. He couldn't find it at first, but he found other things—letters and other photographs of girls, and a notebook full of addresses, and some IOUs and also official papers, passes and so on, and money, including some five-pound notes. And whatever he found he tore up and threw to the wind, until Little Willy told him where the photograph was, and he tore that up too. Then Little Willy begged him with tears not to tear up another of the photographs, so he kept it to the end and without tearing it up threw it up, and as the wind caught it he cut Little Willy free and told him he could run for it. And he ran, and Alastair got into the car and drove away leaving Little Willy running wildly across the moor; and with a ditched car.

'And when he came in again,' said Catherine, 'he was laughing.'

'Yes,' I said, 'I can imagine it.' And as that seemed to be the end of the story I looked towards the window. It was snowing heavily.

'For God's sake don't go,' said Catherine. 'You can't bicycle through that. And Mummy won't drive through it, so she may be hours yet. I'll make us some tea if you like.' She was crouching over the fire, which she had kept blazing with logs, looking at the flames as though hypnotized.

'I don't mind about tea,' I said.

'Do you think you could make some whisky toddy?'

'I expect so.' I made it in the kitchen and put the steaming jug down in front of the fire. When she had drunk some, Catherine got up and pulled the curtains.

'This is better than drinking gin from the bottle in one's bedroom,' she said.

'Do you do that much?'

'I get terribly bored here. I hate the place.'

'You could easily leave it.' Catherine took another drink.

'I'm scared to.'

'What are you afraid of?' She looked at me.

'Patrick—I've always been in love with Alastair.' She spoke in an intense, rather stagy manner, which as a manner was slightly off key, but which over the years I had learned meant that she was speaking the truth.

'Have you?' I said, and in spite of myself I couldn't keep the irony out of my voice. It was lost on Catherine.

'And Alastair has always adored me. You see, we suit one another.'

'It's called an elective affinity,' I said. Catherine looked at me a little suspiciously. But with a couple of glasses of toddy warming her she was not easily diverted.

'When he's with me everything's marvellous. But when he isn't—or before I was sure that he loved me—I do silly things.'

'You have more experience now.'

'What does experience teach people,' asked Catherine morosely, 'except how silly they can be?' She helped herself to whisky. 'If only one knew how long the war was going to last. Tell me—' She began asking me for my views, but since she knew a good deal herself about the progress of the war, and was as well able to put two and two together as anyone else, I did not help her much. Then I saw that the snow was no longer falling. Before I went, however, we finished the whisky toddy, and as I prepared to go out into the cold I was warm and singing inwardly. Catherine must have been the same, because as I was winding my muffler round my neck she said: 'I'm sorry the meal was so awful.'

'Well,' I said meaninglessly, 'things are difficult.'

'Actually Daddy gets all kinds of things—he hates going without, poor dear; he's made that way. . . . I'm indiscreet.'

'It suits you,' I said, and in a way it was a compliment;

it was the easy-going, generous side of Catherine that I was fond of.

'I didn't tell you quite all the story about the Little Willy episode.'

Oh?' I said. There was a note in her voice which intrigued me.

'When Alastair came back . . . he beat me. It was the first time he had ever done it seriously.' Against my will I was somehow impressed and excited. But I wasn't going to let Catherine see she had obtained her effect.

'Was it fun?' I asked.

Catherine thought for a moment. 'It's an overrated pleasure,' she said, and she gave a rather sickly grin. Then she spoke suddenly and seriously. 'It was wonderful afterwards—it gave me a kind of glimpse of what things can be like for people who are truly passionate and violent and don't give a goddam. I swallowed tears till my throat was sore and I *grovelled*. But I couldn't stand it again. I'm just not up to that kind of living. It's what I told you once before—I'm just a canny wee Scotch lassie.'

I saw Catherine again several times during my leave. Once she came to my parents' house for lunch; once she joined me on one of the walks across the moors, which had become one of my main relaxations, as they had been when I was a boy, and for the same reasons—partly because, at Nethervale, there was never quite enough else for me to do. On none of these occasions however did we have much personal or serious conversation. I was struck by the spiritual lethargy which kept Catherine marooned at Kingisbyres when she didn't like being there and when there was an interesting war going on all round her. But I came to realize that along with a kind of perpetual agitation in her nature—a pleasure-loving adventurousness—there did also exist this other strain of dependency and laziness, even of distrust and misanthropy, which, in periods of reaction, was dominant.

But much of the time I spent walking alone. Often I would bicycle to some suitable point, cache the bicycle, and walk a circular route across the moors back to it.

Sometimes I went sketching; I had begun again when I was abroad, and come to take immense pleasure again in my water-colours, which, for an amateur, were really very good. I found myself frequently in the Kingisbyres policies. There was no chance of seeing the Harveys there; and as for the other people, almost all the men, except one or two of the very old ones, had been called up; the place was deserted. In the woods and along the river it felt emptier, somehow, than it had done in Captain Keith's time. The sight of a weasel moving with discreet haste at the edge of an overgrown path, of an owl gliding in utter stillness in a copse of tall conifers, would startle me. I would catch an occasional glimpse of the house itself, blind and as it were maimed by the Nissen huts, old and abandoned-looking; but by a habit of mind I had never lost I thought of it as still waiting for the king who hadn't turned up.

Part Six

MY SECOND wakening was slow and luxurious, but it was the second, and much less mysterious. I knew where I was, and remembered everything, almost at once. It was nearly noon on Sunday. Before going in to see Alastair I had a bath, and shaved, and began making coffee. When I went in he was lying on his back with hair all over his forehead; his beard, against the white of the pillow, was very dark and heavy. When I pulled the curtains he didn't move, but when I addressed him he opened his eyes and said: 'Sucks, I was awake anyway.'

'I've run you a cold bath,' I said.

'That's devilish decent of you. Shows you were at a good school.'

'Thanks.' Alastair got up and made for the bathroom.

'Patrick,' he called as he went in, 'come and talk to me.' When I went in he was standing up in the bath, and as I entered he sat down and thew himself back with a great splash, roaring as he did so at the top of his voice. Then he put his head under and rubbed his eyes and face.

'It's murdered I am entirely with the cold,' he said when he emerged again, but although the water was in fact icy he washed himself with no special urgency. 'Tell me,' he went on, 'if you had a son would you send him to Nethervale?'

'Are you mad?'

'Would you send him to Eton?'

'I'm too doped still to answer hypothetical questions. Sons are your problem.' Alastair was soaping his hair.

'I've only one son,' he said, 'but how very right you are. Now listen—' But in fact I could not wait to listen, because at that moment I smelt burning. I went through and started the bacon over again.

Alastair's son was two. Alastair had spent about eighteen

months in India, and had returned just before the end of the war, very suddenly, to work in the Treasury. Some of the people he had known at Cambridge, and others he had made contact with during his 1941 visit to London, were now powerful, and I suppose they had remembered him. I had been abroad at this time—I was in Italy surveying war-damaged works of art—but Alastair wrote and told me that Catherine had joined him in London. They seemed from his letter to be very happy. Their son was born ten months later.

By this time, however, Alastair, who during his time at the Treasury had worked a great deal with the Americans, was already involved in the train of events which, a year later, led to his being appointed the director of the International Economic Research Organization—'a queer mixture,' as he wrote to me, 'of academic endowment and business investment, which might turn out to be just the place for me for the time being.' The original proposal had been that the Organization should have a London office subsidiary to its New York headquarters, and Alastair was to have been in charge of this subsidiary office only. A violent row between the original director and the founder had led to his being given charge in New York, at first as a stand-in, then after more manoeuvring, in which he himself had played an increasing part, as *de jure* director.

Alastair came in as I sat eating. I put a plate of food in front of him.

'What a fine sight man? Two dinners on one plate, sir. By God it is.' He began to eat like a very hungry man. Businesslike, rapid, his fork and knife carried the food to his mouth and the muscle moved above his jaw. When he had finished he began piling butter on toast in thick slabs roughly pressed down. 'Patrick, let's hire a car and get the hell out of this. Edinburgh on a Sunday makes me die a little death. We could go to Gullane and walk along the shore to wake us up. Uh?'

'Fine,' I said

Alastair was restless now; he had slept and fed, and action of some kind was a necessity. I could see his energies, re-created by sleep, growing under my eyes. When the

car came round I was down first, and the chauffeur began
to go through a routine of explaining the layout to me,
but Alastair stopped that and got rid of him, nicely, but
with the expeditious authority that comes to men who are
accustomed to unquestioning obedience.

'You don't have to explain this model,' he said. 'He
knows it. He was conceived on the back seat of one of
these. He's my eldest son. Now I guess you want your
Sunday dinner. . . .' We were moving before the man had
finished staring.

'I owe a lot to the Army,' said Alastair as we started. 'It
gave me back my natural vulgarity. And maybe America
has helped. There's not much missishness in me, but
Cambridge brought it all to the surface. . . .' He swerved
and squeezed past a van. 'As a successful English barrister
I would have been a stinkeroo. . . . I don't know which is
worse—the real God-given English upper-class arrogance
or imitations of it. I never did like that country very much
Patrick, and now I'm through with it.' He paused for a
long moment. 'I've finally decided to become an American
citizen.'

'I thought you were protesting a lot,' I said. Alastair made
no reply, and we drove for some minutes in silence.

'You mean I was protesting too much,' he then said.
'Maybe so. I had my eye on England, I suppose, for
twenty years. That old Kentish manor-house, you know,
that you could run quite easily with maybe only a dozen
well-trained servants, and an English rose right off the
ice to be its mistress, and a picture in *The Tatler*: "Sir
Alastair Kerr, KC, and Lady Kerr with Jeremy, aged
eight, and Curia, aged ten, on the lawn at Owlets Pastern." Sounds well, doesn't it? But there was a picture
something like that—and Sir Alastair hunting with the
Quorn, and Jeremy opening the batting for Eton, and
Curia leaving St Margaret's on the arm of a duke—in
the minds of the most diverse people, Levantine Jews
and Irish navvies and clever wee Scotties, for maybe a
couple of hundred years. And now we have to give it
up for an apartment on Fifth Avenue. It isn't the same
thing.'

'There are still glittering prizes for those with sharp swords to win.'

'Who said that?'

'Lord Birkenhead to Glasgow students in his Rectorial Address. It was something like that anyway. It nearly brought down the Government.'

'Lord Birkenhead—the man who made the dream come true. If he'd been speaking now he'd have advised them to emigrate, and that bloody well *would* have brought the Government down. But he understood the way things are. There are always some people who want to get into the biggest competition in sight, and they'd sooner die than do anything else.'

'And that's America?'

'Yes. That's America. America is the country that people like myself go to nowadays, like salmon swimming up a river—the way we used to go to England. It was Owlets Pastern we were after then, but England can't afford Owlets Pastern any longer.'

Now we were out on the open road and Alastair began to concentrate on driving the car. As the speed rose I hoped he really did know this make; but I wasn't worried, for I had confidence in him as a driver. The sun was coming through the clouds now briefly, quick and flashing. The wide smooth road was abandoned, and when after we had been travelling for some time I opened the window, I smelt the sea. Soon after Alastair turned down a lane, ran the car on to some turf, and turned off the engine.

'This will do,' he said. We were cut off from the sea by a ridge of sand-dunes, but as soon as we got on top of this we saw the long curving line of the coast, a line of beach backed by more low dunes. Clouds were racing inland faster than aircraft; the sea lay in immensities of green and grey and blue all cold and pure as Hudson's Bay. Somewhere in the distance we saw miniature figures of children, and heard the faintest glass-cracking note of their voices. It was very lonely.

'You know that Cathy and I have been fighting?' Alastair asked the question as we set off along the path that lay on the edge of the dunes and the beach.

'No,' I said.

'She doesn't like the idea of settling permanently in America.'

'She's never been, has she?'

'No, she wouldn't come over.' Alastair kicked at a piece of bleached skeletal driftwood and burst out: 'I made a mistake. I was so busy getting started in New York that I let Cathy get caught in the bosom of her family again. Cathy has this blind spot about her mother especially. God knows why, for she's very independent really, but her mother has an immense influence over her.' As he spoke these last sentences I realized that it was true what Catherine had told me years before, that Alastair had always loved her, because he spoke in that peculiar tone, earnest, reverent, sad, in which people explain the faults of those they love. 'I hadn't time to work out a campaign to win her over. Hell's teeth, I shouldn't have to!' As he spoke Alastair was becoming less guarded, and a note of petulant annoyance that anything should stand in his way, of self-pity when it did, that had been suppressed for years, had suddenly appeared again. He walked on for a time in brooding silence. Then he began again.

'I can't see what's so far wrong with me as a son-in-law! I have as much money as anyone else Cathy was ever likely to marry, and in America I can give her more than a millionaire could give her here. But her parents have always had their knife in me. Anyone would think I was a half-caste beachcomber with GPI.'

'There's something about you that frightens them.'

'I don't blame them altogether. There's something about me that frightens myself sometimes.' We walked on a few paces in silence.

'You and the Harveys,' I said, 'have a lot in common. You have this success bug, this bourgeois, respectable thing about keeping up with the Joneses or getting ahead of the Joneses. You have all the tough competitive outlook of the Scotch middle-class. That's one of the things that draws Catherine towards you. She feels you have a success-potential. It warms her. But there's a difference between you and the Harveys. In you the national subconscious is much nearer the surface. You're apt to be violent or get drunk or lose all your money. No one who knows you doubts that you would watch an enemy on the rack and laugh at his screams. There's something in you that melts Cathy's bones, and it's too much for her.'

'You're an analytical bastard,' said Alastair dryly. 'It must be your theological ancestors.' Without a break he went on: 'When I was away Mrs Harvey and Catherine entered Charles for Eton.'

'Naturally,' I said.

'There's another thing. It concerns my father's death.'

Captain Keith had died a few months before Alastair had gone to New York. He had been in a private mental home for a long time, looked after by Henstridge until finally he had turned against him and Henstridge had gone to live on his annuity. For the last two years, since he had had a stroke, the Captain had been completely senile, recognizing no one. Alastair had nevertheless gone to see him from time to time, and had played a part in looking after his affairs on behalf of the brother in Kenya and the lawyer, old Mr Crerar. It was more or less openly recognized that Alastair was the Captain's son, and at the funeral it was wonderful to see the laborious tact with which people treated him. It was known that he had done very well in the war and that he was then in the Treasury; his brilliance had become a legend; he was married to an heiress. He was obviously worth cultivating; but at the same time he was the Laird's (or 'old Charles's') bastard by a village girl, and as someone in the village put it, 'you had to let him see you didna think he was Lord Muck completely'. Alastair had received friendliness with friendliness, and civility and sly digs with the same urbane indifference, except upon one occasion to an elderly man who went too far he turned for an instant the flame-thrower of his coarsest repartee.

The Captain, although he had left various drafts, had left no valid will. One of the drafts had, however, left 'to Patrick Dalton Shaw . . . the manuscript diaries of my forbear Christian Keith for his private pleasure or to edit and publish as he sees fit'. The brother, an amiable, colourless man, had accordingly presented them to me,

although he was of course under no legal obligation to do
so. He had given the King's Coat and other relics which
were then in store to the Scottish Museum of Antiquities
on permanent loan. So they had come into my hands
again—and how moved I had been to see them!—the
books in which my dear Christian had kept her record
of that vanished civilization, leisured yet responsible, of
aristocratic taste, which for me at least had been part of
the meaning of Kingisbyres.

'Among his papers,' Alastair went on, '—he'd hidden
them about the Grouse Lodge and left little plans and
ciphers showing where to find them, so that it took weeks—
was a package addressed to me. Crerar sent it on. It con-
tained a wedding certificate and a letter from the Captain.
The letter told me the whole story at last quite simply.
Indeed, it's quite a simple story.' Alastair paused for a
moment and then went on in the precise unemotional way
of a good witness in court. 'The Captain had been very
much in love with my mother and married her secretly,
but by the time I was due to be born they had got tired
of one another, and my mother had fallen in love with a
merchant seaman. He went through a form of marriage
with her—he didn't know she was married already. She
only told him she had a lover who would take the child
off their hands but wouldn't marry her. My father gave her
some money. My aunt was willing to do anything to keep
all this dark, even after my mother died. That was in the
influenza epidemic in 1919. So it was concealed. But I've
had everything checked by my own lawyers and there's no
doubt I'm Captain Keith's legitimate son.'

'Keith of Kingisbyres,' I said. Alastair laughed briefly
and threw his mackintosh open; we had become warm with
walking. 'What did you do about it?'

'Nothing.'

'And what do you mean to do?'

'Nothing. The estate when it was settled was worth very
little. And there's nothing else I want. Wall Street won't
be impressed by Keith of Kingisbyres.'

'But you told Catherine?'

'Yes. That's the . . . difficulty. She was mad at me. And

she told her mother and she was double-mad. All the time I've been away the old bitch has been working on Cathy, plugging that she could be Mrs Keith of Kingisbyres and that out of sheer selfish meanness I'm taking her away to be a nobody in New York. She persuaded Cathy to write again and again, trying to get me to change my mind. Then Mrs Harvey wrote herself.' Alastair scowled. 'It was an impertinent letter, and I told her so. I suppose it was then she moved Harvey to decide to get rid of Kingisbyres. I imagine she thinks it might make me give in, even now.'

'She little knows you,' I said. What I meant was that Alastair would never allow himself to be bullied or give way to pressure, but he misunderstood me; or pretended to.

'Quite so,' he said. 'I don't give a damn what happens to the place. I'm not sentimental.'

'So that's what you've come over for—to settle all this?'

'Yes. I'm going to see Cathy and her parents tomorrow.'

I saw now the special significance of the battle fatigue cure. It was to prepare Alastair to dominate the Harveys. It was like Alastair's methodicalness to prepare for a family row by a weekend's drug-taking.

The Harveys had moved out of Kingisbyres not very long after my leave in Scotland in 1943. The War Office, which still held the house on requisition, had moved some administrative unit in, and a dispute which Mr Harvey had already begun about the condition of the place had flared up because the roof over the Harveys' part of the house leaked. The War Office had apparently undertaken to maintain it, and Mr Harvey, declaring that Kingisbyres had become uninhabitable, had bought another house about twenty miles away. This was a much smaller place, a dower-house which had been modernized in the thirties and was suitable for occupation in a post-war world. Kingisbyres had been empty since the end of the war.

'What happened in the end about Harvey's compensation for Kingisbyres?' I asked.

'What do you suppose? He shook the War Office down for everything except a free trip up the Amazon. He'd been turned out of his home, hadn't he? It's true it was going to be inconvenient to run and a financial loss if he sold, but how were the War Office people to know if the slates had been knocked off with a pick and the rain-water that came through was from a bucket?' I laughed.

'That's not true, is it?'

'I can't prove it; but that doesn't mean it's untrue. Oh, hell, I don't know what happened exactly, but I observe that it all worked out very conveniently for papa-in-law, as usual.' At this point the path involved a jump down into a sand-dune, and Alastair found a tin and a couple of sticks and we began to hit the tin along the sand. We ran, shouting childishly, Alastair ahead with his raincoat flapping and his black hair jumping as he bounded forward. Afterwards, when he had worked off some of this effervescent energy, he asked what I should be doing the following day, and I told him about the house I was visiting and where I was to look at some things for which perhaps I might make an offer.

Since the end of the war I had been in a picture and antique dealing partnership. On my last leave before I was demobilized I had dined with Mr Agmondisham, with whom of course I had always kept in touch, and had found him in a state of sad perplexity. He had been offered the directorship of the Heseltine Bequest, an institution which had been founded in 1936 by a millionaire collector, who had left a celebrated country house near London, his own collection and an immense endowment for the buying of paintings. The director's salary was reasonable, but it represented a drop below the income Mr Agmondisham had made before the war by dealing. But that *was* before the war; and were not post-war prospects uncertain? And to have the spending of the Heseltine Bequest! Then, characteristically, he had compromised by inviting me to buy his goodwill. Since it would not have been of any use to more than a small handful of people, of whom I was easily first, and since its value had declined to an unknown extent since 1939, Mr Agmondisham's goodwill was not readily marketable. Nevertheless, he had been determined to get something for it. The negotiations had been delicate, but in the end an associate of mine and I had paid a sum of money and Mr Agmondisham had written a number of letters. The business so far had produced a very unsteady but quite fair income, much anxiety, but also fun and freedom. I told Alastair some more than I had already told him of how things were going.

After this we spoke about other things until we returned to the car. As we walked up to it Alastair said:

'I suppose you've lost the romantic feelings about Kingisbyres you used to have?'

'I think so,' I said. 'They seem unsuitable for a middle-aged man in the atomic age. But perhaps I haven't lost them entirely.'

'I hate that sort of thing now,' said Alastair vehemently. 'Look where it landed my father! Anti-Communist hysteria and senile maunderings about the King coming into his own again. God save us from the romantic outlook!'

TWO

AS HAPPENED so often when I made a professional visit,
I left the house depressed and irritated. I had made my
inspection and had luncheon with the owner, a very
lively, choleric baronet in his eighties, and his heir, an
extinguished-looking retired soldier with a limp. They had
been hoping that, by 'selling the pictures' the major might
continue to live in this house, in which the family had
lived for almost four hundred years. They had already, in
1920, sold their one really good painting for a large sum,
and had been living in hopes of another big killing. As
so often happens they possessed a written opinion giving
some wildly optimistic attributions; the author of this
document, who had been paid a handsome fee for it, was
a notorious crook, since deceased. The baronet and the
major were both naturally angry with me for damaging their
illusions—for it is too much to say that I had done more
than damage them. Indignant, inarticulate, and suspicious
in this field of taste and aesthetics, they had been inclined to
doubt both my competence and my honesty. But I had not
been angry and had not thought it altogether amusing even
when, with his long sad military face red with annoyance,
the major had flapped his hand at a dubious Raeburn and
exclaimed:

'I suppose ten of these wouldn't buy one doodle from
that Communist chap!'

For I knew that while the baronet—he had some illness
—was only facing death, which we must all face, the major
was facing what to some kinds of temperament is
worse, the defilement of sacred places, the cutting down
of the grove, the betrayal of something personally dear and
impersonally significant. Nor, since they had no thinnest
trace of liberalism or egalitarianism in their make-up, would

it comfort them to think that their old home would serve a socially significant purpose as a reform school or Civil Defence depot.

I had left earlier than I should have done if the pictures had been interesting, and I had time on my hands. But even before I had begun my visit I had decided what I was going to do when it was over; I was going to pay a farewell visit to Kingisbyres. For after this I would never go there again; since my father had retired and my parents had gone to live in the south, I would have no occasion to come near it; if possible I would not even think about it.

As I drove I wondered how Alastair was faring. At first I had little doubt that he would win. When he was with Catherine he would soon dissolve her lethargy, reactivate her love, counteract her mother's influence, and carry her off to New York. Obviously when she got there it would suit her, and even if for the moment she found it hard to abandon the English dream, she would do the sensible thing in the end.

But as I got nearer to Kingisbyres (it was a drive of about forty miles), and particularly when the road took me up on to the moors, I began to have doubts about the sensible thing. *Would* Catherine do it? Would Alastair get her to do it? Did he really want to? I believed that he loved her; but in such a case he was not really well adapted to getting what he consciously and sensibly wanted. He was too thrawn. In the mood in which he had gone off in the morning he must, I felt, either conquer quickly or not at all. If he had been going to fight some issue at a business meeting I should have backed him up to the hilt. He had looked altogether a better man than the Alastair who had opened the door to me on Friday—the lines in his face had shallowed, his eyes were clear, his movements exact and unimpeded. He was exuberant, commanding, and young. But he was not going to a business meeting, and I could imagine him, with his energy turned sour, his force blunted, marching out of the Harveys' house, his face white and set with rage, to drive with controlled fury back to Edinburgh, never to see Catherine or his son again.

I reached the Kingisbyres policies at a subsidiary entrance

which opened on to the main Edinburgh road. Here there were now no gates, and the lodge, a tiny thing like a beehive, was in ruins. I turned the car in, but the drive soon became so awful that I feared I would do it some damage. So I left it. Agriculturally the place was in a reasonable state, but I saw that part of the wall of the walled garden had fallen down, and the interior was a wilderness. Inside, a sheep was grazing. What had been gravel walks were now mere tracks, and when I came in sight of the house I saw more sheep grazing right up to the walls. They looked shocking somehow. I walked all round the house. Where there had been flags and crazy paving they had been systematically torn up, and the doors and windows had all gone; instead there was boarding and rusty barbed wire. The house had that misused look which war makes so nauseatingly familiar, and especially so to me, a former specialist on mutilated works of art. It reminded me of a book I had once seen in a cage of monkeys.

I had of course no difficulty in getting inside. It is never difficult to get into a house the size of Kingisbyres, and as I swung up on to the stables and over the roof of the loft that Alastair and Catherine had called the High School I saw that even on this obscure route many people had been before me. I had meant to drop through a sky-light, but where it had been there was only a hole in the roof, and the attic floor below it, where the rain had poured in, was rotten. I had the feeling that I might have gone through, dropped clean through the house and into the cellars. Instead I scrambled over the roof; many slates were missing, and I could see the scratchings of nailed boots. When I came to the ridge of the roof I could see almost the complete round of the view from the house, except where it was cut off by the old tower on my right, and as I saw it I appreciated the site as I had never done before. High, but sheltered by the broad back of the hill, Kingisbyres stood on its little plateau with its park and its trees around it, yet looked out over the moors, while on its right the lawns had run down to the river. It was a beautiful site. But the wind was too cold to stand for long; I made for a little window screened by a balustrade which I found still unbroken; the dusty glass tinkled with a surprisingly loud noise at my feet.

Inside it was worse even than I had expected. Hardly a door was left on its hinges; those that lay about seemed to have been danced upon by maniac giants. The floorboards had been pulled up and the wainscot torn away; all the good panelling had been removed, presumably when the house had been requisitioned, for in these places at any rate the stone had been roughly plastered. But the wood which had been torn up or torn down had not been taken away; the Kingisbyres woods had provided enough fuel for everybody. They had left their records; in a lavatory which had been used for its proper purpose long after it ceased to function Cpl. Geo. Barnes of the (illegible) Transport Coy. had attempted to satisfy man's need to be remembered. Other needs had also been satisfied, I hoped more satisfactorily; of this too there was evidence.

But Kingisbyres had not yet lost its power. I went down into the library where the Captain had received us on my first visit, and often subsequently. It was dark because the windows were boarded up, yet enough light came through where a board was missing to show the wallpaper hanging here and there in strips, defaced and stained, but still reminding me, by being faded in some places more than in others, of the bookcases and pictures which had stood between it and the sunshine. And when I thought of them it was not difficult, in this house so sympathetic to memories and the past, to hear the Captain's voice: 'Kenspeckle—you know what that means?' or 'The King over the water—you know what that means?' And in the drawing-room, which in its emptiness seemed vast and meaningless, it was still possible to catch the echo of Catherine: 'Oh do tell me— are there many young people around here?' It was almost against my will that I went to the King's Chamber at last. It was an act of piety against which my adult mind rebelled, but I had known from the beginning that it was inevitable. When I turned the corner and stepped across the threshold I had a curious experience. For whereas the other rooms were empty and meaningless, the King's Chamber, which had always seemed so to me, now seemed no more so, and thus by contrast occupied and significant. There was nothing at all ghostly about this experience; it was less striking than the vivid stroke of imagination which, years before, I had had on the little lawn; it was just that the room did not seem empty.

I had seen all I wanted to; I went upstairs again to my window. I had not been shocked by what I had seen; Kingisbyres empty and looted, and already half-way, as it seemed, to ruin, the park used for grazing and the roof falling in, somehow did not offend taste or sentiment. I wished only that it might have met what seemed almost the most usual fate of houses in the neighbourhood—to have the roof taken off so that rates were no longer payable, and so left. I could have borne it to think of Kingisbyres crumbling slowly into an immense rock-garden of moorland flowers.

But soon now there would be arriving at Kingisbyres the builders with their thousands of feet of 'softwood', their acres of prefabricated beaverboard partitions, their endless buckets of urine-coloured distemper. From the local towns there would come each morning the bus-loads of clerks, and in the little beaver-boarded cubbyholes, with their cups of tea and their doggy calendars stamp-papered to the partition, there would begin the long little jealous rows of bureaucracy. In the servants' bedrooms the major bureaucrats would sit with their feet upon a carpet and all their dreams come true. And lastly there would come the men with the big machines.

There had been a protest in *The Scotsman*, and a reply from a senior official. He had referred to the economic situation of the country—to the price to be paid for beating Hitler—made the point that although Kingisbyres was doubtless this, it was not the other—and implied that if the owner was sufficiently public-spirited to sell his home to supply our grim necessities, frivolous aesthetes should keep quiet. It was awfully reasonable, even a little wistful, but when you read it you knew that the author would defend, with the same cheerfulness and ability, the demolition of St Paul's to make way for a municipal laundry.

I clambered through my window and over the roof. I had lowered myself down the first stage of the descent and was about to drop again on to the roof of the loft when I realized that there were people in the courtyard below. I looked over: it was Alastair and Mr and Mrs Harvey and they were quarrelling.

When I realized what had happened—and it took me a moment—my first feeling was one of embarrassment. For I was stuck on the roof, and as long as Alastair and the Harveys remained in the courtyard I couldn't get down without their seeing me. But this feeling was quickly merged into something deeper, more serious, a sense of great events, of crisis, a sense almost, although I hardly knew why, of dread.

They were quarrelling about Catherine. I could not make out all that they said, for they were talking in rapid angry bursts which were hard to follow, but from both of them I heard the name: 'Catherine . . . Catherine.' And from time to time I caught phrases which told me clearly enough what was being said: 'her own mind' from Mr Harvey, and 'bullied by you' in Mrs Harvey's more piercing tone—the 'English skirl' that Mrs Mathers had described long ago. And I saw something I had seldom seen, Alastair making a gesture, a kind of slicing movement with his hand in the air. The discussion went on for some time. I was lying stretched out between the edge of a roof and the wall, and some projection was hurting my knee. A shiver or a touch of cramp went through me. Then suddenly, moving with a curious simultaneity, the three figures crossed the yard and were underneath me. I was about thirty feet above them. Unconsciously, I moved back a little; below my face was a precarious gutter filled with dry black mud and pressed skeletons of leaves.

'You must try to understand a mother's feelings.' Mr Harvey spoke reasonably; a dignified, overbearing voice.

'God damn a mother's feelings,' said Alastair. 'What about *my* feelings?' He spoke quietly, passionately.

'You should be asking, what about Catherine's?' Mrs Harvey again, quieter now, passionate too; her love for Catherine and her hatred of Alastair were in her voice.

'Ah!' Alastair made a barely articulate noise of indignation. 'That's too much.' Could Mrs Harvey have been deceived by his quietness? But she said:

'Oh what is the use of arguing? Catherine has made up her mind.' She emphasized each word separately, her harsh voice raised in malevolent triumph. 'You're not going to have things all your own way *this* time.' She was on the edge of hysteria. The moment's silence that followed was charged with the echo of her fury and absurdity, and in this moment she and Mr Harvey turned, and began to walk away. They had almost reached the exit of the courtyard— it was only a few steps—when Alastair laughed and, in a quiet voice which perhaps was not even intended to reach them, said:

'Am I not though?—you screighin' auld bitch.'

When they had gone I waited several minutes before scrambling down. Then it seemed certain that they were not coming back, and it was rapidly getting dark. I stood for a few moments debating what to do. Deep in my mind was the fear of violence. I had a sharp realistic picture of Alastair knocking Mr Harvey down and Mr Harvey catching his head on a boulder. It would be a culpable homicide charge. . . . I started towards the entrance of the courtyard, but stopped. For what if Alastair had some well-laid plan for getting Catherine away, and I interrupted it? I had no business at Kingisbyres at all, let alone a title to interfere in Alastair's affairs. For a few moments I was in a miserable state of indecision, and as I stood looking down at the cobbles of the courtyard, and glanced at the roof from which I had just scrambled down, I felt angry at the place where I had been involved in a situation with which I wasn't fitted to deal. I heard the wind sighing stormily through some crenellation above me; it was an eerie, lonely, sinister sound. I wished I were in London, doing something completely routine, like waiting for a tube. The thought of myself in this position, standing on the platform, perhaps a little impatient, perhaps fiddling with my umbrella or gloves, acted almost magically: I went straight out of the courtyard and made for my car.

I meant, then, to drive back at once to Edinburgh, and it was only when I reached the car that I hesitated. It was now almost completely dark, the wind was blowing cold, and I had the sense of the empty moors around me. The tube platform talisman was still potent, but no longer completely effective. The idea came to me of waiting a little, drawn up at the side of the main road, for Alastair. For the sense of climax was upon me, and if the climax resulted in Alastair's going back to Edinburgh he would be bound to pass this way. After twenty minutes this no longer seemed a good idea; I had wantonly exposed myself to the darkness, the cold, the loneliness, and my own imagination, and they conspired against me. Yet I couldn't quite bring myself to drive away. I gave Alastair five minutes by the clock on the dashboard; then another five. I counted a hundred slowly, and another hundred, and was counting off single minutes on my watch, when at last, with a convulsive effort, I suddenly pressed the self-starter and got away.

How good it was to be moving! I began to plan the evening, thinking of one or two people I ought certainly to ring up. It might be possible to have a small impromptu party in the flat. The road was a good one; I knew it well; it ran away rapidly under the wheels. I had only travelled a mile or two, but in my mind I was practically back in Edinburgh, when I reached a point at which, in winter the trees were bare and it was possible to see the Kingisbyres tower. From old habit I glanced in passing.

Then I jammed hard on the brakes and heard the tyres whine across the road as I pulled the wheel round. For above the trees was a red glow. The house was on fire.

I ran the car as far as I could down the drive, bouncing it savagely over the ruts, then jumped out and ran. This approach to the house curved this way and that through the trees as some eighteenth-century landscape gardener had laid it out, and the fire appeared now on my right, now on my left, flickering and glowing, now strong, now weak, on the upper branches, and then on the dark trunks of the trees themselves. The drive seemed endless; my breath became laboured. I was running as fast as I could, but the avenue was so neglected that sometimes I had to stop and pick my way, and as I did so the fire seemed to gleam more wickedly. When at last I came in full sight of the house I looked up from where I was going and fell heavily, winding myself and scraping my hand. I picked myself up, but for a few moments I could not move, and remained doubled up, gasping as the air tore into my lungs and the saliva burned my mouth, staring at the house.

The fire had taken a firm hold. It seemed to be strongest at the point nearest to me, but the wind was blowing in the opposite direction and it was fanning the fire along the whole length of the house with a roar that I could hear three hundred yards away. In the moments that I watched flames suddenly shot from one of the topmost windows and waved like a great flag. Then I saw a figure moving and ran towards it.

It turned out to be a boy of about sixteen; he had just laid his bicycle on the grass and was staring at the fire.

'Have you seen anyone?' I said, and now I was gasping so desperately that he stared at me in fright. 'Three friends of mine?'

He shook his head, and by the light of the flames I saw his face register my own fear.

'Goad,' he said, 'you're no feart they're in it?' I nodded, too done in to speak.

'Run round,' I said. 'That way. Shout.'

He turned, and bounded towards the house. As I turned and ran too, I heard him shouting. Then the roar of the flames drowned everything but my own voice. I ran close to the house, jumping at one point a blazing beam that had fallen from the roof, and had turned two corners when I saw Alastair. He was standing on a hummock, some way back from the house, so that I was between him and the flames, and I saw his intent still face in their light. There was a moment in which he was caught as in a photograph,

and I saw that he was smiling faintly. Then he saw me and
ran forward.

'Patrick!' He caught my arm and stared into my face.
'What the hell are you doing?'

'The Harveys?' I said. 'All right?'

'The Harveys? They've gone to telephone for the fire
brigade.' Relief rushed into me in a sweet flood; but the
sweetness had gone almost in an instant, so quickly did
my fears seem fantastically unreal. I gasped painfully and
suddenly doubled up.

'Patrick!' Alastair shook my arm. 'What is it?'

'Stitch,' I said. 'Been running.' Suddenly the boy rushed
up and I said, 'My friends are all right.' Alastair looked at
me; the boy stared for a moment, then turned his attention
to the fire. But he was still there, possibly within earshot,
when I rose from kissing my knee and saw Alastair still
looking at me.

'I was here earlier,' I said. 'I overheard you and the
Harveys. I was on the roof.'

'Ah!' Alastair's exclamation was long-drawn-out, but
because of the boy, we both spoke softly. 'So you
thought maybe he was in there.' He nodded to the great
spectacular blaze. Then he took my arm, and moved me
away. 'Did you?'

'I don't know what I thought. What happened?'

'Good evening. I'm told you were first on the scene?'
Without either of us seeing him approach a man had
appeared at our side.

'Yes,' said Alastair. 'I was. That's to say Mr Harvey and
I were. He went to telephone for the fire brigade.' The
newcomer shook his head.

'No use, I'm afraid.'

'I'm afraid not,' said Alastair.

'Any idea how it happened? My name's Mcfarlane, by the
way. Dr Mcfarlane.' Alastair mentioned his name and mine.

'Mr Harvey and I were in the house,' he said. Nothing
could have been more correct, more seriously bland. He
was looking at both of us as he added: 'I'm afraid it looks
awfully much as though one of us had let fall a lighted
match or cigarette end.'

'I'm afraid it does.' The doctor's confirmation was reproving. 'Mr Harvey will be upset about this,' he added.

'We all are,' said Alastair. 'I've known the house for many years. Since long before my father-in-law bought it, in fact.'

'Oh,' said the doctor. 'I see. Nasty business for you.' He moved away, tactfully; and perhaps feeling a little that he had said the wrong thing. We saw him join a group of people; there were quite a number of spectators now. Alastair and I stood looking at the fire in silence. It had made progress even since I arrived. I was astonished at the speed of it. Almost the whole structure was involved now in one vast conflagration, from which, as each minute passed, new flames unfurled and billowed. There was a continuous crackling noise which came through the steady roar of the flames, but Alastair and I continued in silence until I broke it.

'Well?' I said.

'It *does* look as though someone had let fall a lighted match,' he replied, 'doesn't it?'

There was a crash and an immense shower of sparks like a rocket.

'Yes,' I said.

'And then of course the weather has been dry and there's a strong wind. That would account for the speed with which it got hold.' Alastair turned and looked at me, a look of an extraordinary hard directness. When he spoke again it was very quietly. 'I don't think,' he said, 'that anyone would need to imagine that the lighted match had been dropped in a little cache of black-market petrol.' He was still looking directly at me. His words gave me a physical shock which tingled in my stomach and died out very slowly along my limbs. It came to me that there were people who could do things like this, but I had perhaps never met another and never would.

'A fire loss assessor might find some evidence of that,' I said. I still had the tingling fluttering sensation and I was surprised at the calm of my voice. 'I believe they're skilled detectives.'

'He might,' said Alastair, 'but no fire loss assessor will be involved. Harvey never renewed his insurance after the building was derequisitioned.'

'Alastair,' I said, 'he won't fight back, will he? Arson is a very serious charge.'

'No,' said Alastair, 'he won't fight back. It would be lousy publicity.' Alastair smiled grimly. 'In any case he's done very well out of owning Kingisbyres. He can easily afford the loss.' At the word 'loss' we both turned again and looked at the great blazing house. More people were arriving. The fire must have been visible over half the county. There was another rending crash, another blaze of sparks. I looked at my watch; there were still ten minutes at least, I reckoned, before the fire brigade arrived, and then they had to organize water from the river. They might as well not trouble.

The builders would never come here now with their softwood and beaverboard. The drawing-room would not be the scene of conferences in which keen young assistant directors would make their mark, nor the King's Chamber hum with the voices of technicians getting on the blower. Instead there would be a gaunt blackened ruin which they would probably clear away for the sake of the coal underneath it. Where Kingisbyres and its policies had been there would be nothing but the fantastic moon-mountain waste of opencast mining. A thought occurred to me.

'My mother wouldn't approve,' I said. Alastair appeared to think for a moment.

'No,' he said. 'She would see that it wasn't sensible— no—that's not it—was underhand or something.' He paused. I thought he was smiling a little. 'I admire that,' he went on, 'and if I'd lived long enough in England I'd have caught some of it. The reasonableness . . . the gentleness. . . . But I'm not going to live in England.' The heat of the fire was so great that we now had to move back. As we turned to look at it again, the flames dramatized Alastair's face.

'And Catherine?' I asked.

'Cathy will be coming to America.'

'It's goodbye to the English dream?'

'Yes.'

'You might call it the end of an old song,' I said. Alastair looked at me and abruptly laughed.

'You might,' he said. Over on my right the bell of a fire-engine suddenly rang out furiously, and I saw a group of sightseers scatter. Alastair looked at his watch.

'Cathy should be here pretty soon,' he said.

'Here?' I said.

'Yes. In the showdown I had with her parents at the end I sent instructions through her papa that she and Charles were to leave at once. There's a nanny too. I don't know how we're all going to pack into the flat.'

'I'll move into an hotel.' Alastair took my arm and gave me a push towards the drive.

'I'll buy you a drink,' he said. 'And you've lost your eyebrows too. Did you know that? All for the good old cause. How do you feel?'

'I feel rather like a drink.'

'Would your mother put up my family until they get visas?'

'My mother would do anything in aid of the sanctity of marriage.'

'Once I get Cathy into America, I'll keep an eye on her. That'll be an aid to the sanctity of marriage.'

At the point at which the drive emerged from the trees there were several cars parked. Groups of people stood beside them; there were other groups all over the place now. One of the cars was a Daimler, a post-war model. Alastair walked up to it and opened the door. I followed him, and as I came up he withdrew his head.

'Cathy got out to look for me,' he said. 'Charles and Nanny are there. You get in and Mason will drive you round on the road to where your car is. We'll be close behind you.'

'All right,' I said. In the back of the big car I spoke to the little boy, but he paid no attention.

'He's excited,' the Nanny explained, 'by the fire.' The car swung round, and in that moment I looked at Kingisbyres for the last time. Framed by the window, backed by the hill, surrounded by the circle of dark trees, the flames leapt and played, billowed and sank and rose again over the incandescent mass.

'Look,' said Nanny, 'pretty bonfire!' And the little boy strained towards it and laughed with pleasure.

CANONGATE CLASSICS
TITLES IN PRINT